KILLER QUEEN

A Novel

Allen Peppitt

*To Sue
Thank you for your
support over the
years*

Brigand
London

Copyright © Allen Peppitt

The moral right of the author has been asserted.

All rights reserved. No part of the publication may be reproduced or transmitted in any form or by any means, without permission.

Brigand Press,
All contact: info@brigand.london

Cover design & photography
www.scottpearce.co.uk

British Library Cataloguing-in-Publication Data
A catalogue record for this book is
available from the British Library

Printed and Bound in Great Britain by CPI
Group (UK) Ltd, Croydon CR0 4YY

ISBN: 978-1-912978-04-5

Chapter One: Nowhere Man	3
Chapter Two: Not quite Elektra	13
Chapter Three: ABC	19
Chapter Four: Catch Them Being Good	29
Chapter Five: Of Doers and Achievers	41
Chapter Six: Believe in Bitter	49
Chapter Seven: The Damagement	59
Chapter Eight: Get Smarty	65
Chapter Nine: Children First Always	69
Chapter Ten: Community Aliens	77
Chapter Eleven: Shaky Time	83
Chapter Twelve: Exodus	91
Chapter Thirteen: How Candy	99
Chapter Fourteen: Bonny and Clyde	105
Chapter Fifteen: Paul Taker	109
Chapter Sixteen: A Maid with a Blade	113
Chapter Seventeen: Rendezvous in the Pondezvous	117
Chapter Eighteen: How Handy	121
Chapter Nineteen: Love Lies Bleeding	129
Chapter Twenty: A Knight's Tale	131
Chapter Twenty-One: Inconvenience in Store	137
Chapter Twenty-Two: Daredevil	145
Chapter Twenty-Three: Finders Keepers	149
Chapter Twenty-Four: Chop and Change	155
Chapter Twenty-Five: Any Old Iron	159
Chapter Twenty-Six: No Shit Sherlock	165
Chapter Twenty-Seven: Word on the Street	175
Chapter Twenty-Eight: Hancock's Half Hour	177
Chapter Twenty-Nine: Gary Goes Green	185
Chapter Thirty: Friendless Funeral	189

Chapter Thirty-One: Stupid Pawn	195
Chapter Thirty-Two: A Snitch in Time	201
Chapter Thirty-Three: The Beauty of the Moment	213
Chapter Thirty-Four: A Cold Case	221
Chapter Thirty-Five: Common and Proper	225
Chapter Thirty-Six: Grey and Extinguished	235
Chapter Thirty-Seven: *Antiques Roadshow*	237
Chapter Thirty-Eight: If You See Her, Say Fuck Off	243
Chapter Thirty-Nine: Viagra Falls	251
Chapter Forty: Red Herring	257
Chapter Forty-One: Breaking News	259
Chapter Forty-Two: Living Your Values	261
Chapter Forty-Three: Regicidal	263
Chapter Forty-Four: Danglers in a Doggie Bag	265
Chapter Forty-Five: It Was All of Me!	267
Chapter Forty-Six: Flesh Pastures	269
Chapter Forty-Seven: The Hendrix Chronicles	277
Chapter Forty-Eight: Circle of Death	281
Chapter Forty-Nine: All the World's a Jail	285
Chapter Fifty: KTs	287
Chapter Fifty-One: Just like Elektra	289
Chapter Fifty-Two: Sweet and Salty	295
Chapter Fifty-Three: Part of the Union	299
Chapter Fifty-Four: Gordon Brown	305
Chapter Fifty-Five: Goodbye Candy Jane	311
Chapter Fifty-Six: Redemption is a River	313
Chapter Fifty-Seven: Sugar Free	315
Chapter Fifty-Eight: Evil Never Dies	317
Chapter Fifty-Nine: Grave News	319

Allen was born in 1958. A club runner for over forty years, he has the heart of a thirty-year-old man and the knees of a ninety-year old-penitent. Allen now keeps fit by cycling. Following a degree in Economics at Brunel University, he worked in pubs and hospitals but now tries, unsuccessfully, to keep out of both. A teacher for thirty-seven years, Allen currently works with children who have moderate learning difficulties. In 2018, he received a diagnosis of autism which explains a great deal. Allen has never killed anyone and has no idea if he has ever worked with psychopaths – but he has definitely experienced the new-age bullies who now manage far too many schools. He has four children and lives in Woking.

Thanks…Carol for giving me love and that creative space. Dave Ward for believing in me. Professor Phil Tew for editing and coming up with a great title. Peter Holland for organising and encouragement in the final process of publication. The rest of the Brigand crew, particularly Scott Pearce, for giving me a chance. Paula Peppitt for proof-reading and positive comments. Stella Parker Bowles for insight into the condition of anti-social personality disorder. Ed Peppitt for teaching me the value of sending a book to someone, Will Self for bothering to pass it on and Martin Ouvery for analysis and encouragement.

If being at school is your happiest memory, you have never worked in one. Paul and Candy are practitioners who share an unforgettable experience; they find themselves at the centre of the murder of a colleague and allow two vulnerable pupils who are innocent of the crime to be blamed. Education will never be the same. Paul peaks early but Candy becomes the CEO of a multi-academy trust and an ambassador for values-based education; most people she meets discover too late that *Integrity*, *Kindness* and *Fairness* are just words written on a post-it note attached to their P45 – and they are the lucky ones who live to tell. Never in the teaching of history has so much harm been done to so many by just one individual.

Killer Queen

Chapter One: Nowhere Man

In a girl's bedroom on the campus of Stephenson University, twenty-one-year-old Paul McSmart found the words he needed to contain his curdling embarrassment. Despite not really caring about what others thought of him, he was deeply aware of how he felt about himself. Right now, he felt so bad he wanted to be someplace other than where he was. As with his attempt at a sexual encounter, so went his stab at insouciance.

"So that's over and done with."

Having just misplaced his virginity with an understanding young woman of almost compatible innocence, Paul McSmart was determined that nobody else would be allowed to know him being as vulnerable as this. What had he learned? Making love was trickier than masturbation; those living and breathing women did not look or behave like the pictures in his magazines and comics. Real women had blemishes and talked back unpredictably; they made sex so much stickier than he was used to. In so many ways reality was shaping up to be a disappointment. His conjoining act was a mess of poor design and even worse delivery. Theory trumped practice in life and death; everything looked much better on paper.

Covering up her beautiful real body with a dingy duvet, the first real lover in his life had an entirely predictable question for him.

"Is that it?" It was.

"Yes," he said. That kind of feedback was best received flat on your back.

"Nothing else to add in your defence?"

He knew the proper and correct answer; it was his first time – but he was not going to tell her that, thank you very, very much, especially as he was a third-year about to graduate and she was just about to finish her second year.

"No."

The jury was out and so was Paul. Fleeing the crime scene, he pulled on his mercifully dry pants and made a break for the door with his Levis around his knees; it was like watching a man-child failing in a solo sack race across the floor. He was over and out in three failing hoppity hops which would have twisted the ankles of a lesser man.

"Goodbye," he said, as he staggered out of her room in the halls of residence.

The door slammed.

There was a crash and the sound of a man shouting from further and further away.

"Shit, shit…shit!"

She heard him fall down a flight of stairs as he tried to put his denim shirt on. His pain would not be sufficient compensation for hers.

Paul put his shoes down and rubbed his knee. No damage done. He would still be able to go out for a run later on. He put on his shoes and socks, pushed back his hair and walked off into the summer night, still warm and inviting.

Dizzy with rejection, she flopped over and put on the radio. The new Genesis song *'Misunderstanding'* was playing. He was definitely a mistake; all that chat about being a comic-book geek was not him being ironic and witty – he was being literal. In 1980 AD, she had been judged wanting; Dredd really was the law.

And what was her verdict that he did not hang on long enough to hear? A lot of chase and not much pace. Was it the lack of men in her life, or the lack of life in her men? With that final act of abandonment, Paul McSmart considered himself well and truly a graduate of the class of 1980; all he wished for was to be recognized for his powers of invisibility.

It had not quite been her first time and it was certainly

not her best time. Turd class – just like his degree but without any honours. Why did men cut and run after going to bed with you? Perhaps she'd given in too easily, or perhaps she'd held out for too long. Maybe they hated you for being pretty and then despised you for being available. It was a stupid dance, that was for sure. To make herself feel better, she put it down to fear of red heads rather than revulsion.

Dazed by such a visceral rejection, she slept with two further men that graduation weekend just to prove to herself that she could – she was disappointed that Paul was the best of a very bad bunch. A very short while later she was pregnant by at least one of the three stooges. In a world where it was still possible to disappear, that is exactly what all her putative sperm donors did. Reluctant to have a termination, she gave birth to a baby girl a few months before finally she graduated herself. In a life of bad luck, she viewed her baby as her greatest achievement – even if her fathers were a trio of absentee scumbags.

Paul McSmart did not send flowers or comic books; he just got on with the misunderstandings that would dictate the course of the rest of his life, which had been pretty thin up until now. He'd no reason to believe it would get any better. However, he lacked the imagination and practical skills to kill himself, or improve himself. He completed his teacher training in a place far away from where he graduated, lest somebody knew his name, or worse still what sort of a human being he really was. Unfit for the real world, he became an economics teacher where much of his daily reality was defined by the routines of a school classroom. He never understood how the world worked, economically or otherwise – and he never needed to. Reality was for other people. On his PGCE course he became an innocent beneficiary of the immutable laws of demand and supply; a shortage of straight male teachers led to him being as popular with sentient women as he would ever be. Bogusly rebranding himself as a lothario, he also learnt a few rudimentary bedroom skills courtesy of some very patient primary teachers whom he abandoned when something more than rutting was required of him. Whoever suspected that there might be an emotional aspect to sex?

Nobody would ever tell him he was on the autistic spectrum and that he sought out teaching because he required structure. He always hoped he was a psychopath; they seemed to have much more fun than the neuro-typicals he'd met along the by-ways of life.

He had passed through six schools and five and a half relationships hoping to find *the* one. He'd currently paused long enough to father two children and get married. His wife was a blinkered person who had not yet seen through him; probably owing to his passable good looks and her requirement for some sort of rock in her life. As large stones went, Paul was more of an avalanche crashing down the mountain of life. There were no priorities beyond dodging the inevitable; long-term commitment to anything remained an ongoing problem to be approached with his eyes wide shut.

In September 1997, he held a teaching position at Kingswater Comprehensive School – a Surrey institution more flawed than he was. So far he'd been there for three years which was a record for him. The school was in special measures and about to be inspected by officials on behalf of the Ministry of Education to judge its progress; he hoped such a setting would render him invisible to authority, accountability and responsibility. It did not. He found himself responsible for a department of women who questioned his authority, and accountable to another woman who wanted him gone.

He never expected his situation to be much better and that anticipation was to prove accurate enough. All he ever hoped for was not to be remembered for who he was, because he knew he was nobody going nowhere. If only his life was as simple and significant as a cartoon comic strip, where you step out of objective reality whenever you felt the need.

At that point of quiet desperation, he saw the woman of his nerdish dreams walking across the playground to her office. Wearing a scarlet coat, her raven hair flowing around her face, he imagined her as a costumed vixen; like somebody from the X-Men, but not one of the original team.

"Who is she?" Paul asked someone next to him in the

staff room.

"Candy Regent, the head of history and curriculum fuck-ups."

"Is she new?" Paul asked.

"I don't think so. Maybe? Who knows?"

"Why haven't I noticed her before?" Paul asked.

"You live in a bubble."

Paul had no idea who'd spoken those words to him and he had no idea why he'd never noticed this woman teacher before, but the name Candy Regent was now etched on his timid heart, and her image burnt indelibly into his ramshackle, perplexed brain.

On reflection, he deduced he must have been talking to Jimi *'Hendrix'* Brown, legend and hippie art teacher; the only person in the school who ever gave him the time of day without the intention of hurting him afterwards. He looked at the source of the banter. It was Hendrix, the one and only hippie myth-maker.

"You reckon she's hot?" Paul asked.

Hendrix pushed his hands deep into his Afghan coat.

"If you fancy Morticia Addams," he said.

"Do you?" Paul asked.

"Absolutely," said Hendrix through a curtain of hair. "Melancholy and morbidity. What's not to like?"

"I think she looks more like Elektra," said Paul.

"Marvel or DC?" Hendrix was familiar with Paul's addiction to the unreal.

Paul was always slightly saddened that Hendrix did not really get it.

"You have to ask?"

"Be careful what you wish for," said Hendrix. "Now fuck off home and get ready for Ofsted – or do whatever it is you do to yourself in the evening."

"Nothing much," Paul said. He was English misery made flesh.

"Fuck me," said Hendrix. "Hearing about your life is like listening to *Dark side of the Moon* – but nowhere near as much fun."

Paul remembered a line from the *Pink Floyd* album that blew him away in the lower sixth.

"There is no dark side of the moon – it's all dark."

"That, old son, is exactly what I mean." As he spoke, Hendrix held his palms to the heavens.

Paul was still gazing at the woman in red.

"Wish you were her," he said.

"That's nearly funny," said Hendrix. "Now wish carefully and fuck off."

Paul was always up for a clear and concise instruction; it was all the interaction before that he found tedious and most confusing.

Rattling through his secret stash that evening, Paul found her: Elektra the sword wielding super-hero! Elektra Natchios was first drawn in January 1981 – probably why Hendrix, a creature of the sixties, had no idea. Elektra worked as an assassin and one of her listed super powers was low level mind control; maybe that was why he had never noticed Candy Regent before. So why had he noticed her now? Maybe it was destiny. The only drawback to chasing after this dark haired vision of femininity was that he was already married with children, and the very real Candy Regent had never once spoken to him. They were the best ones…those who were unattainable. He decided to keep her in his head with all the other naked women that he would never shag, but fired his libido. He wondered what sort of backstory she had; was Candy Regent anything like the red clad, sword wielding, Elekra Natchios who lay smouldering on the open pages of his comic book? Elektra Natchios. Her surname was one of those words like *insouciance*; he'd read it – but had never heard it spoken. In his head, it came out as *Nachos* which was borderline stereotyping. If he didn't get the meaning and pronunciation of the words – how was it for kids? He'd taught many who used the word or phrase in their forlorn attempt to define the meaning of the said word or phrase. Profit means *prophet*. Whatever means *whatevaar.* Fuck you means *fuck yooo.* Adults were frequently the same when they had nothing useful to say about something. There was box and cox, warp and weft, spick and span; they all meant something to someone, but nothing to him. High and dry took on a whole new meaning in his first year at university. All these phrases were secret codes to a world he just couldn't access.

What was it Hendrix said to him – wish carefully? He carefully wished for safe action with Candy Regent, secure in the knowledge it would absolutely never happen. He'd never lived in interesting times. There was no dark side of the moon – it was all dark.

Hendrix was also a little confused; Candy Regent hadn't been on his radar either – perhaps he did need to get his hair cut and his ears syringed. She just seemed to be there in the school taking charge of some post that had never existed before, and she never seemed to teach any pupils. Hendrix tried to recall exactly when she became visible; there was no precise point, but he remembered her presence being associated somehow with the merger of the school with Jubilee High and the business deal that had been struck with the new consultancy Cradcrock.

That was a frenzied time of staff consultations about micro-economics and other bullshit theories offered by the firm that had no place in the running of an educational establishment. When Paul tried to point out that pupils in a business model could only be items valued at cost – and that they were not goods and services with a price tag, he was told that he did not understand how things worked in this new world order. He carried on by telling Cradcrock's representatives that education was a merit good and as such was under-supplied by the free market because there was little understanding of its economic or social benefit at the point of consumption. A de-merit good was something like heroin where too much was consumed for the social good.

He stopped comparing and contrasting merit and de-merit goods when he heard one of the consultants loudly ask another if the name *McSmart* was a nom de plume, something the lunatic had made up like the voodoo economics he was boring them with.

"Is that a real name?" Those were the words that stuck in Paul's head – he did not have an answer for them. It was his real name, although apart from being forced to teach *Macbeth* to year eight, he was not Scottish in any other way.

All he'd done by speaking out was to make himself a target for wankers and power brokers; when management or their hired consultants asked for an opinion on something, it was not his educated opinion that they wanted – that was definitely a de-merit good far worse than any narcotic available through the free market.

The new school was christened the *Kingswater Academy* in July 1995. Hendrix declared it an exercise in re-branding a turd and everyone he consulted in focus group agreed with him. The new name of the school was never articulated by anybody, including those who were responsible for the change. It remained Kingswater Comprehensive School; and after an indecently short while Jubilee High School was excised as a community memory when the site was acquired by a subsidiary of the Cradcrock consultancy. Cradcrock Construction went on to build several blocks of luxury flats on the land – the first of which was bought by Mr. Duncan Knight, an unpopular rising star in the evolving world of educational mismanagement at the newly re-named Kingswater Comprehensive.

In the first week of the new term, there'd even been a mercifully short-lived campaign to rename the institution in memory of Princess Diana who'd not even been buried by then. Five hundred signatures were collected before compassion fatigue kicked in and everybody continued with their lives. Thankfully, even the hybrid humans who ran the Cradcrock consultancy recognized that potential re-branding as the very worst sort of mawkish, ambulance chasing attempts at publicity. The motion to change the name of the school to *English Rose* was thrown out after a very short discussion to which neither Hendrix nor Paul McSmart were invited.

Chapter Two:
Not quite Elektra

September 1987: Young Candy Regent was in the bowels of an unnamed police station with a named and numbered policeman. His name was Detective Constable Davy Jones and his days were both numbered and interesting. They were in the storeroom where weapons returned under amnesty were kept before being destroyed or sold on. The florescent light bounced off one smirking weapon in particular.

"Here we are," he said. "Davy Jones' lock up."

Ignoring his attempt at being funny, Candy pulled on the man's waistband and found the response she was looking for – Davy Jones unbound. The unthinking male equipment rose to meet her. She always loved that she could do that to almost any man.

"Show me the big blades," she begged. A tired old warrior woke up.

"Are you for real, Angel?" DC Jones asked.

"Yes," Candy replied. "Oh yes, yes, yes!"

He'd met her in a pub. She seemed smaller then. Dark haired and beautiful, but not as dominating as she would later become. Now larger than life, she was a dying man's dream - an enthusiastic practitioner of the darkest erotic arts of seduction and death. All she had wanted was to have manic unprotected sex in a police station with a married man she'd never met before. An older policeman with a smoking habit and a heart condition - anyway he wanted it – everything from swinging off the rafters to being nailed on a cross. That had all seemed very straightforward. But this? DC Jones was not sure where this was going.

"Why?" he asked.

"Don't ask me," she replied. "Just enjoy me."

She pulled up her sweater. Apart from a silver skull on a necklace, she was not wearing anything else underneath. Pre-decimal thrupenny bits. Low hanging fruit. He'd not seen anything like those in forty years. One more ticked off the bucket list. He was pleased that some things remained the same.

"Why the skull?"

"To remind me that death is never far away," said Candy.

"Good point." He opened the cage where the weapons were stored.

"From our last amnesty." Candy eyed up a samurai sword, judged as a blade to die for.

"If you let me have that," she said, pointing to the sword. "I'll let you have this…"

He watched her writhe in fake ecstasy; just more loose change rolling around on the floor. The policeman inside him tried to wrestle control from the sex-starved pervert sitting on his shoulder – but it was no deal, she had his danglers in a doggie bag.

"An old boy brought it back from Japan. Just after the war. They were giving them away then..."

Now bored with his history lesson, she started to unzip her leather strides.

"Aah…watch me…" Then she started to rub against herself, circling her head and gently moaning as she carried out both of these acts of abandonment.

He carried on with his tale of the blade.

"…then he died, intestate…"

He felt a shiver. Same old currency.

The detective in Jones gave way to the bones in Jones.

It would be *shagger-mortis* for him if she carried on like this. He'd nibbled of the insane root. He was up for it. He looked up at her – now a mountain he was about to scale without oxygen or contraception.

That same night, Candy Regent also took possession of an unknown samurai sword and DC Jones sacrificed the rest of his life to lay with her one more time – or three.

"Do you mind if I take these two suits to wrap it in?" Candy said, pointing to the white suits flopped over a chair in the corner of the store room.

"They've been used already," said DC Jones, fighting to catch his remaining breath. "Pre-loved, so to speak."

"I get all moist when you talk dirty!" Knowing there was nothing left in the old man, she stroked him provocatively.

"Please stop," he said. "For the moment, anyhow." Then he pointed to her prize waiting in the shadow. "You need to be discrete with this – it's got previous."

"Of course, darling." She gave him a killer smile.

As she wrapped the sword in the suits, he felt his heart race to the finish line. He remembered the saying, *virtue can't hurt you, but vice is nice*; it was a couplet with a very short shelf life.

"I think we'll call it a day," said DC Jones. "I'm getting too old for this sort of thing."

She was not going to let this one lie.

"No sleep until bedtime," said Candy. "There's a bit of life left in the old dog." Unlike his, her heart was both healthy and black as Newgate's knocker.

He gave himself the thumbs down.

"Not much." He was on the money.

She was not worried about his long-term health. They

shared that much in common.

"I'll bring the oysters," she laughed, "you bring the amorous intent." He looked at this vision of a writhing woman lusting after him. It was ridiculous; he could hear the caustic words of his wife. The detective in him was briefly aroused.

"What does a nice girl like you want with a weapon like this?"

She gave him another killer smile.

"I have a cunning plan." Then he thought better of asking any more questions. Sex was sex. Opportunity was opportunity. Hot was hot.

"Don't tell me anymore, Angel."

"That's the idea – just enjoy me in the moment," she said. "Because that's all we have."

"I am that," he said. Then she asked him a question he was not expecting.

"If you want an illness that will keep you off work and be hard to disprove, what's the best?"

"Inner ear stuff," he said. "Hard to prove you haven't got it – and it's not fatal unless you're James Hunt cornering at 180 miles an hour."

"Is that rhyming slang for something else?"

"No babe. Don't look back if you have Meniere's."

"I never do."

"That's my girl."

He died in her charms three days later. The coroner's report said multiple organ failure.

His widow knew better. Never trust a younger woman who finds you attractive. Write that on his gravestone if you dare. They could barely close the coffin lid on his chemically engorged member. She knew he had been playing away. So did his colleagues. It was what policemen did.

Rather than kill herself or send flowers, Candy found new uniformed playmates.

Several boys in blue visited her flat over the next three weeks; they were not all conducting criminal investigations. She liked policemen; they had enquiring minds, they knew what they wanted and they never gave up the chase. For much of the time, that was all she wanted – to be caught and held for questioning. They also suffered no introspection or fit of conscience when it came to adultery in all its glorious guises – it was all part of the job.

Later that same year, impregnated by one of many uniformed and plain-clothed suspects, she had an abortion, moved to another county and trained to be a teacher. What else could she do with a third in history? She gave herself one rule to live by; wherever she found herself, nobody would tell her what to do, or mark her down. Normal people led such sad and pointless lives weighed down by children and spouses. She wanted to make sure she was so extraordinary that she'd never be forgotten by anybody. She was not going to be normal – even if it meant that normal people would suffer, or perhaps, even die.

The sword from the stir lay dormant for the next ten years, wrapped in two forensic suits and resting happily under the bed of her man-killing lady; it had previous, it was not in a hurry. Faking Meniere's became a reliable standby when any situation got too much. And it all got too much pretty frequently.

Nobody had ever told her she was a psychopath. She always thought she was a messed-up daddy's girl with borderline personality problems. As long as she could remember she'd been prescribed special tablets to stop the voices in her head; when she was lonely she chose not to take them. At this point in her life, she decided she was definitely not lonely enough.

In September 1997, she found herself in a teaching job at Kingswater Comprehensive School. She'd started out as a member of the department, but indecently soon she became Head of History and Curriculum Development. Before she was awarded the post there was no such position as curriculum development; it was just a cover supervisor who booked staff on CPD, or Continuous Professional Development, whether they asked for it or not.

Nobody was sure exactly what happened to the former post holders; it was as if one day they were no longer in the building and there was a cloud of community amnesia. There were mutterings that this was a conspiracy by the newly-appointed county consultants to radically change the school - but nobody was exactly sure what kind of change they were after and nobody left behind had the inclination to find out, partly because they were too busy dealing with the mound of paperwork that all the changes generated.

The school was also in special measures which was fine by Candy – dysfunctionality was her bag and she knew how to climb above the mayhem and harness its random energy; she was the chaos queen and she knew who to seduce to get where she wanted. Her most recent conquest had been the interim head of the Cradcrock consultancy; whilst he could not deliver on all he promised, he did arrange for her a promotion way beyond her experience and competence. He too had conveniently died of a sex-related accident shortly after the take-over of Jubilee High School by Kingswater Comprehensive.

Chapter Three:
ABC

Pupils swirled around the playground – close up it was the worst kind of natural history programme full of blood and gore. From a safe distance, it looked like dirty water circling a drain. That safe distance was the staffroom, two flights up and overlooking the converted tennis courts. From the assembled teaching staff, Hendrix nominated himself to provide a commentary on what was about to go down. He was no David Attenborough, but he knew his topic well.

"If you only kill one person today, Gary…make sure it's you."

Morning break at Kingswater Comprehensive School was often a time of self-actualization - a chance to be the best you could be.

Gary, in year eleven, was recruiting for the *Bad Man Crew*.

Slightly smaller than an average year 10, but taller than a year 9, he shouted out to a bunch of year sevens.

"I'm a nutter! Follow me!" he yelled. "Follow Mr. Bad Man!"

Whooping and screeching like a herd of knob-jockeys, they chased him around the playground.

Hendrix, in his Watchtower, continued with his voiceover.

"The bully's alphabet; Arseholes and Bastards, aspiring to be Cunts."

He said this with no particular satisfaction, or malice. Then added, "Now watch, as one of the common cunts is sacrificed by a Proper Cunt. A cunt above the rest. A cunt for all seasons"

At that point, Gary stopped running and caught the puniest boy in a headlock, twisted his flailing fingers, kneed him in the nuts and threw him to the ground. The predator had found his prey; the law of the jungle was played out in fifteen minutes of unstructured activity.

"ABC, 123," said Hendrix. "There you have it. Tostesterone in action."

"I think you mean *testosterone*," said a dissenting voice from the scientific community.

Hendrix, who was very much an acquired taste, didn't care who listened.

"Nah," he said, "that boy's a tosser."

The beaten boy lay dazed on the concrete as the pain radiated from his groin – small plastic tokens spilled out of his pocket and were picked up by scavenging nerds. He would not be joining the *Bad Man Crew*, a gang guaranteeing, on Gary's geography exercise book, that all members got '*pusey*'.

"Pogtastic," said Hendrix.

"What?" Mr. Kingman asked.

"He's lost his pogs," said Hendrix.

Hendrix provided the closing statement.

"He's lucky that's all he's lost," said Mr. Kingman.

"Cunt club 101," he said. "Master the basics. That boy has a heart as black as coal."

In the olden days, he could have had Gary punished with the cane. Joe would have asked him to choose which one he wanted. It was all a matter of choice. The thick cane that hurt less, and left a mark. Or, the thin version that stung like a bee and left no mark. The one that was not too thin and not too thick that hurt, but not so badly, and left a tiny mark. Kids of old liked to have a choice. But Joe, like hymns being sung in assembly, had disappeared. Now Gary would receive a six-week anger management course, a complimentary cup of cocoa and a book of politically correct blasphemy.

This was not 1974. Things were done differently in the late nineteen-nineties. Disrespect was mandatory and bullying a human right. A grey-haired man looked down his bi-focals at Hendrix, the hippie art teacher whose real name was Jim Brown. Mister grey-haired was the Deputy Head; he'd seen it all before. It didn't work then, it wouldn't do so now and it wasn't going to in the future.

"Mr. Brown," said the Deputy Head, "the enemy is at the gate – do not paint a target on your head."

"Come on Mal, play the game," said Hendrix. "Brown is my slave name."

He offered an old joke worn thin by time, overuse and the fact that it wasn't even funny in the first place.

The Deputy Head, Malcolm, whose slave name was Mr. Kingman, sighed with the stupidity of it all – spending tens of thousands highlighting the issues created by budget cuts made by accountants looking to improve quarterly figures. He'd just been on a leadership course where he was asked to consider if he was a *doer* or an *achiever*. When he said he was a doer, he was told that he'd given an answer of someone who would remain forever in the classroom and never rise to the heights of management. Pointing out that, as a doer, he'd already done so made no difference to the point of view being tendered. Now he looked on a wasteland full of absentee achievers kept from total desolation by the doers. Hendrix was a doer and a dinosaur in this new world. He had a duty to protect such noble beasts as Hendrix from complete extinction.

"That, old son, is what I mean by painting a target on your noggin."

"What?" Hendrix asked.

"You're a dinosaur – those furry little bastards at the gate want to eat you alive."

Dinosaur and proud of it, Hendrix held up his hands, the cuffs of his Afghan coat dropping to reveal skinny wrists adorned with bangles and bracelets, self-awarded for sexual endeavours in the late sixties and early seventies.

"I know," said Hendrix. "I know. Judged by those who can't circumnavigate their own didgeridoos with both hands – a species who manage to be both ruthless and useless. How is that possible?"

"They are motivated by the thought of removing themselves from the classroom far more than you or I," said Mr. Kingman, "and they fear our experience and commitment to a job they could never aspire to…so clearly what you do is you destroy what you fear."

Mr. (Malcolm) Kingman was a working-class man who could turn his hand to anything; so now he was a middle class Design And Technology teacher with a mortgage that had dwindled to the size of his prostate, which had grown to the size of an unshelled walnut, a motor-mower and nobody left to talk to. His most recent project was trying to keep Hendrix meaningfully employed within a modern educational setting; when Hendrix was in this particular frame of mind, it was hard to achieve a work-stress balance.

"Fucking bloody Ofsted," said Hendrix, "with their fucking clipboards and their fucking check-lists. They don't know what room to piss in."

"It's not like we don't have our own clipboards," said Mr. Kingman. "Or our own checklists."

"And our own cunts," said Hendrix.

"They call themselves consultants," said Mr. Kingman. "And what is a consultant? A Cutpurse who'll take your watch and then tell you the time."

"I call them Cunts with clipboards and checklists," said Hendrix. "It's nearly the same."

"I wish you would stop using that word," said Mr.

Kingman.

"Clipboard?"

"No," said Mr. Kingman.

"Checklist?"

"No," said Mr. Kingman.

They then both turned their attention to the small group of inspectors on the playground – grammar school boys about to do the bidding of the public schoolboys truly in charge and apply their fucked-up values to a comprehensive school. Grammar schools creamed off the smart children and public schools the wealthy; neither group had any interest or experience when it came to educating those who were not lucky enough to be born smart or rich. The deluded team of inspectors was greeted by the Head and one of the other deputies who walked them to the safety of the front door.

"There's Ms. Bishop," said Hendrix, "that fucking tour-guide we pay fifty grand a year for. She can't do it alone so she's got our director of directed time, Mr. Shite."

"Yes," said Mr. Kingman. "A supreme achiever if ever there was one."

"Big as Lurch and half as pretty," said Hendrix.

"And probably twice as expensive," said Mr. Kingman.

"He's trashing a childhood memory," said Hendrix. "I loved *The Addam's Family*."

"You're not Cousin Itt by any chance?" Hendrix gave him gunslinger's fingers – both hands rolling with the recoil of the pretend shots.

"I like it," he said.

Mr. Shite was not the lovable Lurch; Mr. Shite had a real name. He was called Mr. Knight and he was not director of directed time; it was one of the responsibilities he never stopped talking about. As far as Hendrix was concerned, Mr. Knight was the Frankenstein monster created by an educational policy of bogus accountability. The unwanted title was one Hendrix had awarded him in recognition for his selfless self-promotion and the vast amounts of time he gave himself to work at home when there was something to be done at work.

"Here comes Johnny Ofsted," said Mr. Kingman, half remembering a song from his youth.

Hendrix sucked his teeth.

"Abscondez yourself, si'l vous plait, or prepare to be judged by pigmies and pig fuckers."

"I think your CSE French leaves a lot to be desired – and many pigmies would be upset at the inference," said Mr. Kingman.

"And a lot of pig fuckers," said Hendrix. "Also I didn't do CSE French. I failed O level – it was something about the oral." It always was with Hendrix.

Mr. Kingman scratched his chin, and asked the rhetorical question of the day.

"How do you get to be an inspector? Not by failing Ordinary Level French, obviously. How does one make the journey from incompetent teacher to judge, jury and executioner of your former colleagues?"

The question Mr. Kingman had actually been giving serious thought to was how a relative newcomer to the school, Candy Regent, had suddenly become so visible within the management team; she'd risen without any trace of where she came from.

Hendrix always had an answer. If he didn't, he borrowed.

"It needs to be damp."

"You stole that line from the lovely Morticia Addams."

"Sue me." Hendrix blew him a kiss and ambled toward the staffroom door. Mr. Kingman chuckled.

"Abscondez-vous yourself. You and your black heart."

He gave a Black Power salute – circa Tommy Smith and John Carlos in the 1968 Mexico City Olympics.

"I'm the man!"

Mr. Kingman raised a hand and responded in the manner of Jack Hargreaves on the television series *How*.

"And I'm the King Man."

Hendrix paused.

"One day," he said. "King Malcolm – it sounds right."

"If you are in a ruddy play," said Mr. Kingman.

"All the world's a stage," said Hendrix. "Was that a Dylan quote?"

"Shakespeare I believe."

"Yeah."

"They're doing *Macbeth* in year eight," said Mr. Kingman.

"Teaching our kids that killing gets you what you want?" Hendrix surprised himself by disapproving on moral grounds.

"It doesn't end well for Macbeth or his wife," said Mr. Kingman. "He was a doer who thought he was an achiever."

"Right on," said Hendrix.

"Too much ambition and too little talent to rule wisely," Mr. Kingman continued, "– like some of our SLT virgins." The Senior Leadership Team; Hendrix hoped he could have a five minute slot on the local news to say what he truly and deeply felt about them. He settled on a few anodyne words.

"Doing bad things to good people," he said.

"That's the problem with violent change," said Mr. Kingman. "Shakespeare lived in treasonous times."

"That's not the bit they'll remember," said Hendrix. "They'll remember the killing and anybody who gets their kit off – but they will not remember why."

"Francesca Annis," said Mr. Kingman. "My first love."

"My point exactly," said Hendrix. "Blood will have blood."

"Just make sure you have a nice data set for the inspectors and maybe a lesson plan for that lovely SLT virgin, Mr. Knight."

"Two bits of data for him," said Hendrix. "Fuck off."

"He doesn't know how to," said Mr. Kingman.

"Maybe we should off him," said Hendrix.

"We could be heroes," said Mr. Kingman.

"Just for one day."

"Oh," said Mr. Kingman, "I think if we got rid of Mr. Knight we would be heroes for a bit longer than that…with all due apologies to David Bowie."

"I shall be that achiever," said Hendrix. "Just for one day."

"If only," said Mr. Kingman.

"Heroes," said Hendrix. "Heroes."

Mr. Kingman sighed with the responsibility of it all.

"I'll touch base with you after your first observation,

old son."

"Power to the people," said Hendrix.

"Catch you later," said Mr. Kingman. "Be good for them…please."

"They'll catch me being God," said Hendrix.

"Please be careful what you say," said Mr. Kingman.

"Right on boss," said Hendrix.

Killer Queen

Chapter Four:
Catch Them Being Good

In the true spirit of free enterprise, teams were allowed to bid for schools they would observe. Inspectors were guns for hire in this Dark Age of educational and governmental reformation. The chosen team swarmed into the school, unsmiling and judgmental. It was as though the world of education was about to be tried at Nuremburg by those who had never fought in the war against ignorance and sloth.

Hendrix strolled off to his ceramics lesson. On the way, he was met by Mr. Knight the newly-appointed deputy head of the school. In the gospel according to Hendrix, Duncan Fucking Knight was the supreme example of a cloned incompetence, his tenure created by a petty, bureaucratic head recruiting another numbskull of a similar aptitude at a grandiose pay scale. Armed with photo-copiers and computers, they were able to generate a torrent of pointless paper work that rendered them irreplaceable and everyone else incapable. Gradually, they would take over the school, and one day, very soon, there would be nobody left to trust. Hendrix, a believer in the wisdom of crowds, knew what he hated – Senior Leadership Team virgins like the one towering over him right now. He was eye level to the virgin-wanker's chosen weapon of mass destruction.

"Nice clipboard," said Hendrix.

Mr. Knight was posh porn to Hendrix's happy hooker. A Proper Cunt who was unable to say anything nice that didn't tick a box, his default was to nit-pick. Mr. Knight recognized that Hendrix was in gross violation of the most recent, unwritten dress code. How handy that he could now put one over on this piece of educational excrescence.

"Mr. Brown?" Hendrix did not give him the eye contact he required from one so lowly. Mr. Knight went into alpha male mode and fanned himself out like a peacock.

"Mr. Brown! Could you look at me?"

"Sorry mate, turns out I'm left eyed and right-eared. I can look at you, or I can listen to you. I can't do both."

"Are you taking the proverbial?" Mr. Knight asked.

Of course he was.

"No," said Hendrix. "My left eye and right ear are dominant. I'm wired the wrong way to look and listen to you properly – or anyone else, so don't feel bad about it."

"What?"

"I can't multi-task," said Hendrix.

Hendrix continued to look away, amused at the partial truth he had unleashed. Continuing Professional Development (CPD) in the wrong hands was a dangerous tool, especially if there was an angry fat bastard near your submissive left ear.

"You're pulling my leg," said Mr. Knight.

"Right or left?"

"Answer the question."

"Is this a question on directed time?" Hendrix asked.

"You need to show some respect," said Mr. Knight.

"You need to earn it." Hendrix the rocking potter was on a roll.

"Why don't you at least look this way?" Mr. Knight asked.

"I can't. It was that course you sent me on about how we learn," he said. "Very informative it was too. Turns out I have a sort of learning disability - handicapping me monster IQ and positive work ethic."

Scuppered on that one, Mr. Knight returned to his original gripe. Faced with a circus riot, he went for the jugular.

"Mr. Brown, are you wearing a tie?" Mr. Knight asked, in the near certainty he was not.

"Why?" Hendrix asked. "Will it make me a better teacher?"

"Head-teacher's dress code," said Mr. Knight. That was his current favourite line.

"Never seen her wear a tie," said Hendrix.

"Don't be stupid," said Mr. Knight. Hendrix looked at him blankly.

"Sorry," he said. "I can't hear you."

"Are you wearing a tie?" Mr. Knight repeated his question a little louder.

"Watch and learn," said Hendrix.

He was wearing a turtle neck which covered some bites from a previous misadventure. He pulled down the jumper. There was a tie around his neck. On the tie was a cartoon character with a knife in his head. The words beneath the character said: -*Oh no, they killed Kenny*-

"What's that?" asked Mr. Knight.

"*South Park*," said Hendrix.

"What's happened?"

"They just killed Kenny."

"Who?"

"Kenny – he dies every week. You should watch it."

"Why?"

"It's what the kids watch – know your enemy."

Mr. Knight was pure *Statto*; he had no idea.

"Keep it covered, Mr. Brown," said Mr. Knight. "Wear it – but keep it covered."

"Always do," said Hendrix. "Never show cleavage on a school day."

Mr. Knight looked with professional despair at the Afghan coat; it was practically alive. It was probably more sentient than the homunculus that was wearing it.

"You could wear your academic gown," he said.

The words formed in his head and were unsaid: *You could give me a hand shandy, you sad wanking excuse of a human being.*

Hendrix chuckled.

"I'm like an art teacher, Man," he said. "I'm a hippie, not a bleedin' drama queen."

He was more like Mr. Benn, thought Knight. Yesterday he was a hippie outlaw – tomorrow he'll be an outlaw potter. Knight had his own Mr. Benn moment; one day he'd be an outlaw woodwork teacher and nail that bastard's balls to the wall.

Knight knew it was check, not checkmate. *Man!* Remember the words – not the tune. Who called themselves a hippie? For Mr. Knight, Mr. Jim 'Hendrix' Brown was a hippie art teacher in about the same way that Charles 'Beach Boy' Manson was a hippie rock star. He scowled and walked the other way, shouting at kids for uniform infringements and general malingering. Life was good with a clipboard and a checklist.

Hendrix walked on past the entrance with the words he never read about the school he taught in and the town he lived in:

'Kingswater derives its name from the legend of the sword of the local king that was cast into the lake after his death in battle. One day, when the world needs a new king, the

sword will be theirs.'

The school badge was a hand, emerging from water, bearing a sword.

'Know the past to plan the future.'

Two world wars and many minor skirmishes were not enough for that to happen, nor was the recent merger with its sworn enemy, Jubilee High – an event in which everybody except the transition team had come away from feeling short changed.

The main school building was a sixties red-brick affair, augmented with more austere clapboard huts abandoned in the early eighties. During the seventies, the Art department had put up seasonal murals that livened up the dull external walls. The work to rule of the mid-eighties had put an end to that – and Hendrix could not bring himself to revive a tradition that wasted valuable dream time.

Along the walls of the entrance hall were the portraits of former head-teachers that Hendrix also never bothered to look at. And the present one that he never bothered to talk to – Ms. Bishop. What with a Knight and a Bishop, his life was turning into a chess board – he was nearly fifty and too old to play games that ended in anything other than carnal pleasure.

He arrived at his classroom. Several year eight pupils were bouncing off each other, waiting for their lesson to start – it would be wanking with wooly mittens. The great un-laid. There was also somebody they did not know. All animals were different – some animals were more different than others. Such was the item before him. It was middle-aged and rounded. It seemed to have very little hair. It had a clipboard and a look of anxiety. It was also, possibly, un-laid.

"Good morning, Mr. Brown," said the man behind the clipboard.

"You have me at a disadvantage," said Hendrix.

"Mr. Castle," he said, by way of introduction.

"Who or what are you?" Hendrix asked. The man appeared to inflate slightly.

"An Ofsted inspector," he said. One of the achievers he had been warned about.

"You're kidding," said Hendrix, standing in front of his door. "Please don't tell me you're first name's Roy."

"Never heard that one before," said Mr. Castle.

"I'll bet."

"May I come in?" asked Mr. Castle.

"Is it a question?" asked Hendrix.

"No," said Mr. Castle.

"Then I suppose you must." Pretending to take it all in, he followed Hendrix into the room.

"Where can I sit?" Mr. Castle asked.

"Keep away from the kiln...and maybe some of the kids," said Hendrix. Mr. Castle frowned. This was not the welcome he'd wanted. He looked on Hendrix with the contempt he clearly merited. If his Ofsted stood for anything, it was skimming scum like him from the profession. He would sit where he liked, thank you very much, you shuffling sixties cliché.

Hendrix watched with a mixture of amusement, dismay and alarm, as Mr. Castle placed himself next to his most autistic child, Ant. The nickname of this particular boy was *'Protest.'* Clearly this man trying to sit next to Ant was also left-eyed and right-eared.

"I don't think you should sit there," said Hendrix.

"What?"

"It was just a suggestion, mate," said Hendrix. "Please yourself." Mr. Castle did not care for the man's attitude. His disrespect seemed to have coalesced too much into contempt for his liking.

"Why?" asked Mr. Castle. "Is anyone else going to sit here?"

Taking a lesson from Knight, Hendrix went light on the detail and description of the probable consequences for this prick who was getting on his wick.

"No," said Hendrix.

"Then I don't see what could possibly go wrong," said Mr. Castle.

"Your call," said Hendrix. "You have been warned."

"And I don't like being called *mate*," said the inspector.

"Check," said Hendrix.

"You're making a joke of this?" The man's irritation grew.

"Whatever," said Hendrix. "But you have been warned - again." This was going too far for the inspector; a line had definitely been crossed by this hairy loser.

"That's the second time you've said that to me."

"Everybody deserves a second chance," said Hendrix.

The inspector was not amused to be told how it was; first the banter and now the downright disrespect. Let the battle commence; he would mark this bad boy down when the time came.

"I think you have said enough, Mr. Brown," said Mr. Castle. The inspector made his chosen move; Castle to Knight's pawn – definitely a rookie error.

There was a hush of expectation; only the pupils and their teacher understood what might happen next; this was going to be one of those occasionally interesting lessons. They watched and waited for the stress fest they knew was about to happen.

Ant was very big for a year eight, but unable to self-regulate his emotional levels. It had taken a half term to get him to enter the teaching room. The list of dangers in the room was so long, he had been scared to go in. *Don't touch the kiln – it will burn you. Don't eat the clay – it will poison you. Don't get paint on your fingers – it might be yellow. Don't. Don't. Don't cry for me, Argentina.*

With *stranger danger* in the room, Ant was already starting to rock backwards and forwards on his chair. Once the inspector started towards him, Ant started humming out the first line of the song to himself. It made no sense to the uninitiated. Ant was somebody who knew the words, not the tune. The music teacher had described it as *crescendoing...* remember, he told Hendrix, you never reach a crescendo - it is just mounting sound. Hendrix was fairly sure that Ant, did in fact, reach crescendos...and was about to do so right now.

"Don't cry for me, ARGENTINA."

Hendrix wasn't sure if this was the Madonna version – but it was a sign of something about to happen.

Mr. Castle looked at his checklist. A class full of distracted children. That ticked the box for poor start to a lesson. Students were *not* given a clear, crisp start to the lesson.

Oblivious to the stress he was creating for another person besides the teacher, Mr. Castle settled in next to Ant who relieved his anxiety in the usual fashion. There was a flurry of punches, followed by Ant explaining his classroom expectations to Mr. Castle.

"You don't sit next to me! You don't sit next to me! You don't sit next to me!"

Hendrix looked at the chaos, defo Julie Covington's.

"I think you'd better leave," said Hendrix.

"Yes," said Mr. Castle, trying to pull himself together. "Get him out of here."

Ant continued to make his point verbally.

"I've got two words to say you. Leave me alone."

"That's three words," said Mr. Castle.

We have, thought Hendrix, a pedantic idiot in our work space.

Ant provided Mr. Castle with the two words he'd been looking for.

"FUCK OFF!"

Hendrix re-intervened. He pointed at the inspector.

"*You* need to leave, mate," said Hendrix, finally finding his teacher voice.

The inspector was not to be moved.

"I think he knows better," said Mr. Castle.

"You need to do one," said Hendrix.

"What?" The man did not get his banter.

"Didn't you read the sign over the door?" Hendrix asked. "This is a school for children who should know better."

"Don't tell me what to do," said Mr. Castle.

"I don't think you understand," said Hendrix. "You need to get out of here, you fucking fruit loop."

There was a hush from the class. Even Ant was moved to silence. Hendrix had called the man a fruit loop! A fucking fruit loop! He was already a legend. What could possibly go wrong had gone wrong. What box had this un-ticked? What could he possibly become now?

Hendrix waited and the class watched as Mr. Castle

and his clipboard dragged himself out of the classroom and into anonymity.

"Goodbye," said Hendrix.

The class cheered him on with a chorus of *'There's only one Jimi Hendrix'*. He bowed to his class.

"Thank you," he said. "Now back on your heads."

At the end of the lesson, as they were packing up, one of the pupils had a question for the teacher.

"Sir?"

"Yeah," said Hendrix.

"What does that mean?"

"What?" Hendrix asked.

"Back on your heads?"

"If I told you," said Hendrix, "I'd have to kill you."

"You really mean that?"

"Of course not," said Hendrix.

"That's a relief, Mr. Hendrix, sir." Hendrix knew he shouldn't – but out came the words anyway. It had been that sort of a day.

"That all depends on your point of view," said Hendrix.

"What?"

"I'd have to kill all of you."

A hand went up.

"Mr. Hendrix, sir…you told us last week."

Hendrix pretended to look confused.

"And nobody died?"

"No."

Killer Queen

Chapter Five:
Of Doers and Achievers

It was confession time. Hendrix plonked himself in Mr. Kingman's office. In the middle of fiddling his records of achievement, Mr. Kingman looked up.

"Can I help you, young man?"

"Yeah," said Hendrix. "I think I have done a silly thing."

Mr. Kingman put down his fraudulent masterpiece.

"You do surprise me," he said. "Have you killed Mr. Knight?" Hendrix looked up at the ceiling.

"No. Not yet," he said.

"Pity," said Mr. Kingman. "I could have got you off that one."

"I had an inspector in my lesson and he sat next to Ant." Hendrix explained his crime. There was no need for any more context. Nobody sat next to Ant and left the room unscathed.

"You did warn him?"

"Twice," said Hendrix, "at least twice."

"I think then that's a case of buyer beware," said Mr. Kingman, leaning back in his chair. Hendrix took a deep breath and let it go.

"I also called him a fucking fruit loop." Mr. Kingman put his hands behind his head.

"That complicates matters slightly, old son."

Hendrix looked at the back of his hands.

"Yeah."

Mr. Kingman jumped up.

"No matter, we are going to sort this one. On holiday, I saw a translation for a bowl of fruit loops as a *cereal crop circle*. You are going to say sorry about the fucking fruit loop business and say that you should have called him a cereal crop circle."

"Okay," said Hendrix.

"Do you have any evidence of the lesson?" Mr. Kingman asked.

"Other than my own personal recollection?"

Mr. Kingman pointed a finger at Hendrix.

"You are one of the doers in this life, they will never believe you."

"What the fuck are you saying?" Hendrix asked.

"I was on a course about the difference between doers and achievers. It's a bit like Chiefs and Indians made over for the digital age," said Mr. Kingman.

"How does that affect me?"

"You are a doer and thusly valuable and expendable in the eyes of an achiever."

Hendrix continued to be baffled by the bullshit Mr. Kingman was alluding to. Doers and achievers? He knew it was wrong. He knew that Bishop and Knight were achievers – and that he was not.

"Where did you get this stuff?" Hendrix asked.

"The wonderful world of continuous professional development," said Mr. Kingman. "When I heard that, I was ashamed of myself for coming so far. I want to be remembered as a doer."

"Let's do Knight," said Hendrix.

Mr. Kingman raised his hand.

"I have a feeling he's going to try and do you for this… we need evidence…"

Hendrix wracked his brains for something more useful than tasteful erotica. Then he remembered the crusade against the battery thieves of Kingswater. It was an idea he tried to get Rocket interested in making a documentary on as part of his year 11 media studies. Rocket, the undisputed evil genius of year 11 had said thank you, but he already had a project filming paint dry.

"There is that video camera in my room…"

Mr. Kingman clapped his hands.

"Does it work?"

"Fuck knows," said Hendrix.

Clearly excited, Mr. Kingman made for the door.

"Well man! Let's find out!"

As they walked to the art department, Mr. Kingman remembered why he had become a teacher, because of the value his self-educated father placed on the profession. He could hear his old man's voice reading him *Animal Farm*. That line of *'four legs good but two legs better'* came back to him. The school pigs had taken over the farm; if he wasn't careful he would be seen as one of them. Hendrix held the key to his redemption. How would his father feel if he knew his boy had taken all that education and then lined up with the pigs?

Had his father and all his mates gone to war with Hitler in order for people like Duncan Knight to patrol this school with a clipboard and an air of entitlement? He knew what the right answer was; fascism came in many disguises. In his own backyard, there were people using data to control and degrade other human beings, and for what purpose? For not being as canny with information as they were, and for putting people before pieces of paper.

He'd come into the educational profession to help the people like his father; the smart ones who never had access to the education that levelled the playing field. And now the bean counters and number crunchers were getting in the way of the prime process, with teachers too busy being accountable to actually teach anything worth knowing. Hendrix taught them something and Knight would have his nuts for just being a bit different from the herd – and that was just what he saw for himself. This was a battle that had chosen him; this was a fight for the heart and soul of the school.

The two teachers, both alike in decency, looked at the VHS cassette before putting it into the maw of the machine.

"Fingers crossed that this has something good on it," said Mr. Kingman.

"Yeah," said Hendrix.

Together they watched a pin sharp recording of the observed lesson. There were two warnings from Hendrix and at least one from Ant himself – all ignored by the idiot with the clipboard.

"I think we have what we need," said Mr. Kingman.

Hendrix had a question.

"Why have you gone to all this trouble to help me?"

Mr. Kingman stopped and looked at him as directly as Hendrix could ever remember.

"Because you are a good teacher – and they've never been good teachers...none of them."

"Do you think you could help Paul McSmart?" Hendrix asked.

Mr. Kingman tried to place him.

"Economics teacher – drools a lot when the head of history comes to work?"

"Yeah."

"It's Candy Regent that really bothers me," said Mr. Kingman. "I can't see how she gets to be where she is in the school with no experience of anything at all, zilch. Troubling."

Hendrix agreed.

"Not here for the mornings," he said, "not here for the afternoons, nobody can remember being taught by her…apart from that she works full time."

The old man had his suspicions.

"It wouldn't surprise me if she was a double agent; she is definitely not one of us."

"Who would do that?" Hendrix asked.

"People in education without lessons to plan and work to mark," said Mr. Kingman. "They find other ways to fill their time, plotting changes that nobody needs or wants; in the seventies, the dictum was to stop teaching punctuation and grammar, next they abolished history, now it's all about accountability and value added. I think our bewitching Candy is part of that process, and for some reason I don't quite understand, she has annoyed Mr. Knight in a very profound way."

"I think she'll be safe," said Hendrix. "But Paul Mac also seems to have incurred the displeasure of Mr. Knight."

"I would have said that makes him one of us," said Mr. Kingman.

"I think Knight really does have it in for him," said Hendrix, "he's not the worst teacher we have in this school."

"You observing lessons these days?"

"I keep my eyes open," said Hendrix. "I hear what kids say."

"And what do they say?"

"Mr. Knight is our worst teacher. He hates kids. He hates lessons. He hates teachers."

Mr. Kingman nodded in agreement – Mr. Knight had the full triad of impairments for being a successful classroom practioner.

"But our Mr. McSmart…not the most likable of chaps, is he?" Hendrix laughed.

"He is so unlikable," he said, "until you scratch beneath the surface and discover that beneath the autistic mask, he is completely and perfectly insufferable. He's so unlikable that he actually becomes likeable."

"You're not selling him to me," said Mr. Kingman.

"What's that line from Nazi Germany? First they came for the hippies – but I did not protest because I was not a hippie…"

"It was the trade unionists," said Mr. Kingman.

"Point taken," said Hendrix, "but they don't care much about trade unionists either. I think the last head of history was the union rep and fuck knows what happened to him."

Hendrix had made his point.

"Gagging order," said Mr. Kingman. "Mediated resignation without prejudice and a backhander to send him on his way to who knows where."

"How convenient," said Hendrix.

"Please don't tell me you have another catchphrase," said Mr. Kingman.

"One is more than enough," said Hendrix.

"Two will put you on a support plan," said Mr. Kingman.

"I think that's what Bishop and Knight are planning for

Paul," said Hendrix.

"You may be right," said Mr. Kingman. "They mostly leave me out of the loop these days on account of my negative wealth of teaching experience and expertise."

Discrimination by experience for the over fifties was a no-brainer. To fight that was to be like King Cnut holding back the tide; with a Cnut or two of his own to deal with, Hendrix focused back to something he could still change in his working lifetime. There were just too many Kings and not enough working stiffs; stopping them from getting to Paul and anybody else of comparable vulnerability was going to be a full-time calling.

"Smartie," he said, "is my go-to guy for understanding how the least-liked child in any class feels."

Mr. Kingman nodded. He believed we should be judged on how we look after our poorest and lowest...not our highest and richest.

"I'll take your word for that," he said. "I am quite busy just looking after you just at the moment – but if he does something really good for the school, like kill Duncan Knight...or find out who has been stealing my petty cash, then let me know."

"I know who has been stealing your petty cash," said Hendrix.

"I know too," said Mr. Kingman. "I just can't catch him being bad."

"Okay," said Hendrix. "Trust me. I will tell you when he kills Mr. Knight and solves your cash flow problem."

"Trust and petty cash," said Mr. Kingman. "That's all we have."

"Yeah," said Hendrix. "I believe that petty cash is one of Mr. Knight's core values."

"See you in the meeting," said Mr. Kingman.

"Meeting?"

"Ms. Bishop has already asked the Senior Leadership Team to be there on the occasion of your public humiliation and possible lynching."

"When is it?" Hendrix asked.

"Now."

"Why wasn't I told?"

"I'm telling you now," said Mr. Kingman. "Just think – a surprise meeting with no given agenda and we are going to provide both the surprise and the agenda."

"I wished I'd baked a cake we could jump out of," said Hendrix.

"Make it a pasty," said Mr. Kingman.

Hendrix laughed – but he knew this was one of those moments when the game changed.

The words of *All along the Watchtower* played in his head. It could be Jimi or Bobby and they could be jokers or thieves…or maybe the two riders approaching.

"Let's do it," said Hendrix.

"Yes, let's," said Mr. Kingman. "Let's make those pigs walk on all four legs for a change."

Hendrix frowned.

"Is that more CPD for achievers?"

"Something like," said Mr. Kingman. "Keeping with an animal theme, we have here what I like to call the elephant of surprise."

Chapter Six:
Believe in Bitter

The head-teacher's office was filled to over-flowing with inspectors and senior staff, many of them hoping to see Hendrix lynched. Hendrix himself was a model of psychopathic calm; he knew he'd done the right thing at the right time – and the elephant of surprise had changed sides. That was all that mattered to him. His current problem was that nobody else in the room was quite as Zen.

Looking at her notes, Ms. Bishop started off the proceedings. The agenda was short; ending in what she hoped was a mediated resignation of Mr. Brown, hopefully by the end of the autumn term.

"Mr. Brown," she said, "would you care to explain yourself with regard to today's observed lesson which has been marked as a failure on every point?"

Ms. Bishop (bitch) fell into Hendrix's *'only shag on a slow day maybe'* category. That he never did and never would was neither here, nor there. All days without a shag were slow days. Hendrix, vaguely irritated by the circus, was sat in front of three random achievers he didn't know, two dodgy achievers he didn't trust – and his trump card, Mr. Kingman.

"I know I shouldn't have bitten the head off that live chicken in my lesson," said Hendrix.

"I think," said Mr. Kingman, "that you need to take this meeting a bit more seriously."

Hendrix started again.

"A man walked into my room and sat next to Ant."

There was a silence, broken by Mr. Kingman who understood the context of the statement.

"Didn't you try and stop him?"

Hendrix, not showing the correct body language, laced his boney fingers around the back of his head and leaned back into his chair in an effort to maximize the distance between him and them.

"I did," said Hendrix. "I suggested that he sat elsewhere."

"And what was Mr. Castle's response?" asked Mr. Kingman.

"He didn't do that," said Hendrix.

"What did he do?" asked Mr. Kingman.

Whatdidhedo? That sounded, to Hendrix, like a song for Fred Flintstone – but he knew the jokes would have to wait a while. He supplied the answer of an achiever.

"He ignored my advice and sat next to Ant. Nobody in their right mind sits next to Ant."

"You let him?" Mr. Knight asked.

"I couldn't stop him," said Hendrix.

"Protest-Ant?" asked Mr. Kingman, a little too theatrically. "Oh dear, oh dear, the man had no idea."

"There was no risk assessment on the lesson plan," said Mr. Knight.

Mr. Kingman looked at Hendrix.

"You wrote a lesson plan, Mr. Brown?"

Hendrix shrugged his shoulders. These words formed in his head, but were denied exit via his mouth: *written twenty minutes ago – along with my mark book.*

Mr. Kingman continued.

"Surely, Mr. Knight, we should have a whole school risk assessment for that young man. What do you think?"

With no clear answer that would exonerate himself, Mr. Knight, the deputy head, ignored the question, pushed his glasses deeper into the folds of his brow and carried on with his interrogation.

"And the swearing, Mr. Brown? I believe you called Mr. Castle…"

"I believe it was the brand name of a breakfast cereal, your honour," said Hendrix in his best mockney.

Mr. Knight looked down at his notes.

"I think you called him," said Mr. Knight, "a *fucking fruit loop?*"

There was a suppressed snigger from one of the people Hendrix did not know. Clearly no two inspectors were completely alike – rather like snowflakes in that respect, or anything in life other than identical twins.

"It was a stressful moment," said Hendrix. "The inspector had failed to recognize the serious personal danger he was in – and a bit of Anglo-Saxon slipped out."

"If you could have that moment over again," said Mr. Knight, "would you have done things any differently?"

In his head a further torrent of four letter words were fighting to be heard in the great outdoors. Instead his mouth and brain working as a team allowed Hendrix to say the following words.

"I might have just called him a cereal crop circle."

"Perhaps that would have been better," said Mr. Kingman.

"Or maybe," said Mr. Knight, "just ask him, politely, to leave the room."

There were collective mutterings of agreement from the inspectors.

"I guess," said Hendrix.

Vaguely miffed at this new collaborative description of Mr. Castle not being recognised for the wit it was, Hendrix would not get hung by his grundies on this occasion.

However, Mr. Knight did not want Hendrix off the hook just yet.

"Your lesson was still judged unsatisfactory by Mr. Castle…"

"In his absence," said Mr. Kingman.

Like a university challenge quizmaster, Mr. Knight tried ignoring the interruption.

"Could you tell us how the lesson progressed?"

Hendrix looked at Knight with a certain amount of suppressed pleasure.

"Very well," said Hendrix. "Very well, indeed."

The scientist in Mr. Knight was annoyed by the subjective emphasis.

"It was judged a failure, Mr. Brown," said Mr. Knight.

"Not by me," said Hendrix. "I was there."

"Do you," he enquired, "have any *real* evidence of that success you are now claiming?"

"Other than my own memory and professional judgement?"

Mr. Knight paused and tried not to smirk.

"Yes. Other than your own memory and professional judgement."

Mr. Kingman spoke again. This was the pincer movement he and Hendrix had secretly worked on – never daring to hope they could employ it so successfully in such a setting.

"Remember that spate of battery thefts, Mr. Knight?"

Knight was thrown by the second change in direction. The smirk crawled back into the folds of his face and died.

"What?"

Enjoying himself a bit too much, Mr. Kingman continued.

"Surely you remember? The battery in all the school clocks was the same size as the battery in a *Walkman*. Bit of a strategic error really."

"How handy," said Hendrix.

"Watch what you say in here," said Ms. Bishop. Then there was a pause as Mr. Kingman gathered himself for the killer blow.

"Ms. Bishop. Who oversaw the purchase of the new radio controlled clocks last academic year?"

The silence was eloquence.

There was nowhere to hide and no-one to blame.

Hendrix and Mr. Kingman watched the blood drain out of Mr. Knight's shiny, red face. Catching the battery thieves of Kingswater was his initiative that term – a considerable budget had been self-allocated for just that singular policy.

Hendrix continued the narrative.

"I finally figured out how to set the video camera yesterday. I set it up for the break, but in the fracas, I forgot to turn it off."

Mr. Kingman got a video cassette out of his bag.

"Ms. Bishop, do you have access to a video recorder?"

Of course she did.

"I'm not sure," she said."

"How handy that I have one in my office," said Mr. Kingman. "Of course, it'll be a bit of a squeeze…"

"I think I can find one," said Ms. Bishop.

Of course she could.

Because he was so handy, Mr. Knight was given the task of setting up the VCR. He did so with the sense of a man colluding in his own doom – this was designed to catch Hendrix out, not exonerate him. And here he was, being observed by the great and the good, as he dug the shallow grave of his own ambition. This proved a point to himself; Hendrix was clearly no hippie - hippies were not supposed to have any corporate survival skills. Hendrix was more like those bastards from Ben and Jerry's ice cream, or Richard Branson; hollow corporate bastards wearing the garments of hippies.

"It's lucky that I couldn't aim it at the clock," said Hendrix, as they were able to see a pin sharp vista of the teaching space.

Mr. Knight groaned inwardly; the man was resistant to instruction of any sort.

The assembled doers and achievers were able to watch Ant's reaction to being sat next to. Then they focused on the lesson delivered afterwards. Every child was involved in the process of making a pot. Some were working clay, some were firing the kiln and some were painting the results of their efforts. It was definitely an occasionally interesting lesson. Mr. Kingman paused the tape just before Hendrix threatened to kill one of his pupils for asking a question at the end of the lesson.

"I didn't see any use of target setting," said Mr. Knight' "or lesson objectives and possible outcomes."

Too little too late. Ms. Bishop gave him the look that

most of the women in his life gave him. The relationship had never been very healthy; now it was well and truly flat-lined.

The leader of the inspection team looked at Ms. Bishop.

"Looks like a blinder," he said. "Sorry about my colleague."

"Is that a technical term?" Mr. Kingman asked.

"It was a very good lesson," said the chief inspector.

Hendrix smiled at the whores of the management. It was better than good.

"Not everyone has what it takes," he said.

"Too true," said Mr. Knight.

Hendrix cut through the toadying. He had decided his boss had taken the trouble to make herself look attractive to him – for reasons he could not understand.

"By the way, that's a nice scarf you're wearing. Is it part of the dress code enforced by Mr. Knight?"

What he had managed not to say was it *'both shows off and conceals your cleavage'*.

In the middle of the most confrontational meeting of his career, Hendrix was still a man who could find the rainbow in an oil-slick.

"Thank you," said Ms. Bishop.

She blushed momentarily; then she got back on her high horse.

"I choose what I wear to school, not Mr. Knight."

Hendrix smiled.

This provoked Ms. Bishop to give him another piece of

unwanted conversation – a short tour of what was important to an ambitious person living an empty life.

"Do you know what we provide here, Mr. Brown?"

He had no idea – but having recently suppressed so much, he was up for making a suggestion in the style of himself.

"Palliative care for those who still believe life is worth clinging to?"

"Hope, Mr. Brown. Hope of a chance for a better world."

It sounded as sincere as a politician's promise.

The tiny chip inside Mr. Knight's head that sometimes functioned as a conscience remembered her saying different in private – *I want for my pupils to live without imagination, hope or ambition – to risk nothing is the key to a life contained. In Kingswater, anyway.* Even his values, he decided, were superior to hers.

Hendrix allowed the rhetoric to wash over him; if fucking Carlsberg sold you a singing crock of shit, it would probably sound like that.

"Thank you," he said. "I will try to work towards a better world."

Listen to me, Hendrix thought, I sound like Bobby Kennedy in '68 – a better world indeed. The better world Bobby wanted shot him in the fucking head in a hotel kitchen. Trust no one - that was the real message of the sixties – death lurked in the shadows of men's minds.

"Remember to stay positive, Mr. Brown," said Ms. Bishop.

Hendrix looked at the would-be assassins surrounding him. He never lost control; he was the man who sold the world. He gave them a gritted teeth Kurt Cobain style smile straight out of *MTV Unplugged in New York*.

"Must I?"

Like the abusers they were, they smiled back at him – face to face.

"Of course you must," said Ms. Bishop.

Hendrix was done with the homilies – he was not for them, he was against them. They shared the same time and space – but that was it.

"Can I leave now?" Hendrix asked. "I have some lessons to prepare."

"You won't be observed again," said the lead inspector.

"That's not why I do it," said Hendrix. "I do it for the kids."

Ms. Bishop looked down her nose at him; he was not one of us. He was one of them.

"You may leave," said Ms. Bishop.

Chapter Seven:
The Damagement

Where Ofsted gave, it also took away. It was a law as immutable as gravity and as unyielding as concrete.

The next day, Mr. Paul McSmart was pulled, by that downward force, into Ms. Bishop's spick and span office.

With the pressure between his shoulders still building, he tried to think what he could do next. He could run away. He would come back years later and meet his children as adults. They would be just like him right now - grown up and angry with their dad. Death was a better option, all things considered. His mind took him time travelling. At twenty-two, all he could think about was getting laid – and maybe doing something useful with his life. He smoothed back his going-grey hair – thankfully it was still there. Different parts of him ached. The stress was there in the background – insistent and invisible like the hiss of a bad quality 70's cassette tape. He could see his father in the mirror – all he needed were the trendy sideburns on his cheek bones. He was thirty-nine and what had he done? Dr. King was dead in Memphis at the same age. Mozart had been four years worm's meat. Dylan had written *Blood on the Tracks*. He wasn't asking for symphonies or sympathy. He didn't know what he was asking for. A moment of connection maybe. Transcendence. Peace of mind. Redemption. Only last week, a fellow runner had died. He'd read the obituary in *Athletics Weekly*. Twenty or more years of not really knowing somebody; a couple of sentences every few months – before and after a race. Never even shared a drink. Now he was gone. Had he been married? Did he have children? Paul had no clue. We had all gone to university. We were the chosen. We were never meant to get this old without getting any wiser.

Ms. Bishop watched him stumble into her office. Some kids thought he looked like Brett Anderson or Pete Murphy, to her he looked like a cartoon of a man caught in some headlights invisible to the rest of the world.

"Good morning. Take a seat, Mr. McSmart."

He caught her sideways on; a flat-chested milk monitor given too much power by her teachers. Also there was nothing good about this particular morning as far as he could tell.

Paul tapped the back of a nearby chair.

"This one?"

Yes. One that nobody is sitting on. That would do.

Paul looked around the room. New broom. Clean. Concise. Cold. On one blue wall was a map of the world and on the other the current values of the school in foot high letters. That was the decoration in this particular torture chamber; it reminded him of the geriatric ward in the hospital where he worked during his university holidays – all the patients were strung out on morphine waiting for the end, and quite unable to see the inspirational writing on the wall. Why did people with no values talk so much crap about values? It was not like you could be in favour of anything other than the values of truth and honesty, so why did you have to pretend you've just invented them as an antidote to lies and dishonesty? In some of the more primary classrooms the words hung from the ceilings and spun in the hot air; those were the text rich teaching spaces that gave him a headache. Then he tried to focus on the purveyors of the truly twisted values who he now guessed were out to get him.

Perched to the left of Ms. Bishop's desk, Paul clocked Mr. Knight – very handy and so far up her kazoo that he needed rectal goggles to maintain his ocular health. What right did he have to judge anybody? As Hendrix said, Knight was a failed teacher looking to recruit others into his less than exclusive club.

Enjoying the fact that he could not see the writing on the wall, Ms. Bishop sat down behind her desk. With a safe barrier between her and her intended victim, she began the meeting.

"I am very concerned by your performance in your observed lesson. When looked at with your examination results, it shows you have a long way to go if you are going to show significant progress..."

Having temporarily resuscitated his working relationship with Ms. Bishop, Mr. Knight was permitted to wield the axe of challenge and inspire. He got straight to the fun business of butchering his colleague.

"According to the residual scores, at least half the cohort under-performed."

"And the other half?" Paul asked.

Mr. Knight glanced at his chinless book of records.

"Some performed to expectation and some over-performed – most likely as a result of poor target setting."

"How handy," said Paul. Using Knight's own catch-phrase was never going to be the most sensible option – but parked here in the head's office it just leapt out of his mouth.

"As a result," said Ms. Bishop, "following a consultation process we will be putting you on a support plan."

"When did you consult me?" Paul asked.

"We consulted each other," said Ms. Bishop, nodding in the direction of Knight.

"So my opinion is not important?" Paul asked.

"Correct," said Mr. Knight, "the decision was based on specific, measurable, objective criteria. That's all you need to know."

How handy. Paul, a little more than crushed, tried to gather himself. His heart began to race and his cheeks flushed. He did not actually know what a support plan was. It sounded alright – but he knew it could not be since he was being put on it.

"Should I inform my union?"

"If you think it might help," said Ms. Bishop. "But to do so would make any future process adversarial." Paul was beginning to understand that one thing this support plan would not be doing was to support him.

"Better to give in now?"

"I think you should trust us," she said.

"What?"

"Don't let your issues intrude in the process," she said.

"My issues?"

Ms. Bishop sensed weakness and confusion squirming in front of her.

"Do you have any strong opinions about anything?"

He went to his default position of alienating sarcasm.

"I don't think," Paul said, "that breast-stroke, back-stroke and butterfly should be Olympic events – unless you add backwards running to the track and field catalogue."

"I hope you think these things on your own time, Mr. McSmart."

He'd been truly delivered of a blasphemy in disguise.

"I shall be your mentor," said Mr. Knight.

"Is that like a tormentor?" Paul asked, not able to give a flying fuck about anything.

"No," said Mr. Knight. That was untrue, the fat bastard had just appointed himself judge, jury and executioner.

"You may go," said Ms. Bishop. "We will schedule a meeting for after the inspection – try to remain positive and upbeat."

The door shut.

Paul remembered the title of a poem he seemed to think might have been funny.

"Good-bat night-man."

Using muscle memory, he walked to the staffroom. At least he thought it was where he walked. Wherever it was, he bumped into Hendrix.

"Everything cool?"

"No," said Paul. "Just been read my fortune by the leadership. And I think she hinted that I was a misogynist."

"She's all silk scarf and no knickers. What did she say?"

Hendrix offered a mental picture Paul liked – but somebody else was wearing the scarf in his fantasy.

"She told me not to let my issues get in the way."

"Issues?"

Paul paused.

"With the opposite sex – I guess."

"Mate," said Hendrix, "you don't have *women* issues – you have *people* issues. People make you anxious."

"What?"

"You're as fearful of parking on a double yellow as killing someone in your car. You can't get over somebody being cruel, or kind, to you. It's what I like about you…"

"Huh?"

"You make *me* feel sane," said Hendrix.

"And these people?" Paul pointed up to the lofty heights of senior management.

"Bunch of control freaks," said Hendrix.

"They said my residuals were down."

"Which meant?"

"I dunno."

"What we need," said Hendrix, "is a polaroid of them and a goat. With Knight giving it a hand shandy."

"Goats have standards," said Paul. "It would try to run away."

"Then tether it."

"That would be cruel," said Paul.

"Doesn't have to be a live one."

"A dead goat?" Paul asked. "A picture of Knight tossing off a dead goat?"

"It doesn't even have to be a goat," said Hendrix.

"I dunno," said Paul, "it sounds like a load of hassle."

"Do unto others before they do unto you."

With his coat sweeping all before him, Hendrix wandered off to make a coffee. Paul watched him move amongst his people. Hendrix, who had told an inspector that he was a *'fucking fruit loop'*. Only a legend could do that. Or a bloke with the right photograph.

Next his mind went to another place. His vision of Elektra - Candy Regent – was that her name? Silk scarf and no knickers – he thought of her - again. He was on top of her or she was on top of him – everything moved in and out with a purpose and was a means to an end. It reminded him of that brief time in his life when he believed sex was easy and consequence free; then he became a father and a husband.

Chapter Eight:
Get Smarty

Half a day later, Paul found himself back at his pigeon hole facing down a dead brown envelope. The missive lay there on top of a pile of junk mail advertising school journeys he would never go on. Before opening it, he gobbled down a couple of paracetamol laced with caffeine.

"Whassup?" asked Hendrix.

"This," said Paul.

He opened it up and started to read.

"Students were not given a clear indication what the lesson was about. The lesson lacked pace and differentiation."

"Apart from that, it was fine," said Hendrix.

"Something about residuals and cohorts," said Paul.

"Sounds like fluent fucking Klingon to me," said Hendrix. "And who has the time and inclination to learn that? Just sad fuckers in *Star Trek* outfits hoping Uhura will give 'em a hand shandy."

"This is a distortion of the facts," said Paul.

"That's the point," said Hendrix. "Any fucker can tell the truth – look at me. You gotta be trained to lie that good."

"There's no evidence for anything," said Paul.

If he had a real mentor, that person would have said he was naïve to think there would be any evidence of anything. Hendrix was the closest person he had to a mentor – and he was not in that line of work.

"It's written by a man who aspires to be an inspector – part of the self-promoting elite who think they know something when they clearly fucking don't. Decency ain't in the spec, probably grounds for dismissal. Have your clipboard broken in two in front of your friends – if you got any. You knew they were conniving bastards before they slithered into your classroom."

"So no big deal?"

"You need to remember that they are inadequate and incompetent. That's why they ran as fast as they could out of any classroom they've ever been put into to actually teach. They don't learn and they don't care. But if there's one talent they have in spades, it's the ability to de-skill others."

"But why?"

"Poor as you are, mate, you cost too much."

"That's it?"

"You're the economist. Find me a better reason."

It was one thing to teach the theory of perfect competition – quite another to be a victim of it. But it was true, governments since before he became a teacher had viewed the public provision of education as something that could be cut when things got tough. That was something he taught as well – only Keynesian theories said you cut spending when the economy was overheating and not when it was in recession.

"Isn't there another reason?"

Paul wanted him to say something re-assuring like they resented competent teachers and bullied them out of envy. Like they were the ones doing the real work – not making up the numbers in a Kangaroo Court.

But Hendrix was bang out of relevance.

"I love the smell of Bandas in the morning."

"What?" Paul asked

"Spirit duplicators…don't you remember the time before photocopiers…loved that smell."

"So I'm about to be fucked over, and you're nostalgic for old technology?"

The bell sounded.

"Coffee break over," said Hendrix. "Back on your heads. And I suggest you do somebody you like."

Paul returned to his teaching rooms, none the wiser about anything anyone had said.

Chapter Nine: Children First Always

In what she now liked to call the Senior Common Room, with her management team sat up and down the long polished table, Ms. Bishop set out her stall.

"The school is in financial crisis..." For effect, she placed her palms flat down on the smooth wood; an autistic image twisted with the rhythms of the wood stared back at her.

Mr. Kingman looked down at the wood. She'd grown another pair of arms in the reflected surface. He now understood why he could not ever grow to like her; she had the whiff of Thatcher about her.

"...and though we have very tight parameters...it does not mean we cannot create a system...which will sustain us into the twenty-first century."

Yes, he thought, Maggie to a *T*. There would be no compromise with this one, no deal struck for the common good.

"Kicking and screaming?" asked Mr. Kingman.

"I hope not, Mr. Kingman," said Ms. Bishop.

"We all hope not," said Mr. Knight.

"But we must not be sentimental," said Ms. Bishop.

Mr. Kingman trusted most of his sentiments far more than he trusted his immediate colleagues.

"I think we need to consider the school brand," said Mr. Knight. "I think we have found ourselves in special measures because we no longer know why we are here."

Mr. Kingman was having difficulty with the concept. He asked for clarification.

"And what do you suggest, Mr. Knight?"

"Look at displaying our core values on a notice board and school headed paper," said Mr. Knight.

"And what might these core values be?" Mr. Kingman asked.

How handy he was asking – he reeled them off. He could spell all of them if it was asked for.

"Resilience, excellence, courage. That sort of thing," said Mr. Knight. "Trust perhaps, maybe respect and responsibility...qualities we would look for in other people."

Mr. Kingman paused and let the bullshit wash over him – this was, after all, the director of directed time who was speaking. Then, being left-eared and left-eyed he looked at Mr. Knight, right between the bi-focals.

"Can we expect to see you showing those qualities, Mr. Knight?"

"Of course you can," he said. "What a strange question."

"And that will lift us up?" Mr. Kingman asked.

"Yes," said Mr. Knight. "That and maybe some new desks and chairs."

"Won't that cost money that could be better spent on staff?"

"I would also be seeking grant maintained status."

"Giving you more control over who stays in the school?" Mr. Kingman asked.

"Yes," said Mr. Knight.

This was too much for the old man.

"We have these values already, Mr. Knight. I was brought up with them and they can be taught using any old desk and chair. Maybe you need to value your colleagues and respect your pupils. I do it already and have always done so."

The man with the soul of a clipboard could not hear the power in the words being spoken by the voice of experience.

"Even with a brand makeover and a change in status," said Mr. Knight, "more changes will need to be made."

"In days gone by," said Mr. Kingman, "the old man would go into the classroom of a teacher he didn't want and hand him a copy of the *Times Ed* with another job circled. He'd say *'We've a good one for you here, boy,'* and that was it. They always got a better job and they knew where they stood. Much like caning boys. I didn't much like doing it – but what the boys hated most of all was injustice and unfairness."

"Are we finished with the nostalgia?" Mr. Knight asked.

Mr. Kingman could see the shadow of a knife about to be used.

"Culling time then, is it?"

"A few strategic cuts will be needed, Mr. Kingman," said Ms. Bishop.

"Blood will have blood," said Mr. Kingman.

"What do you mean?" Ms. Bishop asked.

Mr. Kingman re-phrased his question.

"Either of you going to offer your resignations?"

They were both shocked at the very idea. They had career progression to think of.

"That would not help the situation," said Mr. Knight.

"Oh, I think it might be handy," said Mr. Kingman. "And if you'll excuse me, I have a mark-book that needs fabricating for an inspection I don't really need." When he had left the room, Ms. Bishop spoke quietly to Mr. Knight.

"I think Mr. Kingman will come around to our way of thinking, or he will retire – we can make more immediate changes right now." Mr. Knight smirked.

"You mean our middle management issues?"

"I think you need to keep a close eye on our Mr. McSmart," said Ms. Bishop. "I don't like what I'm hearing from the classroom or the staffroom. I do not want him to succeed with this plan – I want him on a capability plan by Christmas."

"He is a man who defines himself by what he does instead of what he achieves," said Mr. Knight.

Ms. Bishop had been on the exact same course: *Dare to achieve in Education* – delivered by *Cradcrock*, the newly appointed county consultants.

"I think we might sacrifice a bit of doing for a bit of achieving, don't you?"

Mr. Knight nodded in agreement. He would give him the Christmas Tiny Tim would have had if Scrooge had not gone soft in his old age. McSmart's behaviour had not sounded very good when he made it up last week – arguments that never happened and inappropriate remarks that he never uttered. Goodness only knows what Ofsted would make of it.

"I will make him my number one priority," said Mr. Knight. "His lack of achievement will be his downfall."

Ms. Bishop nodded and added a touch of colour.

"His first mistake was to think that his future in this school depends on him being a good teacher. His second mistake is believing that he's actually a good teacher."

Doing and not achieving; they would see he was dismissed. It would be a warning to the others.

"Nobody has any respect for him," said Mr. Knight, "least of all the pupils."

"Quite," said Ms. Bishop.

Mr. Knight took some delight in embroidering his tale.

"They call him *'Mr. McFart'* when they think he's not listening."

"I heard they call him that when they know he is listening," said Ms. Bishop.

"He is mostly hot air," said Mr. Knight.

In a moment of bedevilment, Ms. Bishop put Mr. Knight in his place.

"You should hear what they call you."

"What?"

"It rhymes with Knight – so maybe Mr. McSmart had been teaching them something useful."

Mr. Knight flushed – a feeling similar to rejection rinsed through his system.

"He's an economics teacher – so it wasn't him."

"Maybe our children are beginning to manage their own learning," said Ms. Bishop.

"Economics teacher," said Mr. Knight. "With a small *e*. Not a magic *e*. Mr. McSmart is our not-very-good economics teacher."

"Then you'll need to do something about that rather flattering examination board report from last year."

"I have. It was a statistical anomaly I have now seasonally adjusted."

Completely unsexed, Ms. Bishop was now managing her own amusement.

"If you laid all the economists in the world end to end,

they'd never reach a conclusion."

Mr. Knight now spoke with a lightly clenched anus.

"Not very funny, is it?"

"I've heard worse," said Ms. Bishop.

"I need to get back to my office," said Mr. Knight. "People to remove from the school."

"You do that."

In the quiet of his own room, Mr. *Shite* made a mental note; one day, and one day very soon, he would take this troublesome Bishop out of the game. One day he would tell her what she really was. A woman, another feeble woman who thought she had the right to run his chosen school.

He was determined he would be the new brand of the school and everyone would bow before him. There would be death before dissent. He would kill to get what he wanted – he knew people who did that sort of thing for no more than a teacher's monthly salary. History showed that nothing significant was ever achieved without the spilling of a little blood. On his watch, everyone was expendable. If this Ofsted inspection achieved nothing more than bringing the school deeper into crisis, that would be a good thing. At the very least, they would rid themselves of the incumbent, and the vacant post would be his, there for the taking.

He picked up the phone, rattled through his Rotadex and found who he was looking for. Fat fingers punched out a familiar number. A child answered and then passed him on to the adult he wanted to deal with.

"I have a job for you," he said. "You're doing buy one get one free? Well yes that would be handy. With any luck you might find them together. One male and one female. I'll call again this evening with more details. If you could be here before the weekend, that would be most appreciated."

When he appointed Ms. Candy Regent, she'd given him

such a look of love and longing that he knew she was the one. His time had come. Yet, subsequently, she'd kept her distance and never looked at him that way again. It was a rejection too far, one she would pay for with her life.

He'd a stash of used twenty pound notes in his attic – saved over the years for a rainy day, or a date with a woman. He would use them to kill two birds with one stone. Candy Regent had already refused his primary advances and even had the cheek to say she fancied Paul McSmart more than him. He was less sure about going after Hendrix again, it was like the man had a voodoo doll of him and was sticking pins into it. He would leave him alone. Hendrix, currently carrying the seeds of his own destruction, could die another day.

Chapter Ten: Community Aliens

On reflection, Paul felt something different from sick; it was a total body conversion to a sense of stress and loss. The sensations came like storm-waves, each pounding more frequent and less predictable as the tide rose and the water swelled. His tongue tingled. His cheeks flushed. He was more itch than scratch. He could feel his gut pushing against the waistband of his trousers. Perhaps he just had trapped wind. Fair was foul and foul was fair. The drugs were not working. What were his options? Leave? Die? Shrivel to an imitation of a life. It would be hours before he gained sufficient control of his own mind and body to attempt any answers. He had a wife. He had children. He had the whole *Bittersweet Symphony*. They depended on him to put food on the table. He depended on his job to provide a fragile sense of self. But something about the tone of defiance in Hendrix was helping him forge a notion of destiny – he was going to beat them. He would support those less fortunate than himself (if there were any), and fight for their cause if they had one left to fight for. That notion of destiny would eventually go the way of all of his other ambitions in life – but for a moment he felt like he was in a *Rocky* movie.

In the meantime, he had lessons to torch and a department full of Cert Eds to mismanage. A life in education would be so much easier without having to teach; Mr. Knight had taught him that much with an elegance of economy. Good old *Mr. Shite* with his clipboard and braces. Then (thanks to Hendrix) he re-imagined him, his stomach falling out of a Star Trek jersey, trying to chat up *Wonder Woman* in *Klingon*. There were probably a few sure fire lines a man on a mission could use. *Is that a pen on your clipboard?*

And Paul had his own wonder-women to contend with; they re-enforced his self-belief in his own autism whilst tipping him into stereotypical labelling. They were waiting in the department office, gathered around the photocopier, like the weird sisters, prophesizing his demise – if he failed to do their bidding and suggesting he applied for the vacant job of Head of Sixth. *Lots of free periods, Paul, you'll love it.* They were right of course.

In moments of stress, Paul could feel the walls of the office closing in; all around him were books on typing, applied typing and advanced typing – one of them was written by somebody called Ida Scattergood and called Target Typing Practice. Maybe he was the target.

When he called meetings, they turned up late, when he failed to have meetings they requested meetings but did not turn up themselves. They would talk in riddles to one another – *Have you got the figures for the sixth form vocational course? I put them on your desk with a post-it saying are these the figures for the sixth form vocational course? Oh yes, there they are. I must really try and tidy up my desk sometime.* Trying to follow the line of communication Paul had asked them why the desk had to be tidied up. *Because then it wouldn't be untidy.* Of course! The conversations were pointless to the point of excluding him. And then he was included; *I do hope you are being assertive and not aggressive, Paul.* Perfectly passive aggresse. They were immune to facts and figures; their reality was not his reality – they shared the same space and existed in another dimension. When there was a problem or something that needed to be done, they sat on it like hens trying to hatch stones. He relived one of the great non-meetings of the past when one of them had signed herself out of school but was still in the departmental office when the meeting ended – having done nothing more spectacular than catch up on preparation with everyone pretending she wasn't there. Fuck her! He was the one who needed to be able to pretend that they weren't there – they were as happy as they could be swapping telephone and reception skill stories. He was the one who needed the soft cushion they gave each other – but he was the eternal unloved outsider and that had been the story of his life.

Hendrix, in a rare moment of lucidity and introspection, had explained it all to him; they were just scared people who knew their jobs were on the line. They were not witches with the gift of prophesy – they were just like him –

sad-sacks from another age -and that, in the long run we were all dead. But they still pissed him off; and yet it was a streak of normality that had run through his life – women had always pissed him off. Not all at once usually – and never before in such numbers. Of the three women who pissed him off in his own department, one possessed a barometric talent – like a canary in a coal mine she keeled over when there was a change in the air. The others were strong as horses and would pick up their friend as and when her knees gave way. The problem was that there was not enough work to go round, and the three of them had worked out who needed to leave. It had to be him because he was the last in and the most likely to survive the trauma of being thrown out. Paul had reached the point where he was in almost complete agreement.

It was as if gender roles had been swapped, they got annoyed because he went home to his kids – that was his job. His wife got annoyed because he was not back soon enough. He got annoyed because he felt they bullied him for how he looked, talked and taught. And on it went. They chastised him for not holding meetings that he had stopped because they never turned up to them.

He remembered how one of them had asked him one of those stupid questions.

"What are you passionate about, Paul?"

"Words, adjectives mainly, being used appropriately."

"Really?"

Paul took a deep breath and emoted in the direction of those wilfully blind and deaf to the demands of the new world order.

"No. What I really hate is that we are fobbing these kids off with courses that are worth nothing – that there are no apprenticeships, no jobs and no bloody training because of those fucking Tory bastards. And these courses will fail because everyone, even you, knows what they are – a way of sugar coating educational, cultural and industrial failure. Even the bloody peasants, the ignorant plebs know they are being fucked over in the cause of wealth creation and tax reduction for the already rich."

"I'm not sure that swearing is the answer, Paul."

"Well," asked Paul. "What is?"

"I think that the vocational route is the way forward."

"Yeah right."

As the most recent evolutionary failures of the educational world, they'd taken up the government challenge of disguising youth unemployment with the dead cat bounce of vocational education; they were charged with delivering CPVEs and then its big brother, the GNVQ. The term CPVE was an acronym for *Certificate of Pre-Vocational Education*. According to Hendrix who knew little of these qualifications, a GNVQ meant that you were *generally not very qualified*. They were what a government that educated its own offspring privately felt were okay for the rabble. The recipients of this education knew they were being shafted and responded by doing as little as possible to gain certificates that enabled them to fill out forms for jobs they would never be allowed to undertake because they did not exist anymore. The typists had all gone on three days CPD and emerged as instant experts – respected throughout the county according to their own assessment of themselves.

Apart from that, they were perfectly fine – if this were still 1975 and electric typewriters with golf-balls were the latest thing.

Like the naughty kids they were forced to educate vocationally, the women of the department were easy enough to empathize with - as long as you never had to face them in a working situation. They became a very impressive bullying team. They had words and phrases that annoyed him – *they certainly get their money's worth out of us.* And – *if she didn't exist, you'd have to invent her!* Now with Ofsted in town, one of them was about to fall off her perch.

"What if they see me teach?" Between tears, she forced out these deathless words. That was the question, thought Paul. What if they saw any of us teach? What if I died in my sleep? What if the world ended tomorrow? What if I cheated on my wife? He'd no answers to any of these questions. His chewing gum had definitely lost its flavour on the bedpost overnight.

Killer Queen

Chapter Eleven:
Shaky Time

On his way to his next lesson, Paul saw her. All legs and longing – silk scarf around her neck. In his desperation, he also saw her as the solution to his problems. To do so was hardly strategic. His very thought was hardly a rational one. And, it was hardly hard these days. Yet, there was something powerfully aphrodisiac about the rear view of a black stockinged and skirted, knee-high booted woman you didn't know going about her business, and doing it in such a way that suggested she didn't know, or care, you existed. Apart from being hot, she'd done nothing to deserve this obsession – merely dressed well and been polite. To make matters worse, she'd a name and role, and a responsibility – Candy Regent, Head of History and Curriculum Development. So far, she'd done nothing to piss him off. Back in the day, his mother was always telling him to get himself a girlfriend – maybe now, as a married and mortgaged man, it was time to follow her long-neglected advice. If he'd cared to remember back in the day, he would have recalled how girls who pursued him freaked him out far more than girls who rejected him. If he'd troubled to remember back to 7:30 that morning, he had a wife who looked just like her. If he'd bothered to look back five years before children and date nights, he'd a wife who looked better than her. If only he cared and could communicate with people.

But he was headed for a rendezvous with Liam in Year 8 – a year group and a subject off his radar until the last round of staff cutbacks had hit his department. Knight had given him possibly the worst class in the world – a mixture of high achievers and total losers, it was the only English group not streamed by ability to read. It was justified on the grounds of being control group for a field study on differentiation. Paul concluded correctly that it had been done to make his life more difficult than it already was. It was him who was being differentiated against – not the kids. When he complained, it was made clear to him that as an experienced teacher he should be able to cope with the challenge he'd been given. Even Hendrix was not much help – *be the warrior* he said. A piece of advice Paul put down to one spliff too many. The Head of English told him to screw his courage to the sticking post – he'd only just discovered this was a quote from the play he was teaching them. He was sure that Knight would have tipped off the inspectorate to visit this lesson rather than his sixth form stuff that generally went well. But none of this introspection was going to alter the fact that he was about to experience Liam York in a lesson without any support.

Liam York, the human Halloween mask boy, would be waiting for him to stumble through some more of the Scottish play. Liam, nicknamed *Yorkie*, the boy with the grin that was both radiant and rancid. Liam, who only supported football teams he could not spell from places he would never live. Liam, who looked to Paul like an oversized blonde maggot with humanoid limbs and a brain that was more liquid than solid. Liam, whose head seemed to swivel like a ventriloquist's dummy. Liam. Liam. Liam.

A monster chanting toward his room in seven league boots.

"Man U!"

The sound of a baseball bat smashed upon a car windscreen.

"Man U!"

It was getting closer.

"Man U!"

The mating call of the unwise and unwashed.

Two weeks into the term and they were old adversaries, divided by a common language and both forced to unite in a lesson about under-age sex from a land time forgot. The Head of English had joked that no kid today knew the difference between a proposition and a preposition – although educated in the grammar free seventies, neither did Paul. Hendrix had explained that Liam was a victim of the system – a boy who should have been placed in an MLD provision. He wasn't naughty, said Hendrix – he was stupid. He was a fuck-wit who belonged elsewhere. Somehow, in lesson three on a Monday, it never sweetened the deal for Paul. Neither his professionalism, nor his compassion was that elastic and accommodating.

Liam, already a paid up member of the *Bad Man Crew* had no time for *Mr. McFart* either. That their lives were spent locked in conflict was entirely the teacher's fault – but Paul could never see it that way. Just as the senior management were successfully de-humanizing him, he was successfully de-humanizing Liam. The benefit boy had no past and definitely no future; he was a faulty robot sent from the present time to end his career. But Liam, for all his lack of anything, was getting more out of this than his teacher. And he had heard that Lady Macbeth got her kit off in the film – so maybe *that* was worth waiting for. He'd watch a boy film, or a girl film, if he got to see something happening to somebody. Some tits. Some bum. Something hidden that he couldn't have. Paul was going to rain on that parade – the play Liam would be watching was directed by Orson Welles not Roman Polanski. He wasn't a hundred percent certain that Liam could actually see things in black and white – but that would be his mission impossible...he would try to get the benefit boy to learn something of no real use to him.

Mr. Paul McSmart, a teacher pretending to know about Shakespeare, stood by the door to the classroom and gestured for the pupils, who knew nothing, to enter. This was one of many lessons he could do without an Ofsted visit – although as a nod in the direction of personal survival, he was better prepared than usual and had bought photocopied sheets in lieu of real books that had been missing, presumed read, since the sixteen seventies.

"Got an earring like me," said Liam, pointing at the poster.

That much was true. It was true this lesson. It would be so in the next. It would be true in a future where Liam was either on the dole or in prison.

"He's unisex," said Liam. "Like me."

Who knew?

Liam continued with the scene. Not clear if this was comedy or tragedy, Paul continued to humour the boy.

"Do ya think his bro' done it with a red hot needle?"

"No idea," said Paul.

"Some rubbish teacher you are," said Liam. "Don't even know who done Shakespeare's lug-ole."

He could have told him anything. Perversity prevented him.

"Do you?" Paul asked.

Liam gave the question more thought than most lessons he had recently attended.

"Reckon his mum," he said.

Several kids shouted back.

"Your mum!"

And also.

"Oi, Yorkie, tell Smartie 'ow ya snog ya dog."

Strangely, Liam was wounded by this barrage of peer to peer insults.

"Tell 'em to stop, sir. I don't have no more dog. Benjie got tooken he did. And that's not me nickname no more. I'm *Lump*. I'm a Bad Man."

"Sad Man more like," said another voice.

Lump? Yorkie? A Bad Man? Who in the world gives a toss? Paul moved to the front desk and tried to impersonate a teacher of English. It was hardly inspirational.

"Who can remember where we were?"

Benefit boy corrected his faulty grammar.

"Don't you mean," said Liam, "who can remember where we *was*?"

Always the pedant, thought Paul.

There was silence.

No bugger who knew where they were felt safe enough to say it out loud in front of some of school's more challenging clientele.

"Lady Macbeth has seen an opportunity," said Paul. "She makes Macbeth want to kill the king – even though he really doesn't."

From the class came the familiar sound of nobody listening. Who knew you could make murder and treason this boring?

Liam started to play with his photocopy of the scene.

"Liam," said Paul. "Could you stop that?"

"Stop what?"

"Turning your paper into an airplane."

"It's a football player," said Liam. "It's Ryan Giggs."

"Whatever it is," said Paul, "please stop."

"Why?"

Paul said nothing and wrote the acronym NFI on the whiteboard.

"What's that mean?" Liam asked.

"No fucking intelligence," shouted someone from the back of the class. There was a ripple of laughter that washed all over the poor kid.

Liam was distraught.

"Sir?"

"Not following instructions," said Paul.

Liam was pacified. He unfolded the paper.

"That's alright then," he said.

Paul's thoughts fluttered back to Candy Regent; the cartoon character of his wanking dreams. How he wanted to kiss her and how he knew it was a despicable and treacherous thing – a betrayal of his family and more besides. He would even settle for snogging her in a cupboard somewhere – as long as his knees held out. What did Liam say he was? Unisex! You could listen and listen and never know.

Then he remembered he was back in a classroom and there was an inspector peering through the wire-reinforced glass of the door. He could make out a face – just a clipboard and a black eye. This was the end. In desperation, he tried to reach one of the reasonable ones.

"Sean," he said. "What do you think about Macbeth?"

Sean barely looked up.

"He's a bit like Noah Claypole." Sean was not giving him any context here. Who was Noah Claypole? What scene was he in? Why could he not just answer: the question put to him? Paul played teacher's bluff.

"Sean, in what way is Macbeth like Noah Claypole?"

"He's a dick."

"In what way is he a dick?"

"He should man the fuck up and not let his old lady give him GBH of the lughole."

The inspector was in the room.

"What's that wanker doing in our room?" Liam asked. "He should fucking knock."

Killer Queen

In that moment, Paul understood that Liam had given him at least a little more respect than he gave the Ofsted guy. He was about to say *thank you* when the fire bell rang. In a heartbeat, the class emptied onto the playground.

Paul approached the inspector. On closer inspection Paul could see he'd taken a bit of a pounding. He realised this was the poor bastard who'd sat next to Ant. He was probably a little wary of Liam who was harmless by comparison with Ant.

"Good morning mister, I don't have your name," said Paul.

"Mr. Castle," said the inspector.

"We was doing all about castles," said Liam, who was actually following instructions and waiting for a member of staff.

"Were you?" Mr. Castle asked.

"What's it to you?" It wasn't a question you were required to answer.

Paul pointed to the sign that said *Fire Exit*.

"This way," he said.

"What happens now?" Mr. Castle asked.

"They try and find out who done it," said Liam.

"Are they like the Mounties?" Mr. Castle asked.

"What?"

"Do they get their man?" Liam considered the question.

"Usually someone takes the blame and we all miss the rest of the lesson."

"Good job all round then?"

"Suppose," said Liam.

It was just how it was.

Paul tried to remember if anyone had been missing from his class. He was the only person he could recall. He looked back and the inspector had disappeared – decided to run away before Liam turned vicious.

Chapter Twelve:
Exodus

In the playground, Mr. Knight had augmented his clipboard with a megaphone. Happy as a pig in shit, he was walking up and down the assembled pupils barking out the bleeding obvious.

"Be quiet in the ranks, everyone."

Dissent was everywhere.

"What about you?" asked Hendrix.

Mr. Knight spun around and saw Paul smirk.

"Mr. McSmart. Do I need to remind you that the fire drill is for everyone?"

"Everyone," Hendrix whispered, "except you, you fat bastard."

After five minutes everybody had settled down so that in the event of a real fire the screams from those dying in the fire might be heard by the senior management.

All that was left was to catch the culprit. Mr. Knight made his opening and closing offer to the multitudes.

"If the pupil who set off the alarm comes forward now, everyone else will be allowed to go back to lessons."

Mr. Kingman groaned inwardly. The sun was shining and it was nearly break. Nobody wanted to go back inside. Knight would need to manage his expectations downwards. He walked across to Mr. Knight and whispered in his ear.

"Offer them a longer break, if the boy steps forward."

"It might not be a boy," said Mr. Knight.

"It's always a boy," said Mr. Kingman.

There was a pause while Mr. Knight considered his options.

"If the pupil who did this comes forward, then all of the school can stay out for an extended break."

Not everyone knew what *extended* meant.

"Extra break if you give up the boy," shouted Mr. Kingman.

Somebody tried to push Liam forwards. Paul stopped them. There was a bit of kerfuffle as Liam was quite keen to take one for the team.

"Not this one?" Mr. Kingman asked.

"He was in my class when the bell went," said Paul.

Mr. Knight was losing patience. Rather than risk threatening a whole school, he singled out Paul for harassment.

"Mr. McSmart! We need to maintain silence!"

Eventually, Gary pushed his way through the ranks of the unwashed.

"It was me! I done it!" He faced the assembled school and bowed. There was a cheer from the Lower Sixth lads.

"Off to the *'cooler'* for you, laddie," said Mr. Kingman.

"Thanks sir," said Gary.

"By the way," Mr. Kingman asked, "did you do it?"

"No sir," said Gary.

"Good boy," said Mr. Kingman. With his favour to the school community done, Gary felt he could ask Mr. Kingman a question.

"Why don't you call it the *'inky'* like Mr. Knight does?"

The *'cooler'* was renamed the *'Inclusion Unit'* by Mr. Knight in a fit of re-branding. He then tried to give it an affectionate nickname: the *'inky'*. Nobody was fooled, but the nickname *'stinky'* gained universal currency. Anybody calling it the *'stinky'* within Mr. Knight's earshot was put in there as a punishment. Paul had lost many non-contact periods that way. It was proof, as Hendrix said, that you could try and brand a turd – but people would still know it was a turd whatever else it was called. Gary was only referring to it as the *'inky'* out of respect for Mr. Knight who had once done a school visit to his house and said some nice things about him to his mum.

"Because, boy, I don't like Mr. Knight." The answer seemed to please Gary.

"Blinding," he said. "You know what his new nickname is?"

"I don't think I do," said Mr. Kingman.

"Doughnut," said Gary. "Like in dunkin' doughnut."

"That's very funny," said Mr. Kingman.

"You're coming with me, young man." Mr. Knight said, intercepting Gary and Mr. Kingman.

"Where?"

"Three days internal for you," he said.

"It used to be a half day," said Gary.

"Not now I'm in charge," said Mr. Knight, allowing for inflation.

Gary sang from a different sheet.

"I didn't fucking do it," he said.

"I think you did," said Mr. Knight.

As they were walking back to the building, a secretary ran up to Mr. Knight.

"Technical fault on the school alarm," she said. "All sorted now."

"See," said Gary. "I didn't fucking do it." The facts were not going to save him. Mr. Knight fished in his pocket for his little black book.

"Three days internal exclusion for wasting my time and swearing."

"Fuck off, Doughnut." said Gary. The nickname was out.

"That's four days."

"Fuck off."

With five days on his scoresheet, he then made a home run for the fence. He had a lot of practice. On the other side, he looked back and gave Mr. Knight the finger – had to be half a day at least. He ran off and lost himself in the grey council estate that lay beyond the wire and concrete posts that marked the boundary of the school.

There was now a football chant coming from unidentifiable members of the sixth form ventriloquism society.

'Duncan Doughnut, he didn't do it, he didn't fucking do it...Duncan Doughnut, he didn't do it, he didn't fucking do it.'

"That was a bit unfair," said Mr. Kingman.

"He needs to know who is in charge," said Mr. Knight. "He's wasted my time and called me a doughnut in front of the whole school."

"Now he really will be wasting your time," said Mr. Kingman.

"He'll learn," said Mr. Knight.

Mr. Kingman kept his counsel. He thought they were, possibly, the stupidest words Mr. Knight had ever uttered in his short time as a member of the senior leadership team.

As the school descended into the chaos of a premature morning break, Hendrix and Paul walked towards the sanctuary of the staff-room.

"Somebody should kill that bastard," said Hendrix. "Chop off his fucking head and put it on stick." A woman's voice cut through the air, cool and controlled.

"I heard that."

Paul and Hendrix looked behind them. It was her. She was smiling at Hendrix.

"Me and my big mouth," said Hendrix. Paul was about to say something he hoped would be witty and charming when Mr. Knight called out on his megaphone.

"Ms. Regent – a moment please." The request delighted her as much as it would anyone else who was phobic about ugly talking animals.

"I have heard," said Hendrix, "that Mrs. Knight has a gag reflex that stops her giving him a blow-job on his birthday."

"Is there a Mrs. Knight?" Paul asked.

Nobody knew.

"Maybe his mum," said Hendrix.

"It's not his birthday," said Candy. "Much as he might like it to be."

Hendrix continued the improv in the hope of impressing her.

"And that he has a framed doughnut in his room with a label that says in case of emergency break glass."

"Probably a pasty," said Paul.

"He's a temple to carbs," said Candy.

While she waited for Knight to come to her, Paul and Hendrix kept walking.

"He's a prime cunt," said Hendrix.

"Divisible only by himself?" Paul said.

"Some fucker should step forward – take one for the team."

"Since it's your idea, why don't you chop off his head?" Paul asked.

Hendrix had clearly given the concept headspace.

"I would – but I would be the first fucker fingered."

"Might still be worth it," said Paul.

"Yeah."

Back on the playground, Ms. Regent met Mr. Knight's Frankenstein gaze. Looks and words did not mesh together.

"I need you to go over the new syllabus details with me." Such a rigmarole was the last thing she needed. She knew exactly what he wanted. She also knew he would *not* be getting it from her.

"Can it wait until after Ofsted?"

"No." She could sense him salivating and stiffening up.

"Thursday after school?" she suggested. She looked down at her boots and waited for it to end.

"Okay." As he spoke, he looked down at her boobs and looked forward to it continuing. "So, my office?" She looked up to the sky and read his mind.

"Where else?"

"See you then," he said. Although nothing physical had

happened, she did not want this to rumble on towards a shared table in some shitty restaurant where she would be picking his dandruff out of parmesan cheese all evening. She'd played this game before with dirty old lecturers - and lost. They had promised her at least a 2:1 and delivered her a third because she wouldn't give head – wouldn't work the pig through the python. She wasn't going to be sucking anything she didn't like – not now, not ever...for anything less than a headship. This was not even going to be a means to an end. He was not an attractive man. He was a deeply unattractive one. He was genuinely repellent. She wanted him out of her life. She'd a plan that involved stepping over his dead body - not lying under him while he was still breathing his foul stench all over her. She wanted him gone. Surely such an outcome was really not that much to ask for.

Curiously it might have actually cheered her that he wasn't planning to sleep with her, rather he was planning to kill her and Paul. He fully expected Burke and Hare to be on the premises no later than tomorrow evening. They'd do a quick sortie and then do their thing – no need to give either of them a copy of the *Times Ed* or take the time and effort to find them both better jobs. No need either to look at ways he could make their working lives better here – they didn't fit with his brave new world so they could fuck off and die as far as he was concerned. Such was to be the price of her failure to collude and for showing him disrespect.

On her way back into school, Candy passed beneath the school mission statement – *Know the past to plan the future*. She was about to give the whole thing a makeover in her mind; for her it was going to read – *Know the future to plan the past*. She was planning to do a very bad thing and then provide herself with probably the best alibi in the world. The very thought of the possibility made her feel warm and tingly all over. She just had to make sure she picked the right person to do her bidding; she had a sense of the weakness of Paul McSmart – a man looking for something he was too scared to find. Yes, Paul would be the easiest person on the staff to nudge into executing the bad deed she wanted done; she just had to wait for the right moment to present itself.

Chapter Thirteen:
How Candy

Paul could feel his hair turning grey. Like toothache for an Eskimo, failing to teach Shakespeare was a unique and unexpected pain in his life. The fact that he was doing so in order to protect the jobs of a team who would stab him in the back at the earliest opportunity was an additional irony. Being humiliated by Clipboard Man was merely an unexpected bonus. He was gasping for a cigarette, but he didn't smoke.

In the staff room during the next break, Paul took his place at the back of the queue. He moved forward, slowly, to where Mrs. Alverstoke, the old lady who served the coffee, stood. Clad in what seemed to be an old shower curtain, she was a friendly soul who always failed to learn the names of the staff:

"Morning, John," she said to Paul. "Coffee then?"

"Thank you," said Paul. He couldn't remember her name either. He picked up the steaming mug and put his money in the saucer by the side of the serving hatch.

He then turned to walk toward the rows of easy chairs. Wham! He bumped into her. Up and down he went, like a drooling nodding dog. He felt the eternal tingle of anticipation. She had all the right notes in all the right places. She really was just like Elektra. She'd the scent of something lost and found.

"...hello," he said, having tried to choke off some other less appropriate noise.

He'd the crumpled look of man still shopping in Next, ten years after it had ceased to be cutting-edge style for the reluctantly middle-aging male. However, faced with an imbecile on heat, she appeared to do what many attractive women feel duty bound to do – she humoured him, as her cunning plan presented itself fully formed and perfectly proportioned. She gave him the close up once over. He had all his teeth and his own hair. He didn't even have a beer belly, builder's bum or food stains on his tie; she could shag him at least once before she gave him his P45.

"Hello," she said.

She said, *'Hello!'*

"Hi."

"You smell nice," she said. "What is it?"

"Just the same as yesterday," said Paul.

"*Just the same.* Is that CK One?" He knew his underpants were Calvin Klein. The smell was probably the Chicken Kiev he had last night.

"Why haven't I seen you much before?"

"I have been ill for the last two terms," she said. "Meniere's. It comes and goes. Mostly it's been coming recently."

Comes and goes! If only. He pressed his thumb against the hot porcelain rim of the ramshackle mug. He was not to know this mug had been thrown by Liam York when he was in year seven. How it got to be fired was a mystery. How it got to the staffroom was an enigma. How it got to Paul was kismet. There was a crack. The detached body of the mug dropped like a steaming bomb, like the lump of clay it once was. Made of strong stuff, it did not break on impact, but lolled on its side, spewing out dregs of drink. So much for a cool greeting that might get him a look in.

"Sorry, sorry, sorry," he mumbled to those around him.

Based on this display of ineptitude, he was certainly not a man she wanted splashing his excess juices around her en-suite bathroom. The very sense of dodging that bullet made her smile. She'd a better use for this clumsy, elbow-patched specimen of a jobbing teacher. She checked him out again. Was he up for everything? He was just about tall enough for the job she wanted, and dark enough for her to bear intimately – for as long as it would take anyway.

Perversely, Paul thought, she was finding this funny.

"Nice finish," she said. "I was expecting you to just drink it."

"Everyone does," said Paul.

"I'm Candy," she said. "The new head of history."

"Paul. The old head of business education."

"That's all the interesting stuff about work over and done with," said Candy. "I can tell by your drooling that you want to *fuck me hard.*"

The last three words were whispered. Paul looked around – perhaps she really was a telepath like Elektra. Nobody else had heard the words. Maybe he'd not heard the words.

"What?"

"You heard me."

"Sorry."

"Don't be," she said. "I'll catch you at the end of the day." With that, she walked off.

"Where?" Paul asked.

By then, she had finished talking to him. This, Paul decided, was why men never won arguments with women, was why they should never pick arguments with women; once they have said what they want to say, they stop. They close for business. End of. No amount of logic would raise the shutters until they were good and ready. You could see the same dance happening in the playground as in the staffroom.

Hendrix, alerted by the way she'd moved away, sidled up to Paul.

"That didn't go well, mate," he said. "She seems to have blown you out."

"My life in a shattered moment," said Paul.

He looked Paul up and down in a male-on-male way.

"You're shaking. She must have read the runes to you."

"She said," he whispered. "She wanted to *fuck me hard.*"

"I think you may have got that wrong," said Hendrix.

Paul thought again. He knew what he'd heard.

"She said I wanted to fuck her – but that was okay and she would see me at the end of the day." Hendrix whistled.

"Do it, but tell nobody," he said.

"Not even you."

"Especially me."

"And…"

"If you do get your leg over – and you get caught out, you deserve everything you get. Death, divorce, diabetes."

"And the upside?"

"If you're lucky," said Hendrix, "she's a classy woman looking for a zipless fuck."

Paul was all about the downside.

"And if I'm not?"

Hendrix knew the score.

"Just enjoy that priceless moment of satisfaction… before the girl of your dreams becomes the woman of your nightmares."

"Have you seen this movie?" Paul asked.

"There will come a moment," said Hendrix, "when she hands you back your limp dick and bites off your head."

"And if it was you?"

"Well," said Hendrix, "my ideal woman is a porn star who likes me for who I am and is never disappointed when I eventually let her down in the trouser department – owing to her being able to make up the numbers another day – or get off with her hot occasionally lesbian soulmate."

"You're not answering my question," said Paul.

Hendrix had lost the plot.

"Which one?"

"Would you give her a seeing-to?" Paul repeated, but varied his question. The words fell out of his mouth sounding alien to both of them. But Hendrix was now back on track.

"Like a rat up a drainpipe, old son. Like a rat up a bleedin' drainpipe."

Paul was slightly upset that Hendrix did not counsel caution.

"I thought you were supposed to be setting an example," said Paul.

"I am, mate," said Hendrix.

"Huh?"

"I'm setting a bad example – I'm the romantic who brings flowers to a key party."

"I don't know what you are on about," said Paul.

"Me neither," said Hendrix. "I think it's about swinging – or wife-swapping."

"I just wanted a second opinion," said Paul. Hendrix laughed.

"Coming to me for advice. I wouldn't come to me for advice. I'm not that stupid."

"Cheers," said Paul.

So he was on his own with this one, just him, his lust and that pea sized vestigial entity he called his conscience.

Chapter Fourteen: Bonny and Clyde

Paul was outside her office at the end of the day. Semi-aroused, he knocked on the door. It creaked open.

"Hi," he said. She did not seem as pleased to see him.

"I said *I* would catch up with *you*."

Then, without looking, she grabbed him and kissed him hard. Strangely her lips became bones. She pulled him into the room and locked the door. Inside, the blinds were down. Outside, there were the sounds of children going home, with laughing, teasing, the sibilant sounds of adolescence, distant, as if filtered. With one hand she pinned him to the wall. With the other, she rummaged around in his trousers until she found what she wanted. He didn't hear the clicking of a hidden camera.

"There!"

She pulled down her knickers and swung him around. Now she was against the wall and he was supporting her body as she crammed him into her. The movement hurt him somewhat.

"Yes!"

She pushed and pulled until it was over. What was done would not be undone. Paul, who was hoping for a little foreplay and maybe a candle-lit meal had been reduced to a finger buffet. Now she owned him. He felt used and more than a little sore.

"Is that it?" She looked at him with what he took to be contempt:

"For now," she said. "I've had better." *Me too*, he thought, *me too*.

He'd not seen any part of her that he couldn't see in the

staffroom. What was revealed was anger and manipulation, her breasts still remained off limits and he was a love rat. The scenario was all very unsatisfactory.

"I'll put a note in your pigeon hole next time *I* want you."

And that's you – silk scarf and no knickers.

The only person he told that day was Hendrix.

"She sounds like a cunt," he said, scratching his chin, "But then again, I've never met a cunt I didn't like."

"I really wish you wouldn't use the 'C' word. Melissa says it's misogynistic."

"Melissa's not listening," said Hendrix.

"I think it's rather harsh, even unpleasant," said Paul. "You could find another word. I quite like quim."

"Me too," said Hendrix.

"You know what I mean," said Paul.

"I've never met a vagina I didn't lick." Hendrix cleaned up his act. *Hendrix and the Vaginas*; it sounded like the title of a novella written about a sex addict adrift in his own wet-dream.

"You're not helping," said Paul.

"Not trying to mate," said Hendrix. "I told you *not* to tell me." That message was lost in translation.

"What now?" Paul asked.

"It's all gone a bit existential, hasn't it?"

"What?"

"You're lying by your own rules now."

"Thanks."

"Don't mention it," said Hendrix.

"I gotta go," said Paul.

"Hope you saved a little for Mel," said Hendrix. Her name being spoken out loud sent a spasm of guilt through Paul's body.

"Mel?"

"Melissa. Your wife. The majority provider of quim in your miserable life; the blonde and beautiful mother of your children, James and Sarah."

"Oh yeah, sure."

Paul walked out of the building. What now? What now? What now?

Just as he left there was his red Polo where he'd left it, just as if nothing had occurred between him and the woman earlier. The driver's door opened the way it always did. He got into the vehicle in the same manner he always adopted. He started it in the usual fashion.. He didn't notice the smell of leaking fuel. The sound of *The Verve* greeted him as he turned on the ignition. What *Urban Hymn* was he writing for himself? What drugs could work for him now?

With his world changed forever, Paul went home to his family – home to his two lovely children and his beautiful wife, home to where he knew all of their names and even some of their birthdays.

Before he got home, it occurred to him that perhaps he should clean up. He went to his gym, changed out of his work clothes and ran twenty minutes on the treadmill. He worked up more of a sweat than he had with Candy. He then had to weigh up whether to shower there, or at home.

As Paul was driving home, Candy was walking to the lake. She was carrying an artifact wrapped in a towel. Certain she could not be seen, she unwrapped a samurai sword and placed it in the shallows of the lake where the blind bough of a weeping willow grazed the surface. She would need to be careful not to step on it tomorrow. Then she went home and wrote the best seductive doggerel she could summon up for a weekday.

Chapter Fifteen: Paul Taker

At home, all was much the same. Jamie had chicken pox and Sarah was bugging him.

"Talk to me, Daddy," she said.

"I want Biker Mice from Mars," said Jamie.

"I want to be left in peace," said Paul. "I have lessons to plan." He really meant he had comic books he wanted to read as an escape from his wife and children.

"You need to spend some time with them," said Melissa, touching his shoulder. "They need you." He needed time alone; it would not be for many years that he properly understood why – that he was on the spectrum and masking it was hard work.

Paul held Melissa's hand for a moment.

"Did you see *Our Price* are selling things called CDs? I have no idea what a CD is."

Paul's was an intimate gesture too far.

"She's my mummy – not yours," shouted Jamie. "My mummy!" Paul backed away from the family that was encircling him, Indians around a wagon train.

"Where are you going?" Melissa asked.

"Work," he said.

"Oh," she replied. On the lounge wall there was a Jack Vettriano print called 'Dance me till the end of the love.' This time, as Melissa looked at it, the message and the tone was much clearer. The light of the painting was very subdued violet – somewhere in the sky was an obscured un-shining sun. Melissa looked at the lonely couple who were joined at the groin waiting for their moment. The woman was looking up at the man. The man was looking into the middle distance.

That was them; she and Paul had reached the end of love. She'd given everything and was waiting for something in return; now she knew that reciprocation would never happen. The issue was not that her husband had gone out; it was just the realization that he'd never properly been there for her, and she was a fool to expect that would ever change. He could never feel her joy or pain, he could only ever feel her anger.

Melissa taught kids with speech and language issues. Only today she'd broken up a playground spat between two year nine girls. The argument, as ever, was over a boy. One girl was accusing the other girl of stealing him away from her. Sad they thought so little of themselves that they considered a dismal cheating boy worth a fight. But somehow they always did. The boy in question was called Paul – just like her husband. Instead of calling the girl a cheating bitch, she accused her of being a *'Paul taker.'* A Paul taker! You could work a lifetime in the field and never predict how impaired language would come out sounding. She wondered who her *Paul taker* was; it might not even be a 'who'.

Whatever was pulling them apart, animal, vegetable or mineral, she understood in that moment she would have to divorce him. The marriage was over. Beyond the legal requirements, the reason was not going to matter much. She'd be happy to give him half of everything if it meant she could be free; it wasn't as if he'd cheated on her, he was simply unable to be any more than himself.

Retreating to his inner psychic space, Paul had more important things to ponder. And what things they were! Things such as what it was to be a man. Matters his father should have taught him. Contexts far more exciting than mere offspring who wanted conversation and feeding – maybe even nurturing and teaching about the way of the world such as he understood it. He also read a bit more about Elektra and her fight with Daredevil; they were friends, enemies, allies and maybe even lovers.

That night, Paul slept badly – like a child on Christmas Eve.

The next day in school, Paul picked up a note from his pigeon hole.

When the world was magical and places had no names, there was a silver lake fed from a diamond stream. The lake was girdled by a wood and hooded by a hill. One Dark Age day, a defeated King threw his sword into the lake and the place found a name. Be by that lake, my King, at 5:00. Please sit next to me – your Queen - and we can watch the wind on the water; it alone knows eternity. Don't forget to bring a towel.

Fangs Candy.

A picture of a set of upper and lower case teeth were drawn underneath the words; she had really got her teeth into him.

A shiver ran down his back.

Paul was being taken way out of his depth.

Chapter Sixteen:
A Maid with a Blade

The day dragged. The towel sat in his bag. The sun shone. Lessons came and went on the tide. He only saw inspectors in lessons he was competent to teach – A levels and GCSE. Such was his focus that he had no concerns for their opinions whatsoever. If he could have given anything other than shagging Candy headspace, he would have understood just how angry this was making his mentor. He'd done so well that Mr. Knight would be required to take him off the support plan and claim the credit for turning him around – unless he could find some way of failing Paul in a lesson or two the next day. Paul had no idea. All Paul hoped for was warm water and minimal shrinkage. Adultery was the perfect short term distraction for inspection anxiety.

Eventually, the school emptied into the estate. Paul made no excuses for being late. He walked down to the lakeside. The trees hid him from the world. She was there.

"You came," she said.

"I did," said Paul.

She started peeling off her clothes.

He watched her disrobe. Of course he did. To do so was to be a man. He'd missed such moments of revelation because he was married and in that relationship nothing was novel.

"Don't be a wuss," she said.

Now naked except for her silver skull necklace, she dived in. He'd no idea how deep it was – but it swallowed her up. She surfaced again near the willow, swimming freestyle. Treading water, she righted herself and spun gently around. He could finally see her breasts – only slightly concealed by her dark hair and the muddy pond weed hanging off her nipples.

"Jump in!" She shouted out to him."Okay." He pulled off his *hush-puppies* and paused for a moment.

"Now take your Smarty-pants off!" Without any obvious physical injury, he got through the comedy that is a male undressing for hurried sex.

Looking around to check they were not being watched, he waded in – completely out of his shell. It was not quite as cold as he had feared – but chilly enough. The breath flew out of his body. As he adjusted to the new environment, she swam towards him.

"Take me!" Barring any shrinkage issues, there was going to be a great deal of taking in this relationship.

"In the water?" He was not certain this was the right sort of place for this kind of activity. She laughed like a mermaid giving him the *come on*.

"Where else?"

"On a bed?" He had been thinking of at least a rented room in a *Premier Inn*.

"Come on, Paul. You need to experience life." There was living and there was living.

She caught hold of him and kissed him. He felt her take control again. Another unsatisfactory sexual experience was about to happen. She broke off and dived under the water; the last thing he saw was her perfect bottom chased by her long legs.

"Where the fuck are you?" Paul shouted.

She surfaced moments later, holding a sword.

This object looked, to Paul, like something from a *manga* comic. It seemed old but not as rusty as it ought to be. He thought back to his cartoon fantasy of Elektra with her two swords; he needed to be more circumspect about what he wished for.

"Look what I've found," she said, swishing it through the water.

"Careful," said Paul.

"I think this means I have a Kingdom to conquer!"

"Or maybe you just found a sword in a lake." He'd almost forgotten they were here to commit adultery.

She held the sword above her head. The blade shut out the sun for a second. He saw her in diabolical silhouette – the lady in the lake.

"I shall be Queen!"

"And me?" She laughed at him.

"Finders keepers."

"I think we should get out of here." Paul was starting to shiver. They eased themselves onto the bank.

"Do you want to dry me off?" Candy asked. "I am a Queen, after all."

Her skin had taken on the look of uncooked chicken – it was not even a footnote in his fantasy. With that puckering, he thought, he didn't enjoy the rubbing down quite as much as he had hoped.

"What's with the skull on a chain?" Paul asked.

"To remind me that beauty is only skin deep," said Candy.

"Nice," said Paul.

"Look," she said, "it's got a note attached to it." Candy gestured to the sword from the lake. Even for a sucker like Paul, this was beginning to seem a bit fucked up. Without looking, she read it out to him.

"Once upon a time, I knew why I was here. Once upon a time, I ruled my classroom wisely and justly. Once upon a time, I believed that anybody, armed with good intentions, could change the world for the better. That time has gone. All

we can do is cut back the dead wood and wait for spring to come."

When they were dressed, Candy wrapped the sword in her towel.

"Wait to be called tomorrow," she said, carrying away her sword but not his sense of guilt. She left him, lonely by the lake, clutching her note. It made sense. Sort of. The time had come to change the world for the better. Maybe.

Back at her house, Ms. Regent planned her alibi for the day that was to follow. A few calls later and it was all done and dusted as her dozy cow of a mother would have said.

Chapter Seventeen:
Rendezvous in the Pondezvous

High up in the science building, Mr. Knight had been following the exploits of Candy and Paul with the school telescope. He would normally use it to spot pupils running for the fence or smoking behind the trees. Today there'd been a more exciting show in town. His heart raced as Candy Regent stripped off and plunged in. Although occasionally unable to see the boobs through the bushes, he'd the best seat in the house. To see her reveal everything to somebody other than himself was to be a lovesick teenager again – to experience the suicide dive into despair and longing and not have the language to articulate the journey. His heart was broken by her betrayal. He would definitely kill the two of them for this treason against his will. She was so perfect and so cold towards him. It was as though she'd been created to torment him. And McSmart was a married man – he wasn't even supposed to have sex with his wife. The whole thing was immoral – Mr. Knight, when much younger, had learnt that at school along with a deal of other bigotry and an eternal sense of delayed gratification. Now he knew it to be completely derailed gratification. The pleasures of carnality had passed him by. He thought of several soppy girls who'd shown an interest – he'd shown them the door. Always waiting for the one who would turn him inside out – and when she had, she turned him down. He always felt there was something better out there. But there wasn't. There was just Candy Regent and her magnificent breasts frolicking in a rank school pond with an underachieving excuse of a human being. Even the morons in this school got laid – some of the dozy girls thought they could only get pregnant if they were in love. Some of the idiot boys thought you couldn't get a girl pregnant if you did it up against a tree. He wanted to be that moron, that fuck-wit, that underachiever who finally got the girl.

    Why was he never the one? He was in such pain and turmoil that introspection would have twisted his black soul. Always rejected; he was never chosen.

And there she was, being defiled by this other man. And enjoying it! She was truly the spawn of the devil. The scriptures never lied. He knew that now. Maybe all women were of the devil. All the vaulting ambition in the world could not mend his heart or fill the Tardis-sized void within. He was nothing and nobody. He hated them and he detested himself. But rather than kill himself or do something to improve the wasteland that was his own personal life, he would hurt those who were having more fun than him. Applied universally, he could destroy the planet. There was not an organism, or a part of one that was more miserable and hateful than he was at that very moment. All the clipboards in the world could not mend his heart or soothe his soul. He could look into the evening sky all he wanted – there was nobody out there like him. He was the saddest, loneliest planet in the solar system. Bold, bloody and resolute, he put away the telescope and walked back to his office to plan a murder or two.

In the sanctuary of his office, he turned off the closed circuit cameras that he'd personally and privately installed around the room with the battery-theft budget. He remembered what happened to President Nixon after the Watergate break in – he was the most powerful man in the world and still he was hung out to dry. Nobody was going to hang Duncan Knight. If he was going to plan and execute a murder, being caught on candid camera was not going to be the best thing that could happen to him. Hendrix had shown him the dangers of twenty-four hour surveillance.

Meticulously, or so he thought, he began to plot the deaths of those who had considered sinning against him; the feelings of sweet vengeance took the edge off his personal pain. He felt somewhat hungry. He looked at his pastry stock. He really fancied a doughnut, but after that child had ripped into him in front of the whole school he felt uncomfortable eating one. The little bastard had spoiled one of his few sensual pleasures. He picked up a pasty and carefully inspected it; he generally preferred them a tad moister than this particular specimen. But it had been a long day and he was hungry. He wolfed it down – but still wanted more. The second one in the packet…that was the one. He would take this a bit slower…let himself become one with gloriousness of the whole experience. He closed his eyes and chewed slowly. A vision of Candy Regent baked in a pie came into his head – he'd no idea which end he would eat first. He peeled the crust away from his lips. His one true love would never let him down.

Chapter Eighteen: How Handy

The next day, there was another note. These were worse than those from Ms. Bishop.

Hi P,

The sword has given me an inspiration. Just like us becoming lovers, this must be for a reason. Meet me at 4:00 pm – my room. Bring flowers and fuck me – if you dare!

XXX

Putting the note into his pocket, he could hear Hendrix laughing in his head:

"Mate... be careful what you wish for!"

And where would he find flowers before the end of day?

Armed with only a bunch of freesias, Paul entered the lair of his lover. She sat reading a book.

"Hi, lover boy," she said, not looking up. "Just reading up about old swords."

"One of my favourite things," said Paul.

"Old swords were hammered out of pig-iron. It was a tremendous skill. Some tribes would deliberately lame or maim their smithies so they couldn't work elsewhere."

"Is there a point to this?"

She picked up the sword and put the sharp end against his throat.

"Did you know that *'scabbard'* is Latin for vagina?"

"No," he replied.

"And there are some letters on the sword." Paul was still looking down the blade, it had grazed his skin.

"Could you put it down?" he suggested.

"As the Knight said to the Bishop."

"Very funny." She laughed.

"That's my inspiration," she said. "Use the sword to kill a Knight and blame it on the Bishop."

"Are you crazy?"

"Depends," she said.

"What on?"

"I could do Knight's job better than he can – and nobody will miss him. Not even Mrs. Knight – if there is such an unfortunate person alive in this world. In fact, least of all, Mrs. Knight."

"This is just a school," said Paul. "If you don't like it – then leave."

"I like it here," said Candy, now stroking the sword. "I just don't see why *I* should leave to get a promotion."

"Because…"

"Because doesn't do it for me, mate." Candy leapt in.

"Screw you," said Paul.

"You have. And I have the proof." Reaching into her desk drawer, she pulled out an envelope. "Amazing what they will let you get away with these days. It gives a new meaning to that phrase *puss in boots*."

She laughed and presented Paul with some very clear photographs of him clearly up to no good with a very nice looking woman. All her bits that he never quite saw at the time were in perfect focus; the male gaze came easy. In a different life he might have asked for framed copies to give to his friends; in that other life he might have had friends he could offer them to.

"Where did those come from?"

"Like they say in the teaching manuals – *Catch them being good*. Although being good is a relative concept in this case – but I guess you have been well and truly caught out."

Paul reached for an indignation and pity combo.

"I am a married man," he said. "Please don't show them to anyone." She punched him on the arm. "Finally!" she exclaimed.

"What?" Paul asked.

"You remembered you are married…and doing this is wrong." He looked down at his shoes. "Yes," He admitted in a whisper. She paced around the room, swishing the sword.

"Did you think of *them* when you were with *me*?"

"Who?" There were a lot of thems in the world.

"Your wife. Your children. Your vows of fidelity."

"Well…" Of course he hadn't

"I know their names and what breakfast cereal they like. I know where they go to school. I know the way they walk home. What do you know about me?"

You're not just a pretty face, he thought.

"…erm…" Less and less by the second.

"You know how my breasts look in a push-up bra. I think that is about it."

"It was a push-up?"

"Come on. What do you know?"

"You teach history and you have a responsibility." He went literal.

"I am head of history and curriculum management. If it wasn't for Knight and his magic frigging clipboard, I'd be a deputy head." She knew that was not strictly true – she was only where she was now because she'd form for this kind of sexual entrapment, and she operated in a world of boy scouts who never in a million years could see what they were getting into.

"Is that what you want to be?" Paul asked. Sometimes men still surprised her with their stupidity and lack of drive.

"Why not?" she asked. Paul shrugged.

"It's just a job," said Paul. "It pays the mortgage." Mortgages were not Candy's bag.

"No," said Candy. "Not for me. I want to be in charge, and I can't wait for the idiots and pigmies to give me the chance. Knight always works late on a Wednesday. You, I, and the sword are going to surprise him."

"What?" Paul asked. "Scare him with the sword?"

"You really are a slow learner," she said, laughing. "You and me…we're going to kill him *with* the sword."

She really was Elektra…or Lady Macbeth. But who was he? Yet, apart from one thing, it seemed to Paul like a very good idea.

"What about our fingerprints?" She laughed again and then asked the right question of him.

"No guilty conscience then?" she asked, as Paul considered slowly the pros and cons of a potential murder.

"What if he has cameras all around his office?"

"It's very unlikely," said Candy.

"What if?"

"You are being paranoid," said Candy. "Who has cameras in their office?"

"You do," said Paul. Candy laughed again.

"But that's because I was expecting you, silly" she said. "He won't be expecting us, will he?"

Paul stopped and processed all the details she'd supplied. All his life, he'd worried about being caught out. Not enough love. Not enough preparation. Not enough contraception. Too much guilt by disassociation. Now he knew, it was never the deed that bothered him – just the thought of being discovered doing the deed. Now somebody else was taking on that responsibility on his behalf. It was a load lifted.

"I don't like him," said Paul.

"I know," said Candy, "that you hate him."

"How?"

"Hendrix," she said. "What that man will say to get laid."

"Have you?" She looked wistfully at the blade.

"I'm considering his options."

"Can I go home?" Paul looked at the time. Candy swished the sword some more.

"Not yet," she said. "We have work to do." She handed him a cloth and some gloves.

"Rub the handle with this," she said. "The prints will disappear."

"How do you know?" Paul asked.

"A policeman told me," said Candy.

"Did you do him too?" Paul asked.

"Of course," she said. "Why else would he help me with my enquiries?" She interrupted the conversation abruptly, to go to her cupboard and take out two white disposable body suits.

"Wear one of these," she said, tossing the suit at him.

"Where did you get these?"

"From the Police of course. I have always found them very helpful." As instructed, Paul put one on. He caught himself in the mirror. He looked like a sperm under a microscope.

"That's better," said Candy. "Now phone your wife, say you are working late. It is Ofsted season, after all. And when we kill Knight, your alibi is you were having crazy office sex with sweet Candy."

Mired in the shallows of manslaughter and mayhem, Paul had pretty much forgotten the inspection.

"What?"

"Kill a man nobody likes. I'm sure his mum and dad won't miss him all that much."

"This was only supposed to be about sex," said Paul.

"Everything is about sex," said Candy. "Except sex. Oscar Wilde said that so it must be true."

"Oh."

"And just to show you what a good sport I am," said Candy, "you can actually do it to me now." Paul felt a pang of adolescent self-consciousness. He looked at himself again in the mirror – now he looked like an extra in *Quincy*. His self-image was changing by the moment.

"Not sure I'm in the mood."

"You want soft lights?"

"Yeah...maybe." Candy laughed. Paul thought she was enjoying this rather too much.

"Be the serpent, not the flower."

"What the fuck are you on about?"

"Note to self," she said. "Find a real man next time. Knight made you look like a naughty little boy out there on the playground." No need for any Arthurian nonsense, Shakespearean bollocks or caped crusader shtick; she'd hit upon just the right tone required to motivate the workforce.

"Is the blade sharp enough?" asked Paul, being at heart practically-minded, task-driven.

Like a teacher delivering an outstanding lesson, Candy had anticipated everything. From her cupboard, she produced the long dead leg of a farm animal. He figured it was part of a pig and chosen because it most closely resembled the man they were going to kill. She placed it on her desk. Then she raised the blade a few inches. In an instant, it had cut to the bone.

"Think what it can do in the hands of a big strong man like you, Paul. You could chop his head off in a heartbeat."

Now he wasn't thinking, he was out of his suit and they were on the floor of her office rutting like wild creatures who knew no future. So he thought.

This time he saw everything from her exquisite dark pink nipples to her perfectly manicured lady-garden. She lay on top of him letting him do all the heavy lifting. He didn't care. He saw it all. He was the man! The cheating lying man!

And here he was, looking up at the whole deal. And how could you describe it? How could you remember it? It was like explaining gluttony to the starving; it couldn't be done – and if you could not enjoy the moment, you were really fucked. For a time the closeness became too much and it was as though he drifted to a place distant from everything, where nobody could touch him. He could sense that he would have very incriminating carpet burns when all of this was over. Then he was on the edge – at that point where you tried to remember something to take your mind away from thoughts of the inevitable. He was trying far too late – which only meant he would be coming too early. Immediately, he felt that gentle explosion that told him his time was up. That *petit mort* was all he ever wanted, and he was scared it amounted to so little.

Candy felt the warm invasion and understood that today of all days she needed to give him some value added in this particular exchange. She began a crescendo of moaning… never quite getting there until that moment she would have him suckered in.

"Oh…oh…oh…ah…ah…" Her orgasmic sounds were so soft and beautiful and yet an utter fabrication.

As she pretended to climax, shuddering and screaming, she knew she'd corrupted him body and soul.

She lay on top, her hair masking the look of boredom on her face. After she had rolled off him, she lay on the carpet by the coffee maker.

"How was it for you?" Paul asked. Being with him? Why do they ask? Don't they know? With all the shrinkage, it was as gripping as tube socks.

"Perfect," she lied. "Just perfect."

"Great," he said. Paul appreciated a good lie about his sexual prowess as much as the next man.

That was the truth; tell any man he is good in bed and he really will kill for you – tell him anything else and he might kill you. She had his danglers in a doggie bag; the rest would be panting by numbers.

Chapter Nineteen:
Love Lies Bleeding

Mr. Knight had arranged a super day for Paul to stumble and fall. He'd two sixth form classes and an assembly in front of Key Stage 4 scheduled to be inspected. That would mean inspection by the angry amigos of year 11, Rocket, Rambo, Gordie and Vinnie. Get that right and you were home and dry. Piss them off and life was an obstacle course leading to an abattoir of teaching ambition.

    Sat at home, Paul looked at the assembly from another time, school and key stage. He would tart it up. But this was what was going down tomorrow morning.

    Good Morning Year 9.

    Today's assembly is about forgiveness.

    What does forgiveness mean?

    Pupil answers

    When somebody has done bad things to you, you are able to let go of the pain it has caused you.

    Who might you forgive?

    Pupil answers

    Why should you do this?

    Suppose somebody does a terrible thing to you.

    For a while you will feel angry and maybe hate that person.

    Your mind will be taken up with that person and the bad things they have done.

    What happens if this never changes?

    Let's pretend this whiteboard is the space in our head.

Have black pieces of paper to put on whiteboard.

These are the angry thoughts about people who you hate.

Have white pieces of paper.

These are the happy thoughts about people who love you.

If you have this much hate, you will never have the space in your mind for the people who really care about you.

Your mind will be taken up with the people you hate.

A famous man called Nelson Mandela was put in prison for twenty-seven years.

When he was released, he forgave the people who put him in prison. He said if he had not done so, he would still be in a prison in his own mind.

Put bars on picture of Nelson Mandela.

Who might you forgive?

I forgave my father for throwing me out of his house when I was still a teenager.

I did not speak to him for ten years.

It took me a long time, but when I became a father, I understood it was a waste of my time and energy to hate him for what he did.

Thank you for listening.

If something was worth planning, it was well worth over-planning.

Chapter Twenty:
A Knight's Tale

In school, next day, Paul felt he was ready for anything. The line from one of Dylan's songs popped into his head. It was definitely *hanging day* and he was definitely the *Jack of Hearts*. On his way to death or glory, Paul met Mr. Knight, clipboard at the ready.

"Good morning, Mr. McSmart. How are we on this defining day of days?"

Paul knew this was Knight's effort at small talk. But fuck that, he was a dead man walking. He would try and say what he felt, short of saying he felt like killing him.

"It looks like you have asked them to pay me special attention," said Paul.

Mr. Knight gave him a smug smile that truly sealed his fate.

"I expect they'll be very keen to see how challenge and standards are in the upper school," said Mr. Knight. Paul bit down on a desire to ask him whether Paul might force his management speak clichés back down his fat throat. There would be time for that later.

"Of course," Paul said. Mr. Knight, though by no means an empath, picked up on the greater than normal hostility in the man's voice and his body language.

"Is there something you need to say to me?" Paul looked back. *Hill Street Blues* the early days of Big Phil was what was needed.

"Be careful out there."

"Thanks," said Mr. Knight and walked off. Paul remembered Jabo from the later series.

"Do it to them before they do it you," he added, the

words only for himself. Paul walked on to a place where he really could hold his own. A-level economics – where it started and ended for him. Show me where the money goes. None of that *Is this a dagger I see before me?* bollocks. This was facts and figures – stuff that might even really matter.

Lesson one was upper sixth macro, the Philips Curve – piece of piss - unemployment traded off against inflation, as long as the measures were passive and the data retrospective. The place where the Keynesians and the Monetarists fought their holy war, and forgot the good advice of the great Lord Keynes: in the long run we are all dead. Next he'd a break and an assembly to deliver. In the break, he sat quietly going over his notes – actually not notes but a word by word account of exactly what he would say and who he expected to answer any questions.

Paul strode up to the front of the assembled. He knew he had something good to give. Like most things in his life, he was good for a few minutes. Two minutes if you were running 800 metres, four minutes if it was 1500 – and keep quiet if idiots confused a sub-four 1500 with a sub-four mile. Easily done.

He took a deep breath, held it three seconds and let it out. He felt a little flushed around the cheeks – nothing to worry about. He'd delivered this one before.

Good old dad! Who knew that being out on his ear at eighteen would prove so useful when it came to delivering assemblies in the white heat of Ofsted? Forgiving people was really a selfish rather than a Christian thing because it released you from the hassle of hating somebody who one day might soon be dead – and who might actually like being hated rather than being forgotten. Carry on hating them and they live forever in your mind. His mother had shown him that lesson – still angry over those who had died more than forty years ago and were now immortalized by the rage of their enemies. Just like the dead of two world wars, they were remembered at the height of their powers – no getting feeble and incontinent for them. No lessening of their ability to hurt you from the grave – it was as if they crossed the line between love and hate and became something altogether greater like Obi-Wan-Kenobi in *Star Wars*. He wasn't sure if he would ever stop hating Mel Bishop and Duncan Knight dead or alive – but it was probable he was about to put it to the test. He could probably better forgive Duncan Knight dead than he could forgive him whilst he was still alive and making his time at work as miserable as he could.

Paul put his hands on the lectern; in that moment he felt completely at ease – it was something that never failed to surprise him. Talking for five minutes on a random topic fully prepared was his superpower – he would have preferred to be one of the X-Men, but you don't always get what you want in this life. Given he could never be Scott Summers, he went with the closest thing – being good at talking to a captive audience for five minutes.

"Yo Smarty!"

Rocket gave him a thumbs up. The emperor of the rats had delivered his verdict; Paul would live to fight another Ofsted. He hated groups and he hated talking. Yet he could talk in front of a group about anything. Paul possessed a superpower of no particular consequence. And to do so put him as near to some sense of wonder as anything else he had done which included adulterous sex. He was at one with the universe in a way he could never quite understand. Assemblies were so much better than lessons in school and better than life in general, which when you considered the matter closely, was hard and confusing with too many rules and conventions – many of which were unwritten and unspoken unless you broke them as regularly as Paul did. In assemblies, it was just speak and be listened to. As long as you gave them a piece of yourself – a slice of vulnerability and failure you were fine. That was the secret that the narcissists never learned – no matter how eloquent they were. Nobody wanted to hear how happy and complete your life was – they wanted to hear about the struggle and the pain. Don't talk about putting up your tent on holiday – tell them about it coming down in the middle of the night during a lightning storm. Leave your ego at the door. Don't tell them you passed your driving test the first time, tell them you crashed the car and only finally passed the third time on April 1st. His narrative was true and, as he understood from its reception, it was funny. All they ever wanted from an assembly – other than not having to be there in the first place – was struggle and misadventure. Paul could detach himself so completely from the pain, it was as though he was listening to somebody else talking when it was actually him.

What really cracked him up was that Ms. Bishop had made him do assemblies in the reasonable hope that he would crash and burn. She was the one who pointed the way to his destiny. Thank you for listening to my pain, Year 11. They gave him a round of applause, probably just relieved it was all over and nobody got hurt.

At the end of the assembly, an inspector rushed up and shook his hand. He had obviously ticked all his boxes.

"Where did you get the idea for that from?"

Paul looked at him. How do you answer an idiot? Yet, basking in the glory of his oration, he would give it a go.

"I'm a practicing Buddhist," he said. "I cure my inner rage by forgiving myself for anything I might have done, or might do in the future." The inspector, slightly scared, stepped back a pace to give Paul the distance he appeared to be asking for.

"Very convenient if you are up to no good," said the inspector.

"You should try it sometime," said Paul.

"I might just."

The inspector walked away to inspect somewhere else in the school. Paul wondered what damage he'd done and concluded he was spending too much time in the company of reckless people like Candy Regent and Hendrix. The trouble was that they were too much fun and he was easily led in his early middle age; they were also the only people who would actually talk to him without an obvious agenda concerned with doing him personal damage.

His final lesson of the morning focused on the theory of diminishing marginal utility for a lower sixth who enjoyed tales of debauchery. Without an inspector in the room, he went low and hoped for the best. Full Buddhist. Micro-economics in the shadow of a micro-brewery.

"So," said Paul. "It's like this. One drink at the start of the evening is great – it yields you a massive total utility. The second drink, depending on the capacity of the individual will increase your total utility although you may find that the extra enjoyment of the extra drink is not as great as the first. By the time you get to your ninth pint and the vomit is streaming out of your nostrils, you may have encountered the theory of diminishing and then negative marginal utility. You would be better off doing something else."

Front loading your lesson was a risk since you never knew when one of the thought police would find their way into your classroom. With a trusted class, you might even save your best stuff for that moment when the inspector walked in – that was real high-wire stuff not to be attempted unless you were brilliant, or had a death wish.

"Sir!"

A friendly voice and a helpful finger alerted Paul to the shadow in the window. He realized he was about to be observed – again.

The inspector walked into the room. Paul wrote some stuff on the whiteboard. She saw a group of students thoroughly engaged and listening to every word being spoken. She'd now seen this teacher described as 'marginal' teach four goodish lessons. It occurred to her that somebody in the school might have an agenda worth looking at. Who had tipped her off about this failing teacher? Mr. Duncan Knight – Deputy Head in charge of Raising Standards. The hippie art teacher had referred to him as the director of directed time. She liked him and yet he did not like this man Knight. This seemed to be a pattern throughout the school – nobody liked this man.

Generally you were universally unpopular for a good reason. How high were his own standards? The thought was enough for her and off she went to discover what the classes of Mr. Knight might look like when scrutinized professionally.

Chapter Twenty-One:
Inconvenience in Store

In Science 11E, Mr. Knight was facing a mutiny of Gary's mates. An unwritten law had been broken by Mr. Knight. Gary hadn't set off the fire alarm and the correct punishment for owning up was a day in the *'inky'* tops. His earlier punitive sanction of the boy was unanticipated inflation of the worst sort. In front of the whole school he'd broken that social contract – it was also their job to torment and mock Gary, not his. Mr. Knight had stepped over the line. The balance of events meant that although they hated outsiders like Ofsted making judgements on how their school was run, they now hated Mr. Shite even more. And they'd a cunning plan to take him down.

Mr. Knight had assumed charge of the lesson. He was the general, and they were the grunts. The start was to be swift and decisive. The various outcomes had already been written during the eternity of free time he had during a working day and the video segment was ready to go. All his sheets were differentiated at least by pupil name. He would show the world military precision in lesson delivery.

There were to be no good mornings and how are you? There was to be no explanation of why anybody else was in the teaching room. He would simply be a whirlwind of educational expectations.

Mr. Knight began with a re-cap of the last lesson.

"Can somebody tell the class what a molecule is?" A hand went up. It belonged to a long sleepy looking boy, already exhausted with the business of just being an adolescent.

"Yes Gordie?" Mr. Knight thought this would be a neat touch – show he knew their nicknames and hope they didn't use his.

"Is it what you have on the end of your nose, sir?"

"No." He nearly added *boy* to his response, but reined

it in.

Another hand. This one had energy to spare and a flair for organization in matters of teachers trying to be down with the kids. If Rocket wanted your lesson to succeed, it would do so. Rocket did not want this lesson to flourish.

"Yes Rocket?"

"Is it an animal sir?"

"We're not doing biology," said Mr. Knight. Another hand went up. The class clown – up for anything short of classroom homicide provided it got a laugh.

"Yes Gonzo?"

"Does it make holes in the ground?"

"I said we're not doing biology."

"Didn't you say mole?" Gonzo asked.

"No. I said molecule."

There followed a distracting question, one tried and tested in a number of science lessons.

"Sir," said Gordie.

"Yes," said Mr. Knight.

"Do you think a vegetarian would eat a Venus Fly Trap?" Mr. Knight groped for an answer before he realized he was being played by an expert.

"Are you being serious?" Mr. Knight asked. "Are you really being serious? It's a really stupid question." Gordie had a counter argument ready.

"You said there were no stupid questions, sir."

"Well I think you have just asked one," said Mr. Knight. Rocket tapped his pen. Rocket was well prepared for the lesson and had instructed the class not to talk if he tapped his pen. The class said nothing. They watched Mr. Knight start to get red in the face.

Rocket then placed his pen on the desk. It was time to take back the classroom. Another hand shot up. One all the staff were careful about. Not the leader, but a sleeping dog best left alone.

"Yes Vinnie?"

"Is it a part of something?"

"Yes. Yes," said Mr. Knight. A returning hand. In for a second bite.

"Yes Gordie?"

"Is it a vegetable?"

"No." Rocket smiled inside; he wasn't expecting such standards of improvisation in such a high-stakes game.

"Can you buy it in a corner shop?" Gordie continued.

"No." Mr. Knight looked around. Every bugger in the room knew what a molecule was. They'd danced around the hall last lesson and pretended to be molecules smashing into each other and setting off the fire extinguishers – *Accidentally sir*! It had nothing to do with blind burrowing mammals, Venus Fly Trap eating vegetarians, or skin blemishes and they bloody knew it.

Another familiar hand went up. Rocket was making a solo run. This time the boy had a grin. He was looking at an open and maybe consequence free goal.

"Yes Rocket?"

"If you could buy it in a corner shop, what would the corner shop be called?"

"What?" Incredulous and angry, at this point, Mr. Knight would have had them all kettled – but this was a lesson observed so he had to play it out. But he couldn't – the laughing hyenas had him surrounded and isolated.

"You all know what a molecule is!" Mr. Knight shouted. "You all know! I told you last lesson. I told you. . . ." His voice trailed off in defeat, he slumped like Robbie the Robot with his power pack pulled out. The hand went up again. Mr. Knight looked around. There were no other hands to choose. He knew the silent futility of picking on another pupil at this point – they would all feign mute exhaustion.

"Yes Rocket?"

"I know a good name for a corner shop..." This was the killer blow.

In his interrogations, Mr. Knight would book-end any self-serving excuse or story that extricated a pupil from a spot of bother with the words *that's handy* or for a change, *how handy*. In Year 11, it was always in the dark tales of the dealings with Mr. Knight. That's handy that the door to the tuck shop was open just as you were passing. That's handy that the boy fell on his face after walking over your foot. That's handy that you forgot your detention. It was the stuff of legend.

"...it could be called *that's handy*." Rocket had the self-anointed honour of blowing him out of the water. Laughter followed. The children, boys mainly, who understood the joke, infected those who did not and several who had been on the point of slumber. There was no record of how long it lasted.

Eventually Mr. Knight shouted.

"ENOUGH!" The class were cowed into silence. The disguise of reasonable caring teacher had been ripped off exposing the monster that lurked beneath, just like the scene in *Basil the Great Mouse Detective*, where Rattigan a cartoon manqué mouse is exposed as a rat who wants to kill the Queen of England. Mr. Knight was Rattigan, and inconveniently he'd forgotten his audience was not remotely those items of mortality he could bury with support plans, capability procedures or just good old-fashioned lies.

The Ofsted inspector looked at him. She was scared by what she'd seen and was preparing to leave the room. She gathered up her clip-board and handbag and fled the scene. Everybody knew this would not be good for Mr. Knight – but nobody was sorry they'd reduced him to a big fat zero. When she had gone a hand went up.

"Yes Rambo?"

"Is a molecule the smallest physical unit of an element or compound?" Mr. Knight tried not to scream.

"You knew that all along boy. You knew that!" Rambo kept his composure.

"No sir. I only just remembered it."

"Sir, isn't a quark smaller than a molecule?" asked Rocket, adding a touch of colour. Mr. Knight, mainly a chemist, was not one hundred percent sure what Rocket was on about. Half a moment ago, he was talking about the convenience of corner shops. He wanted the boy dead – but his dad was a governor. He had to go along with the game.

"Can you tell me what a quark is?" Mr. Knight asked.

"I seem to have forgotten," the boy responded.

"Are you sure?" Mr. Knight asked.

"Yes, sir," said Rocket.

"We could look it up in the dictionary," said Gordie. Mr. Knight felt grateful to be offered a lifeline. Good old Gordie – just goes to show it doesn't matter how many times you put them in detention. Mr. Knight reached for the science dictionary.

"Rocket."

"Yes."

"How do you spell it?" Mr. Knight asked.

Rocket bit his lip. This was nearly too much.

"I don't know," he said. Throughout the known universe that was this science lab, no bugger knew what a quark was, except Rocket who always did his best to conceal his own formidable intelligence.

"I think you do," said Mr. Knight.

"It might begin with a 'K' sir."

"Are you trying to make fun of me?" Mr. Knight asked.

Rocket, no stranger to GCSE Drama, gathered himself and gave Mr. Knight a practiced look that said he had been hurt to his core. He might even have popped out a tear.

"Sir?"

"Look at me when I'm speaking to you."

"I can't sir. Hendrix... Mr. Brown told me I'm left-eyed and right-eared. I can look at you, or I can listen to you. I can't do both."

"I've never heard so much rubbish in my life," said Mr. Knight.

By saying so much and no more, they shut him down; it was a lesson somebody should have observed and given to teacher training establishments everywhere. It was a lesson on the importance of at least not being actively hated by those you wish to teach - otherwise known as *Rocket Science*. Rocket Science 101: Own up to your own ignorance and inadequacy, because it will always catch you out if you don't.

"Let's watch the video," he said. Mr. Knight was waving the white flag of defeat. A video that would have lasted him until the end of term was used up all at once. *Molly the Molecule* took over and the class had the bonus of a *'doss'* lesson, courtesy of the lads of Year 11.

Mr. Knight walked out of the classroom as a man

with an ego so shrunken and diminished that it would have taken an electron microscope to make it visible to the school community. He'd been rendered no more important in his own observed lesson than a fly caught in a carnivorous flower. He had an associate who became a merchant banker; he delighted in telling his ersatz friend that the Thatcher tax breaks in the eighties meant that his own pay increased in one week by an amount greater that Knight's salary for a whole year. Not just that he earned more in a week than Knight did annually. He thought that one through and broke off all contact with the man – it was that humiliating. He should have been a merchant banker – he struggled to find a reason to remain being a teacher. It was as close to introspection as he'd ever come and he wanted no part of it ever again.

He also decided it was time to rebrand his catchphrase. From now on, it would not be *How handy*; after much thought he hit on the words *'Fancy that'*. Catchphrases rejected included *'Well I never'* and *'That was a stroke of good fortune.'* After the battering by year 11, he was looking for that stroke of good fortune himself; it would be very convenient if his plans to get rid of those inconvenient items bore their bitter fruit.

Chapter Twenty-Two: Daredevil

That same Wednesday, Gary and one of the *Bad Man Crew* had planned a revenge night raid on the school. The extent of their plan was they were out to nick whatever they could find that they thought might be worth nicking. As it became dark, they slipped over the fence, past the lake and onto the playing field. At that point, they were picked up on camera with their *Bad Man Crew* t-shirts clearly visible.

Parked outside the school, a couple of men in an unmarked white van watched how the boys got into the school building. The man in the passenger seat trained binoculars on the window – just in time to catch the end of the Paul and Candy show. Knight was on the money about them being shag-buddies. Shame to kill the girl, but needs must, that was the job.

"So," said Binocular Man, "this is where Paul McSmart and Candy Regent work out. We'll do it tomorrow."

"After we get the cash?" Driver Man asked.

"Of course after we get the cash," said Binocular Man. The van drove off.

A few minutes later, Paul and Candy, now dressed in forensic white and carrying a medieval Japanese sword, walked along the senior team corridor. Paul, post coital, felt as though he was dreaming. He hoped he was. They both knew where they were going, there was no need for talk.

They entered Knight's office where he was hunched over his records, eating another beloved pasty. Eyes half closed, he was in a state of half-baked ecstasy...deep in his pie zone. One half of the pasty was in his mouth and the other in his hand. They'd no idea what he had been looking at – it would have paid them to have taken a look. Duncan Knight was going through Paul's paperwork, dropping flakes of pastry all over it – but more importantly taking him off the support plan. He was next going to find out what a quark was – nail those little fuckers in year 11 the next time he crossed swords with them. And check out that nonsense about left ears and right eyes. Once he had done that, he intended to firm up the verbal contracts he had on Paul and Candy – Romeo and Juliet must die, but well before Act Five.

All Paul knew was that he hated the sounds people made when they ate food and thought nobody in the world could hear them. He remembered how much his father detested them too – and how he would shout at his children for not eating with their mouths closed. Duncan Knight was about to pay the ultimate price for poor table manners, a general lack of awareness about his personal space and being a total bastard to one and all.

Candy gave Paul a loving look that seemed to hint at childhood summer memories filtered through the eye of Ridley Scott. It was killing time. She gave him an almost imperceptible smile of encouragement – in that moment he could do no less than exactly what she wanted. Breathe in. Hold and count to three. Breathe out. He could hardly believe he hadn't noticed them in the room – not like they were invisible to the human eye.

What comic hero was he in this moment? Then he saw himself; mild mannered Dr. Don Blake finding Thor's hammer in that cave in. Three strikes and he was a cripple no more…he was the god of thunder who owed nothing to the mortal world. Channelling his inner Norse, Paul then raised the blade and brought it down as hard as could on the neck of the deputy head – his less dominant ear as it happened. No more megaphones for you fat boy. Killer instinct took over – he was Mac the Knife. Whooshing through the air, the blade bit through flesh and bone. It felt so clean and so right. There was only the noise of Knight's head hitting the floor about a yard from his shoulders, the pasty bitten clean in half and his clipboard cut in two. In Japan, Paul would have lost a few marks for coarse cutting – the head was supposed to hang by a thread of flesh – what he'd done would have been considered somewhat vulgar. No matter, mayhem had been accomplished.

Through the alchemy of mixing his bodily fluids with Candy, he'd found his inner psychopathic Norse god. With the arteries in Mr. Knight's neck fully exposed, there was blood spurting everywhere – it covered the walls and ceiling - any colour you wanted as long as it was red and clotted. The truth had been revealed; he was human after all. It was not the stroke of good fortune Mr. Knight had been hoping for – but it got year 11 off his case.

"Crumbs," said Paul. "I think we are a bit late for a tourniquet." He was definitely a boy scout with a first aid badge. Candy laughed the same laugh she produced before and after having sex with him. It was from a time that now felt long ago and far away.

"How handy," she said.

"I think I may just have come off my support plan," said Paul.

"You've got a knack for this," said Candy, wiping her face clean of spots. "Well done."

"Beginner's luck," said Paul. Beginner's luck! That was something he had in spades. Always good for a bit, but no follow through. As a runner of some promise, he was under two minutes for 800 meters at sixteen, then zip. A good start to a teaching career followed by a steady decline into mediocrity and borderline incompetence, exacerbated by a lack of curiosity in the workings of his own mind – and a lack of attachment to anything else. The general sense he had, until now, of never being in the moment. He was astounded that he felt no guilt. Mirroring a psychopath, all he had required was the instruction to kill - and then to not feel bad about it afterwards. Candy, ever full of surprises, said something surprising.

"We never asked for his forgiveness."

"What?"

"An executioner," said Candy, "would always ask the condemned person to forgive them for the deed they were about to do."

"I doubt he would forgive us," said Paul. "I wouldn't."

"It's because you don't get it," said Candy.

"Get what?"

"Death," said Candy. "Something we should all plan for."

"If you say so," said Paul. Candy was pleased at how well her plan was working out. It was another thing to tick off the bucket list. She looked at the mayhem they had caused and became a little wistful.

"That's the way I would rather go," said Candy. "As long as it was done properly – and I was still beautiful."

"I think once a night is quite enough," said Paul. That attitude was why this relationship was never going to be forever. Candy ignored the very poor play on words and considered the positives.

"You have what the Japanese call *zanshin*."

"We make a good team," said Paul.

"Better at killing than kissing," said Candy.

"Whatever," said Paul. He was beginning to worry about being caught for this one; he knew he was guilty and that was all that mattered. What he most wanted was for someone else to get the blame. He could live with the guilt, minimal as it was, but he did not want to go to prison. It sounded like school only much worse.

Chapter Twenty-Three: Finders Keepers

Further down the hallway, there was the sound of breaking glass.

"Fuck!" Paul whispered. Candy held his free hand.

"Don't panic." She went to the door and looked out. She recognised the boys. This gave her another idea. She turned to Paul.

"Wipe the sword down and put it outside the door." Paul couldn't think on his feet. He did not see the same opportunity that Candy did.

"What?"

"Just do it." So, with his sleeve, Paul wiped the sword clean of most of the blood. There was still some on the handle. He then opened the door and put the sword into the hallway. After Paul had withdrawn, Gary was the first to see it, ghostly in the moonlight.

"Look Lump! It's a bleeding sword!" He picked it up and raised it above his head. It smashed against the corridor ceiling lights. It was all Paul could do to stop himself telling Gary to be quiet. In a second Paul saw them as a debuting pair of deadbeat DC villains, *Benefit Boy* and his sidekick *Loser*. All it needed was a vigilante like *Batman* to take them down.

"Look at me," he shouted. "I'm a Nutter."

"It's like in that play we done with Smartie – *Blackdeath*," Liam responded excitedly.

"What?" Gary had bunked most of key stage three and knew little of the recommended texts. Liam gave him a crash course.

"It's a play by Shaking Stevens where they all get shivved because a queen wants to be a king." Gary gave it some thought.

"Does she give tit-wanks?"

"I hope so," said Liam. "Next lesson maybe."

"Take it to one of Smartie's classes," said Gary. "He'd crap his pants he would." Liam laughed and became serious.

"What's a sword doing in a school? It could hurt somebody," he said. In response, he was given the ultimate insult by Gary.

"Are you a pussy?" Liam manned up and asked the correct question.

"Are we gonna steal it?" Gary considered the proposition and remembered Mr. Knight's old catchphrase.

"That's handy." Again Paul resisted an urge to correct their malapropisms and let them get on with the business of stitching themselves up for a murder they did not commit. Malapropism! A word he'd only just learned since joining the English department – and yet another word he could barely say in his head, let alone speak. And as for Benefits Boy and Loser picking up the tab, he was sure that something similar had happened in the Scottish play.

"What?" Liam asked.

"Victimless crime, in'it?" Gary had self-justified his intended robbery.

"Do ya fink it's worth anything?" Liam asked. Gary looked at it carefully.

"Got defo scrap value," he said. "My mate's dad does scrapping."

"We could sell it to 'im," said Liam.

Gary held the sword and considered its future; it was much too good to scrap. Fuck his old man, he was going to keep it for himself…maybe scare somebody with it one day…

maybe that cunt Knight…show what a real bad boy he was.

"Be good for the Bad Man Crew to have something," he said. "Ya know, in the shed."

"How we getting it out of here?" he asked. Liam was more concerned with the logistics of the crime.

"Take off your sweatshirt, Lump," said Gary, pointing to the garment around Liam's waist. "We'll wrap it in that."

"Why not yours?" Liam asked. "You're bigger than me."

"Because, Lump, I'm the number one *Bad Man* here," said Gary, successfully pulling rank. Armed with the sword, the two boys walked down the senior corridor, pausing only to empty Mr. Kingman's petty cash box and then strolled back out onto the field where the CCTV cameras lived wild and free in trees and bushes.

Back in her office, Paul and Candy had taken off the forensic suits. Candy picked them off the floor and put them into *bags for life*; then she covered them with paperwork she'd completed earlier in the day. Since it was a response to Mr. Knight's agenda for their head to head, there was no need to worry about the random spots of blood.

"I'll get rid of these," she said. "You go home to *wifeypoo*."

"She has a name," snapped Paul.

"I know she does," hissed Candy. She gave him a kiss and pulled a note out of his pocket.

"What are you doing?" It was the note she had put in his pigeon hole that morning.

"I don't think Melissa needs to see this," she said, waving it in front of his face.

"No," said Paul, as he stepped away from her. "Good

thinking."

"Someone has to." It was almost as if they'd never murdered anyone in the first place. Just to make sure they had, Paul went back to look at the severed head.

"Shoes and socks off first," she said. He blindly obeyed and squelched across the blood soaked carpet.

One half of a pasty was still in the man's mouth.

"He looks quite content," said Paul.

"Pastry was his one true love," said Candy.

"Perhaps they'll bury him in a pie...or bake him in an oven." Candy huffed. Even in the business of murder, Paul was very easily distracted. She wondered how Melissa put up with him. Any man was too much hassle and he was more so than any man she'd known.

"I think we should leave him to rest in peace," she said.

"Or pieces," said Paul.

"Killer joke," said Candy. "Now scoot." As instructed, Paul left the premises first. Because Mr. Knight had put all the spare CCTV budget into checking petty theft in the classrooms, there was no evidence of any adults leaving the premises that evening.

After three days breaking all the rules, Paul felt he'd no more adultery or murder in his heart. And who would care that Knight was dead and that a pair of innocent children would be blamed? He had applied a principle of Benthamism – the greatest happiness would be delivered to the greatest number. Nobody would have Gary or Liam in their class, and nobody would have Knight on their case. Two wrongs definitely made a right in this instance.

Half an hour later, Candy left with the forensic suits in lieu of marking. Her new log-burner would have something different to incinerate tonight. What a piece of luck! Those two little twerps were almost as simple as the one she'd just bonked. She would succeed where Lady Macbeth had failed, because she, Candy, was strong enough to be alone.

At the school gate, she saw Paul's polo. He was standing by his car, waiting for her. She pulled up in her topless MG.

"See you at the motel," she said. "Room 55."

"I just need to check we're cool about this."

"Check your car," said Candy. "It smells like its leaking fuel."

"Like you would know," said Paul, who would definitely not be checking for leaking fuel after that piece of passive aggression disguised as helpful advice. She looked at him, idiot that he was. He looked to her for reassurance.

"Are we cool?" he asked.

"Are we cool!" She raised her voice. "Of course we are! You stupid man! Now go there!" She looked around to check nobody had seen them. Invisible random thoughts flew out of her head. What a loser he was. At least Hendrix knew what he wanted – gatefold muff and plenty of it - Paul was the sort of man who would turn up at a gang bang with a bunch of flowers, a box of chocolates and no condoms.

Chapter Twenty-Four: Chop and Change

Candy drove home and disposed of everything she'd worn for the past week. As planned, her hairdresser and manicurist turned up an hour later. As far as Candy was concerned, the girl was gorgeous until she opened her mouth. Candy would have changed hairdressers but she was good at what she did. The banter annoyed Candy to a point that did not quite extend to murder, but sometimes came close.

"Hello," she said. "Have you been a good girl?"

"Depends on your definition of good," said Candy.

"As long as no-one died."

"No, then I have," said Candy, enigmatically.

"You are a funny one," said the hairdresser. "What's it to be?"

"Make me look serious," Candy said. The hairdresser had no idea.

"How do you want it?"

"Cut it short and make my nails nice and long – and purple." The hairdresser sounded upset. She held up Candy's limp fringe.

"All this gone?"

"Yes," said Candy.

"And long nails?"

"Yes," said Candy. "Long enough and hard enough so as to gouge out someone's eyes." The image sat uncomfortably between them.

"I'm not sure I like what you're saying," said the hairdresser.

"Call the police then," said Candy.

"I think I'll just do your hair and nails." The rest of the transaction was completed in silence which is what Candy had always wanted. After she was finished with Candy's hands and hair, the hairdresser looked at the decimation.

"What about this beautiful dark hair?" the hairdresser asked politely enough. Candy shrugged and tapped her new nails on the side of her chair.

"It's yours if you want," she said.

"You could sell it for charity," the hairdresser suggested. Candy had no room in her soul for anyone worse off than herself. She pointed to the pile of dead cells.

"Take it. I have no need of it anymore."

"Like I said, it's beautiful." The hairdresser commented, picking up the cut hair. After the hairdresser had packed away and gone, Candy drove to the local motel. Nobody looking to be discrete in Kingswater ever went there. On the way there she was spotted by at least twenty children she recognized as pupils of the school. Paul had already checked in and was hopefully waiting for her on the bed.

"Love the new look, *Mein Fuhrer*." Like the despot she was, she gave him his marching orders.

"Get out and go home," she said.

"But, I thought…"

"It's never going to happen again. You have a knob of butter and I'm lactose intolerant."

"And, what about yesterday?"

"This is our alibi," she said. "Now leave."

"That's it?" Paul asked.

"Do you want flowers and chocolates?"

"No," said Paul. "I just want to know why."

"Why? Because you have given me all I needed."

"What about me?" He hadn't expected a role reversal quite so soon

"You're a cheating husband. I think you'll deserve exactly what you get. Go home before I tell Melissa where you are and what you've been up to."

"Why would you do that?" Paul asked.

She remembered her father coming home late most nights when she was a child. When she discovered he didn't actually live in his office, she understood the betrayal. With married men, she tempted them to destruction and afterward despised them for their intrinsic weakness. As a predator she knew where all weakness could be found and she honed her skills on vulnerable males. A pattern repeated itself, always the same. She never gave up the chase and she always hated them once she won. She'd undergone therapy for the problem – but once she understood why she did it she had sufficient motivation to carry on doing so. Therapy was good like that. She gave him the short answer.

"Because you're not enough of a man to do it yourself."

"Right," said Paul, "so that's over and done with."

"All over, for good."

"I'll be off." Paul said. She stopped talking. He was going to be screwed over. He could have the last word. Paul went home to consider his clichés.

Stick or twist?

Frying pan or fire?

The devil or the deep blue sea?

Chapter Twenty-Five:
Any Old Iron

Armed only with an incriminating photograph of Gary carrying the murder weapon off the school premises, DC Grissom pushed the doorbell at the boy's given address. As he waited, he patted his pocket; the manila envelope felt pleasingly full of the folding stuff. There was no sound. He banged on the door. A large man appeared at the door, one hand holding it slightly open, the other hand rummaging around for something in his underpants that he couldn't quite find until the exact moment he made eye contact.

"What d'ya want?""I am a Police Officer." DC Grissom leaned in a bit too close

The large man locked eyes with him.

"Obviously," he replied.

"I need to speak to your boy. Is he in?"

"How the fuck should I know?" Clearly, the large man did not care much for the conversation.

"I need to speak to him," said DC Grissom, "he's a suspect in a murder at the comp."

"Can't be my boy," said the man. "He's been expelled."

"They call it excluded these days," said DC Grissom.

"Whatever." The Detective ignored the last exchange.

There was a standoff for a less than a minute. The man spoke again.

"You still 'ere?"

"Yes," said DC Grissom. There was always a dance with a geezer like this one; it was a cultural thing in Kingswater – waste the old bill's time so that they could nick fewer of you. "Your Gary?" DC Grissom had started again.

"What about him?"

"Is he in?" The man leaned back into the house.

"Gary! The old bill's looking for ya. Somefink 'bout a murder." A few minutes later, Gary came to the door.

"Could we speak inside?" DC Grissom asked. A smell of stale sweat and chips further colonised his personal space.

"No filth in this house," said Gary's dad. Filth indeed! The house had dust on top of dust. To DC Grissom it looked like a place where you wiped your shoes on the way out. The alternative he was about to propose was a much better one for both his health and safety.

"Then you need to come to the station," he said. Gary understood some sort of game was up. He prepared his defence. He was going to throw Lump under the bus. He was going to squeal. Quick as.

"It wasn't me. It was Lump. He said he found a sword. Made me keep it in the shed, or he'd do me in, he would." A murder weapon! Thought Grissom.

"Could you show me this sword?" DC Grissom asked.

"It's in the shed," said Gary. "I was going to scrap it."

That was not how the family did things. Petty cash was one thing. An antique sword was something else.

"I'm the scrapper here," his father said, pointing to his chest.

"I was gonna show you later today," said Gary. DC Grissom noted the dishonesty between thieves – a free and frank discussion between father and son might have meant there was a murder weapon on the premises. The investigation was ticking all the boxes.

"Well fuck off and find it," said his dad. A few minutes later, Gary was back with the sword.

"You had better give that to me," said DC Grissom.

"We use shooters in this family," said his dad. On any other day, thought DC Grissom, that would have been incriminating.

Gary's dad went to hit him on the head. But Gary darted behind the Police Officer.

"Shooters," said his dad. "Did you hear me son?" He paused. "Shooootazz." He stretched out the last word for effect and made his right hand into the shape of a gun.

"Like I said, it was Lump made me do it," Gary said, trying to throw the blame onto somebody else. .

"Lump? Lump? Who the fuck is Lump?" His dad frowned

"Lump," said Gary, "is Liam York."

"Fuck off," said his dad. "Liam's only just out of shorts – girls at primary used to nick his lunch for practice."

"He's fucking scary," said Gary.

"He's twelve years old," said his dad.

"He's really tall for his height," said Gary. A white trash code of honour had just been breached in the most profound way – murder was one thing, on this animal estate being a pussy in front of a pig was totally unacceptable. It was game over for Gary.

"You should go down just for saying that," said his father. "Take him away; he's no son of mine."

"I think," said DC Grissom, "that the two of you need to come down to the station."

"What if I don't?"

"I just go around the estate telling everyone you're helping me with my enquiries," said DC Grissom.

"I'm no grass."

"Who are they going to believe," said DC Grissom. "You or me?" That was the motivation the man needed to grow a lawn.

"You need to wait a moment," said his father. "I got guests. Cousins from up north. They need to know we're going to the nick."

"Alright," said Grissom. The man hollered up the stairs.

"Oi, Burkenhare, I'm off to the fucking nick with me boy. Something about a murder."

There was a shout from upstairs.

"Who got murdered?"

"Fuck knows," said Gary's dad.

"It was a man called Duncan Knight," said DC Grissom.

"A fucking fat teacher," Gary's dad shouted upstairs.

"That cunt," said Gary. "He excluded me yesterday."

"You seem to be self-excluding," said DC Grissom. "And who are the men upstairs?"

"Don't you tell him nothing," said Gary's dad. "It's enough that you're a pussy without being a grass." But DC Grissom already had his boy. He did not need the complications of real life clouding his case.

Burke and Hare, the driver and passenger of the unmarked white van watched as Gary and his father got into the back of DC Grissom's car.

"I think that's us out of here," said Burke, who was the one with the binoculars.

"What about the money?" Hare asked.

"In the coat pocket of that copper," said Burke.

"Why?" Hare asked.

"He didn't ask anyone where the money was," said Burk.

"What went wrong?" Burke asked.

"I think our boy thought he was Billy Big Potatoes, tried to punch above his weight and got took his self. I reckon he bit off more than he could chew trying to kill that girl."

"I'm glad we didn't," said Hare. "I don't like killing women."

"Nah, me neither. They don't shut up no matter what." Burke and Hare got into their van and drove off into the sunset – none the wiser and none the richer.

Chapter Twenty-Six:
No Shit Sherlock

Ms. Bishop had her lightbulb moment; with Ofsted cancelled, she came to the understanding that what she really craved was power without the responsibility that came with being a head of a struggling comprehensive. With an idiot husband in full support of her inherited wealth, she immediately resigned her post, took a leave of absence and trained to become an Ofsted inspector. Mr. Kingman became the acting Head. He said privately that what would have been his first two acts on becoming the head were already accomplished at no cost whatsoever to anybody – with the bonus of a 100% decline in gang related crime. The death of Mr. Knight and the resignation of Ms. Bishop had given the school community a lift that would have seen them through the inspection and all the way past Christmas.

A police officer knocked on Ms. Candy Regent's office door. If he'd any previous knowledge of her, he would have been surprised to see a stern looking young woman with short dark hair and a floppy fringe that was too much Adolf H. for his taste.

"Come in," she said. She assessed him as a man in early middle age, aware of his own mortality, but sound enough for a sustained shagging that might change his point of view on matters of guilt and innocence.

"Good morning," he said. "I'm DC Grissom." She knew she could. But she knew she wouldn't even try.

"Good morning Mr. Grissom."

"I am here," said DC Grissom, "to talk about what happened last night."

"It was me," she said. "I killed him." They shared a moment.

"That makes it easy," said DC Grissom.

"Icebreaker," she said. "My little joke."

"Okay…"

"I was in school," she said. "I was preparing for the inspection, but I left quite early."

"Is there anybody who can verify that?" DC Grissom asked. She nodded, allowing a few strands of her new fringe to fall into her face.

"I booked a room with Mr. McSmart, the Head of Business Education."

"Why?"

"I share a house and Mr. McSmart is a married man." He'd checked that she did not share a house, but he nodded. He was a married man; it was what he did when he needed to.

"Understood." With nails too long and pretty to wield a blade, she pointed to the door.

"Mr. McSmart shares an office just down the hall."

"No taking him there then?" DC Grissom failed to suppress a smirk as he spoke. She laughed.

"I'm not sure he has ever serially satisfied four women."

"I'll catch you later," he said.

"Looking forward to it," she said. As the door shut, Candy Regent reflected on what was a very successful encounter – with maybe the bonus of potential encounters to follow. DC Grissom knew she was something more than she presented. She seemed to see through him – all the way to his loins. She had done something, even if it fell short of murder on this occasion.

The next person he called on was Hendrix. The potter was in his potting house counting out his pots.

"What can I do for you?" Hendrix asked.

"Do you know Mr. Knight is dead?"

"You hum it and I'll sing it."

"No," said DC Grissom. "You don't get it. He really is dead. His head was cut off last night."

"I'll have to get a new catchphrase," said Hendrix after he'd stopped laughing.

"I take it you didn't like the deceased," said DC Grissom.

"I think," said Hendrix, "this will go down as the most popular cut in education."

"A bit harsh," said DC Grissom.

"The only people who didn't hate him were people who had never met him." Hendrix expanded on his point of view.

"So he was killed by somebody he knew," said DC Grissom.

"He was a Cunt who gave other Cunts a bad name," said Hendrix. "I'm glad he's dead."

"Did you kill him?" DC Grissom asked.

"No," said Hendrix. "But I often thought about it."

"Do you know who might have?"

"Yes," said Hendrix.

"Who?" asked the policeman. Hendrix threw his arm out theatrically.

"Anybody in this fucking school. Anybody who knew him well. Anybody who met him once. Anybody with a social conscience."

"That doesn't help much," said DC Grissom.

"I never said I would," said Hendrix. DC Grissom left Hendrix and carried on with his enquiries.

In his shared office, Paul McSmart sat and considered the wrecking ball he'd just introduced to his personal and professional life. Even for a person of minimal self-awareness, this was a cosmic mess. He'd killed one human being and shagged another. Or was it shagged one human being and killed another? Difficult to know which was worse. Neither of them was his wife. His alibi for murder was adultery. The adultery hadn't been all that – and neither was the alibi. He was pleased that Knight was dead – not so happy that the deed haunted his conscience. He tried to live in the moment, but that failed and he found himself mired in the recent past. Down the hall, it was still a murder scene and he was still a suspect. He'd read that most murder victims knew their killer. Despite all of this, he'd enjoyed the best night of sleep since before the birth of his children. His somnolence was because, as he'd predicted, he was no longer on a support plan following the death of his proposed mentor, Mr. Knight. Hey-ho.

There was a knock at his door, followed by a voice at his door.

"Mr. McSmart?"

"Yes."

"May I come in, Mr. McSmart?"

"Yes." Paul McSmart saw a man with bad skin and a large nose. DC Grissom saw a guilty man who was squirming in his own skin.

"Good morning, Mr. McSmart," he said. "I am sure you know why I am here."

"Yes."

"Can you tell me where you were last night?"

"I was here working…then I left…" DC Grissom filled in the gaps.

"With Ms. Regent?"

"Yes." Paul responded immediately. DC Grissom paused a moment.

"How would you characterize your relationship with the deceased?"

"I disliked him intensely," said Paul.

"As good as that?"

"Yeah."

"Any reason?"

"He was a bully," said Paul. "He was responsible for putting me on a support plan. He enjoyed hurting others."

"What's a support plan?"

"A procedure that pretends to help you do your job, but it's really all about getting rid of you."

"So, the opposite of supporting you?"

"Yes," said Paul, "it's like being thrown a lifebelt full of lead. Unless you are Harry Houdini, you sink like a bloody stone and everyone says good show and goodbye."

"Would that have been a reason to kill him?"

"Of course it would."

"Did you kill him?" There was a deathless pause. DC Grissom looked around the room. He saw an X-Man comic book. DC Grissom was more of a Batman kind of guy. That stuff made sense, no superpower nonsense, just good old vigilantes enforcing the law in a lawless world.

"No," said Paul.

"Who do you think might have?"

"You have a school full of suspects," said Paul. "Nobody liked him. I am sure I wasn't the only person who was placed on a support plan."

"So the teachers mostly didn't like him?"

"I hated him," said Paul. "Really hated him. Support plan or not, I'm a teacher."

"And the pupils? They felt the same as you?"

"Oh, yes," said Paul. "He excluded a boy yesterday for owning up to setting off a fire alarm. Turned out it was an electrical fault. He gave the boy three more days for wasting his time. Punished him in front of the whole school. There's a motive."

"Gary Smith?"

"Yes," said Paul.

"Thank you Mr. McSmart," said DC Grissom. He paused, before adding, "In my experience, it's best you tell your wife before she finds out. She might not forgive you…but if this goes public, I'll probably be investigating your murder as well."

"It would be much easier to solve," said Paul.

"Yes," said DC Grissom. "With a more than good chance she'd serve less time than she did in her marriage."

"I'll bear that in mind," said Paul.

"She might even get off."

"I'll tell her my truth," said Paul.

"You be sure to do that, Mr. McSmart…if I went on *Mastermind*, my area of understanding would be adultery. Men are fuckwits when it comes to relationship politics; think they can fool women. I don't know why. A woman might allow it to happen – she might tolerate a man who roams - but she'll know it is happening. Oh boy, will she know what you're up to."

"Thank you," said Paul.

"Goes with the job," said DC Grissom. "I'm on my second marriage and it's not going that well."

"Get out early as you can," said Paul. The Detective said nothing. "Poem by Larkin," said Paul. The Detective knew that – but wasn't going to let on.

"I see. Well I'll leave you to your poetry and adultery."

"Catch you later," said Paul. Just as DC Grissom got to the door, he paused, before speaking again.

"Just make sure you don't kill anyone else. "The electric tingle of guilt jumped from Paul to the policeman. He registered the alarm.

"What?"

"Humour, Mr. McSmart. Humour. You have to laugh at human nature in this job. Bit like yours but with more dead bodies and less paperwork. Apart from yesterday of course."

"Oh," said Paul limply. The Detective left with his hunch intact. If he was asked to make a guess, he would have said it was done by those three people. The only thing that didn't make any sense was the tax free *'Archer'* he had found in the deceased's top drawer earlier that morning. The money was in an envelope marked for the attention of Burke and Hare. Two grand in used notes was enough to kill at least one teacher, maybe more. If the motive was robbery, it was a piss poor job all round. In fact, the whole money thing made so little sense to him that he decided to tell nobody about it. He put it down to a couple of boys with learning difficulties who got over-excited with the whole killing thing that they completely forgot the robbery aspect. Never try to multi-task when you're an idiot. The economics of stupidity happened quite frequently in his experience – buy a gun for a *grand*, rob a man for a *monkey* and throw the shooter in the cut when you ran off. If he had a *pony* for every time that happened – well he'd have a great deal less untraceable paper in his pockets than he had right now. Real life: it all added up to a paint-by-numbers Squeeze song written for a remaindered episode of *'Only Fools and Horses'*.

After the police officer had gone, Paul watched five minutes crawl by before he steamed into Candy's office.

"Best to knock," said Candy, "no telling what I'm up to in here."

"Do you think he bought it?" Paul asked.

"Well," said Candy, "we were definitely doing something wrong last night. Policemen always know if you've been naughty or nice."

"You know what I mean," said Paul.

"Of course I do," said Candy. "It's just best not to go over it."

"Not something I do every day," said Paul.

"Me neither," said Candy.

"What now?"

"I'm going to be applying for the vacancy," said Candy.

"Dead man's boots?"

"I'm a shoe in," said Candy.

"That's a bit cold," said Paul.

"It's practical," said Candy.

"And me?"

"Now that you're off your support plan, I suggest you apply for my job."

"And us?"

"There is no more us."

"Why?" He was one very slow learner. She tried being nice this time.

"Anyone who hooks up with you needs to be brave, blind or besotted – and where you are concerned, I am none of those."

"Harsh," said Paul, secretly pleased to be off the hook.

"Relax," she said, putting her hand on his. "You're a dick, somewhat shriveled and pathetic, but it might not be a lifelong condition." It was one of the few judgements she made about Paul that was wrong. He was definitely a dick and it turned out to be a lifelong condition.

Killer Queen

Chapter Twenty-Seven: Word on the Street

As in all times of stress, Paul went to see Hendrix.

"Good news," said Hendrix. "Was it you?"

"Yes," said Paul.

"Fuck my old boots," said Hendrix. "You have done the world a favour – but don't tell anyone else, they won't see it the same way as me and the rest of the school community."

"I did it after I shagged Candy Regent," said Paul.

"Fuck me," said Hendrix. "Fuck me! You were only supposed to blow the bloody doors off. "

"Doors, windows, walls and ceilings," said Paul. Hendrix laughed again.

"I used to think you lived in an unconvincing manor," he said. "Detached from everything…but adultery and murder…you my boy have moved up the property ladder."

"She put me up to it," said Paul, "but it seemed like an okay thing to do at the time."

"Bit of a laugh?" Hendrix asked. That was the excuse with the highest currency if you were under sixteen.

"No. Exhilarating I would say. Definitely worth it. But not many laughs."

"Never a good thing when someone is laughing during sex," said Hendrix, "or murder I suppose."

"Yeah," said Paul. "She put me up to it and we took it all very seriously."

"Not the best defence I've ever heard," said Hendrix. "Find another one if you can."

"Don't tell," said Paul.

"Who's going to believe me? The old bill thinks it was me anyway on account of me not liking him."

"Tea break over," said Paul. Hendrix laughed like the maniac he wished he could really be.

"Yeah," he gasped, "back on your head!"

But Hendrix understood enough about proximity and blame to go home that evening and write a long note to his future self. He decided he would detail everything he could recall about all the people involved in the crime. He gave the whole thing a grand title: *The Hendrix Chronicles.* It was, he decided, only to be opened and read in the event of any unnatural death in his family. Having committed himself to the project, he was then not sure what to do next. There were very few people of sound mind he could discuss recent murders in the community with. Eventually, he hit upon the idea of leaving it with a solicitor. All he had to do now was write the thing and find a solicitor. He eventually settled on asking Paul McSmart to give him the number of the solicitor he would be using for his divorce. Then he was worried that he might not now be bothered to actually write the document.

Chapter Twenty-Eight:
Hancock's Half Hour

In the staffroom later that morning, Candy sat and had coffee with Angela Phipps, a science teacher she might have some use for one day in another cunning plan. She was just on the brink of losing all the looks she had – and Candy guessed, a husband with alcohol issues and erectile dysfunction who was beginning to look for a younger model to stiffen his resolve. Angela enjoyed Candy's company, if only for the random stuff she came out with and because she was unbelievably beautiful. Today she looked like a warrior, fierce and sexy with cropped hair and purple talons.

"I think," said Candy, "it's time for a change. What do you think?" Angela was surprised at the calm tone. This had not been the most normal of weeks so far. But that was Random Candy. Someone dies and she gets a makeover and considers promotion possibilities.

"I was thinking of working for the union," said Angela. "Helping those people who get let down by the system – like your friend Paul – Mr. Semi-Detached."

"Not my friend," said Candy.

"Tell that to the jury," said Angela. Worried that Angela really did know something, Candy became a bit more forensic.

"What do you know?" Candy asked.

"I've seen him with his tongue on the floor when you pass by." The danger for Candy had passed. Same old.

"Occupational hazard of being hot," said Candy. Angela laughed.

"I never found it to be a problem."

"I find you very attractive," said Candy, sensing a vulnerability she might exploit.

"Flattery will get you most places," said Angela, feeling a little more internal heat than she expected.

"I know," said Candy. "And men are such coarse beasts, is it any wonder we chop their heads off?"

"What?"

"Only kidding," said Candy. "But I think they'd make a lot more fuss if we lopped off their low hanging fruit."

"So," said Angela, "what's your plan – other than mass castration of the male population?"

"After we fuck them?"

"Obviously."

"Firstly I think people should be made to look out for themselves and not rely on unions."

"That's not a plan," said Angela, "that's more of a philosophy."

"I want to run a school like this and make proper decisions about who stays and who goes."

"So," said Angela, "one day we might be frenemies."

"Looking forward to it," said Candy. "But I promise I'll be gentle with you." They both looked over to the staffroom door.

"Watch out," said Angela. "Here comes Hendrix."

"He's alright," said Candy, once you have his rocket in your pocket."

"I don't have any pockets," said Angela.

"Then watch where his hands go," said Candy.

"What about his pecker?"

"That goes where it wants," said Candy. Hendrix sat

down next to them and gave them his best jazz hands.

"Guess what," he said, "schools out."

"Tell us something we don't know," said Angela.

"Secretly you want a threesome with me."

"Nice try," said Candy. "I would hate to see you cry."

"You really are old school," said Angela.

"Is that a compliment?" Hendrix asked.

"No," said Candy.

"No," said Angela. Others joined in. By the end of the break there were no women on the staff, apart from Mrs. Alverstock who were up for it – she was insistent she kept her overalls on, but in many other ways she was flexible.

"I'll take my teeth out, if it turns you on, Hancock" she said.

"Hendrix," Hendrix said. "My chosen name is Hendrix."

"I think you are in danger of being labelled as a sex pest," said Angela.

"Or getting yourself a very silly new nickname," said Candy. "Hancock – rather more retro than you might want. And as for toe, knee, hand, cock…well that's a pretty good game of charades all by itself."

"Sorry," said Hendrix.

"I think you're more Sid James than Tony Hancock – all that leering at women dressed as schoolgirls."

"I know," said Candy, "a far more innocent time."

"Sorree," said Hendrix. He was regretting he'd even walked into the staffroom.

"Nothing worse than ageing Lotharios," said Candy. Hendrix went for a reality check; talk about blowing the bloody doors off, this was coming from a woman who'd just conspired to kill a man in cold blood.

"Ageing?" Hendrix asked.

"You are a fifty year old man acting like a twenty something outlaw." Candy continued with her verbal decapitation." You own property. You have a wife. You have children. You need to have some respect for yourself and others." This comes from a woman who had no fixed values, and a rap sheet for murder.

"Outlaw?"

"I know, because you told me, that along with a massive heat seeking penis you also have an extensive property portfolio worth over a million. *Millionaire Outlaw* is something of an oxymoron – what do you think?"

"I dunno," said Hendrix. The black animal in Candy's soul caught a glimpse of the small child hiding in Hendrix. There was weakness, shame and vulnerability in plain sight. She could not help herself. She went in for the kill.

"You've got a mind like that Jimi Hendrix album cover." Hendrix knew the one; his favourite song was on it.

"*Electric Ladyland* – it wasn't his choice of cover. It was the idea of the record company executives."

"Whatever sells shit," said Candy.

"It's got a great version of Dylan's watchtower," Hendrix said, exposing his inner geek. Candy liked Hendrix the rock bore less than Hendrix the sex pest.

"Who cares?"

"I do," said Hendrix. "Some things matter." Now that he was on the defensive, she skewered him.

"Maybe," said Candy, "this rock star philandering is because your mummy didn't love you enough when you were just a little boy – and all this is just to have some female contact – seeking out a mother's hug in another's vagina." Hendrix bit his lip; he'd been outfoxed by a Foxy Lady. The bitch had seen through him and into the howling void within him. It was one of those naked moments like when that sixth former practically gave him a lap dance as part of a musical – picked him out of the shadows and ran her hands all over his face and chest. He tried to cover the pain of being stripped bare in territory he had once considered safe.

"School's out," said Hendrix.

"So," said Candy, "this sex-addicted hippie meets a goddess of change and transformation; she offers the hippie a single wish. The hippie tells her he wants to up-tight, out of sight and in the groove. There's a bang and a flash as she turns him into a tampon."

Angela felt slightly ill and uneasy with what had been said. When all was said and done, she rather liked Hendrix; beneath the façade she thought he was a decent sort of chap. At the very worst, you knew what you were getting with him. Now here he was, on the wrong end of something she'd not seen in another colleague – and from a woman come to that.

"Very funny," he said. Hendrix had been out-cunted although he tried to pretend otherwise. "I first heard it before you were born – but worth a second outing."

"Never mess with gash on the lash," said Candy.

"I'm off," said Hendrix. Normally he would add – *does anyone want to join me?* Today he left the staffroom quietly with his danglers in a doggy bag. To complete the humiliation, Candy shouted out after him.

"Just remember…two's company, but three's a non-starter."

"Wow," said Angela. "That was harsh. Borderline sexual harassment even. Remind me never to get into an argument with you."

"He's a man. He shouldn't give it out if he can't take it."

"I'm not sure," said Angela. Candy touched her knee. An electric shot ran through Angela's body. Candy – the sweet that didn't rot your teeth or make you fat.

"Knock, knock," said Candy.

"Who's there?" Angela, her knees trembling, responded automatically.

"Duncan," said Candy. Angela knew this was bad.

"Duncan who?"

"Duncan make the flowers grow."

In that moment, Angela understood that Candy had killed Duncan Knight; maybe not on her own – but she'd been part of the deed, Angela was certain. She could not conceive of Candy playing a supporting role, or being an innocent bystander. She was sex and death dressed up to seduce whatever came onto her radar – and she knew she was going to get away with it.

Looking back through the window, Hendrix could see what Candy was capable of in less than twenty four hours - seduction, murder and metaphysical castration. He could probably add physical castration to the list – all he lacked was evidence rather than capacity. He knew she would go far in this fucked-up world as long as she didn't get caught early on. He had a flashback to the early seventies, he could see the old man coming into his classroom with a copy of the *Times Ed* and a circled job vacancy – *got a lovely little earner for you boy*. It had never actually happened to him, but he'd heard Mr. Kingman talking about the old head teacher so many times that it seemed it might have. He knew his time here was up.

At that moment he understood he was ready to change schools and maybe try to be a better person – or convince those in a different school that he was a better human being than he really was. He'd only a few years of working life he decided – surely he could pretend to be anything, even a decent human being which is what he became. He would keep his sixties ideals of peace and free love – but he would try to be less of an arsehole and recognize there was a difference between consent and capitulation. It would be a challenge that he might not be up to – but it was less of a challenge than being at home, trying to dodge housework and balance his diminishing portfolio of extra-curricular shenanigans whilst staring into the abyss of his own mortality.

Chapter Twenty-Nine:
Gary Goes Green

DC Grissom, two thousand used pounds better off, knocked on the door of another shithole house on the same estate next to the school. With the cash in his pocket he could probably buy the place and have change for the chippie.

"Liam York!" Liam was up in his bookless room playing *Sonic*. He figured it was a truant officer he called *Eggman*. The tactic was to lay low. Another louder knock followed.

"Liam York! I am a Police Officer!" A chill of fear ran over Liam. Was this about the sword they nicked last night? He remembered Gary's words about it being a *victimless crime*.

"Hang on," he said. He jumped off his bed and put on some track suit bottoms. He didn't recognise the face at the door. Not one of the juvees - an occupational hazard for a serial bunker. DC Grissom was much larger and less friendly than a juvee.

"You are Liam York?"

"What if I am?"

"Just answer the question."

"Yeah."

"Where were you last night?"

"I was at home playing ma Sonic." Liam gave the well-rehearsed answer. Ironically to DC Grissom's ears, it came out as *'masonic.'* He should be so lucky. DC Grissom shook his head.

"No my lad. You were over at your school at the wrong time of day."

"Prove it," said Liam. They always wanted proof that their lie was the truth. Today it was very easy. DC Grissom showed him a blurred CCTV image.

"Could be anyone," said Liam. The officer showed him another enlarged image of boy in a t-shirt with the legend that clearly said:

LUMP

BAD MAN CREW

"Spellings pretty good for a school refuser," said DC Grissom. Liam lost his bottle.

"It wasn't me spelling. It was Gary's. He's the one what nicked the sword. I only wanted the cash from Kingman's office." DC Grissom put the pictures back in his pocket.

"I know," he said. "Gary already gave you up. All he wanted was the cash from the office. Said you made him steal the sword."

"Fucking grass," said Liam.

"He cried a bit too," said DC Grissom. "Said you bullied him into it." A bigged-up Liam regained some of his composure.

"What if I did?"

"It was used to kill a teacher." DC Grissom replied, delivering the killer blow.

"Who?"

"Mr. Knight."

"That cunt?"

"Language," said the detective.

"Sorry, that fucking cunt?"

"Yes." The years fell away and Liam became a sobbing thirteen-year-old kid caught in somebody else's web of lies.

"I only stole the sword. I spent the cash on fish and chips for Nan. Gary said it was a victimless crime."

"You and Gary need to get your stories sorted out."

Liam had one request.

"Please don't tell me Nan."

"I think she will get to hear about this, one way or another." Liam sobbed some more.

"Not me Nan. She still believes in me." Liam's mum came home. She did not believe in him. On her doorstep was a very familiar sight.

"What's happening here?"

"Your boy is in a spot of bother," said DC Grissom.

"You been nicking from school again? You won't go there to learn but you will go there to thieve."

DC Grissom got her up to speed.

"Liam and his friend Gary are suspects in a murder that happened last night at school."

"Who?"

"Mr. Knight."

"Could have been anyone," said Liam's mum. "And that Gary, he's a bad 'un."

"I'm beginning to get that impression myself," said DC Grissom.

"And," she added, "my boy...well he's not up to doing something like this...he's not exactly brain of Britain." DC Grissom nodded, involuntarily, in agreement. This boy was too special to carry out a murder like this. He was just a small link in a very big chain of circumstantial evidence that DC Grissom was unwilling to unpick in the name of justice – Liam of York was a mere pawn. Unfortunately, the available evidence placed him at the scene of the crime with the murder weapon and a motive. Liam was going to be learning a lesson that would have been valuable had he not been facing a near lifetime behind bars. Whether guilty or innocent, he was going to be sacrificed in this particular game.

Chapter Thirty:
Friendless Funeral

Two and a half weeks after Duncan Knight's death, Kingswater Comprehensive was again closed for his funeral. In hindsight, it was unnecessary since nobody really wanted to attend. A staff meeting was held to plan out the staff response to this. Hendrix was the first dissenter.

"I don't want to go," he said. "I didn't like him when he was alive and being dead has not changed my opinion. I would rather teach Year 9E all day long."

"Perhaps we could have a show of hands for those who feel the same way." Ms. Bishop said, surveying the room. This was too much for Mr. Kingman.

"Ms. Bishop, this is a man's funeral. It's not just a PR exercise. He's got family…" Mr. Kingman paused. "….he has got family, right?"

"A mother, a father and a twin brother."

The silence was broken by Hendrix laughing.

"He's got a fucking twin…oh my good gawd. What does he do?"

Ms. Bishop found herself in the role of straight man.

"He's a Deputy Head." Hendrix tried stuffing his coat in his mouth. He choked, spat it out and laughed some more. Other staff were trying to hold back guffaws.

"At least he's not a bastard," said Hendrix.

"I think," said Mr. Kingman, "we need to take a break."

"Fifteen minutes," said Ms. Bishop. Mr. Kingman wandered over to Hendrix who was still catching his breath.

"I know you didn't like him," said Mr. Kingman, "but

it's beginning to look to the others that you might have done him in."

"Sorry," said Hendrix, "but he was a fucking bell-end." Mr. Kingman looked down his bi-focals in a paternal way.

"That's about the kindest thing you have ever said about him," Mr. Kingman said.

"But do I have to go to his fucking funeral?"

"Nobody here wants to go to his fucking funeral – but everybody is going to his fucking funeral – just to show willing." Mr. Kingman was explaining how matters were going to go.

"Why?"

"So that nobody becomes a suspect."

"Are we suspects?"

"We all hated him." Mr. Kingman drew the same picture but gave it different shading. "We'll be drawing lots to see who has to speak at his funeral – short straw gets it."

"Can I have a word in private?" Hendrix decided to play his joker. "Yes," said Mr. Kingman. Hendrix walked with him to his office.

"So, what's the big secret?" Mr. Kingman asked. Hendrix opened the door and looked down the corridor. He closed the door again.

"Between you and me, right?"

"Yes," said Mr. Kingman. Hendrix gathered himself.

"Paul McSmart and Candy Regent killed Duncan Knight."

"This better not be a joke," said Mr. Kingman.

"On my old dear's life," said Hendrix. "She put him up

to it – and he fucking did it."

"This means I've to watch out for him as well?"

"Only in this world," said Hendrix. "Hard not to laugh, isn't it?" At this comment, Mr. Kingman summoned up a guilty grin.

"We'd better get back to the safety of a crowd… don't want those two chopping off our heads when we're not looking." A few moments later, they were back in the staffroom. Ms. Bishop went back to the front desk and called the assembled staff to order.

"It has been agreed by the senior team that all staff should go, along with pupils from the school council. There will be no further discussion on that." He paused. "Now we come to the question of who will speak for our staff," Mr. Kingman explained next. "Ms. Bishop and I will say a few words…but it would be fitting if somebody from the middle management of the school also spoke." There was the silence you might find at a miser's convention when the topic of who was going to get the next round cropped up.

"I will." Paul's mouth dropped. Candy Regent was volunteering herself to speak.

"Fuck my old boots," said Hendrix.

"Mr. Brown," said Ms. Bishop, "anymore obscenity and I will ask you to leave."

"Ask me to leave then," said Hendrix. "Please ask me to leave."

"You may leave," said Ms. Bishop, "boots and all." With Hendrix excluded from proceedings, a plan of sorts came together. It was agreed that no children would speak at the funeral unless they had something good to say. Several minutes later, it was agreed that no children would contribute. Ms. Bishop and Mr. Kingman had a free and frank discussion about topics that could be spoken about at the funeral of Duncan Knight. They settled on a couple of readings from the

Old Testament. Candy Regent agreed that she would talk about Mr. Knight's contribution to pastoral well-being and the raising of school morale. After the meeting Paul went over to speak to Candy.

"What are you doing?" She gave him that look.

"What needs to be done," she said.

"But..." However, Candy had an answer.

"If not me, then who?"

"I dunno," said Paul. "There must be someone."

"Look around," said Candy, "it's all they can do not to put on funny hats and start telling jokes."

"Jokes?" Paul asked.

"You know," said Candy. "What goes ha, ha, ha plonk?"

"What?" She touched his knee. This time he felt nothing.

"A man laughing his head off, silly."

"You're off your rocker," said Paul.

"You have any better jokes?" Candy asked. There was nothing. "Well then," added Candy. "Just go with the flow."

At the funeral, Paul tried to count the number of people he didn't know and weren't from school. There were three. One of them was Duncan Knight's twin brother. The other two looked like his mother and father – the family resemblance was scary.

"The bride of Frankenstein," said Hendrix. There were no tears to be seen anywhere in the crematorium. The whole effect was not lost on anybody. It looked like Duncan Knight was there to watch his own cremation – just to make sure he was really dead. Paul tried not to take any of it in. The whole affair was gruesome in the extreme; he was at the funeral of a man he'd killed and looking at another man who was the exact likeness of his victim.

"No songs?" Paul whispered to Hendrix.

"Something to do with him being a Scottish Miserabilist," Hendrix whispered back.

"I think it might be Calvinist," said Paul.

"Whatever," said Hendrix. "He's going somewhere hot."

There was a reading from a minister about total depravity and limited atonement. Ms. Bishop said something to send the congregation to sleep and then it was Candy Regent's turn to speak on behalf of the middle management of the school. The same middle management that the deceased himself had plotted to kill. Paul would have watched through his fingers, but Candy looked so radiant, so regal, it was hard to remember what she really was – a real life Lady Macbeth. From the podium she had the balls of the world in her hand. The speech was amazing, although nobody remembered a word.

Duncan Knight became dust and ashes, but all they saw was Candy Regent at her beautiful best – full of the semi-skimmed milk of human kindness and ready to chance the turkey crown. The lies that poured out of her mouth dazzled like diamonds and danced in the sky like stars on a clear night. Everyone wanted her; this was the prologue to her coronation and she killed it.

Chapter Thirty-One:
Stupid Pawn

I am Paul McSmart. I am an idiot. I am a pawn in another person's game. My cast-iron alibi for murder was adultery. I did not take the good advice of the kind detective. I waited until it came out in court. I waited for my wife to properly despise me for what I really was. I waited for the Clinton-Lewinsky scandal to be the number one international news story; it turned what I imagined was a simple process of separation into a freaking circus of female empowerment. I was a material witness. Candy Regent was a material witness. We condemned those boys to time in prison and I condemned myself to court-imposed poverty. In my defence I would say I was happier with them going to jail rather than me; a bleak divorce and a custodial sentence would have been rather too much for a murder that did more good than harm. I would say it was a nasty divorce, but that seemed to be stamped through the process in the same way as 'Blackpool' is tattooed through a stick of rock you buy from Blackpool (Ha Ha).

From a starting point of 50/50, I lost a further 25%. Quite an adultery tax I am sure you will agree – and had I known, a definite disincentive for any kind of cheating. I carried on paying off the mortgage of a house I never liked that much and will neither now own nor live in. It was nothing I had ever read about in any super-hero comic book. A lot of super-heroes are widowed, there is even one called *The Black Widow*. As far as I have read so far, there are no divorced super-heroes of any sort whatsoever; I would consider that to be a major gap in the market.

Without a divorced super-hero role model to light my way, I fetched up in a one-bedroomed cupboard in Kingswater with a commanding view of the local Pupil Referral Unit. I got over that. I even applied for a job there. I was very lucky to be unsuccessful in my application; I discovered almost every pupil who ever tormented me was on their roll. If Liam and Gary hadn't gone down for murder, I'm pretty sure they would have been there too.

There are some good things about the single life. Less to keep clean. Bob Dylan lyrics start to make sense again. An evening can last a year. You choose the length of your curtains – or if you even have curtains. If you don't want a saucer with a cup, it's your call. And when you do break the rules of good housekeeping, it's like my experience of murder…nothing bad happens other than food poisoning and friends not calling round.

What does change is the grinding sense of being alone – wanking yourself off to sleep – something I never needed to do whilst married. You just fall asleep next to somebody whether you've ejaculated or not. Laugh and the world laughs with you. Masturbate and you masturbate alone.

I would see the kids at the weekend – sometimes during the week. Melissa was pretty good that way. They never asked the obvious question and that was good too. I guess, for the children from the end of the century, having divorced parents is the norm. You get rinsed if your biological parents still live with each other.

In school, it all changed. I think I came off my support plan when I did because the outgoing Head was genuinely worried I'd really killed her deputy for what he'd put me through and that she might be next. Before she ran for the hills she said something about everyone coming through a community learning experience – or some such bullshit. I don't buy that. Say what you like about the threat of personal violence – it definitely puts some people in their place. She went down the line of if you can't beat them, join them – she became a lead inspector in her own consultancy and probably destroyed more teaching careers than she ever would have done as a humble head-teacher.

With old Kingman in charge of the school he steered a steady course through the next few turbulent months. For the first time in a long while I felt safe…yeah I know, I'm a murderer, but it was true all the same. Pupils and teachers knew where they were – which is really all you can ask of a Head. At the end of the summer term, he took early retirement and converted his promotion into a much enhanced final salary pension. When he left, more people missed him than didn't – which is the mark of a successful head. I now know that is harder than it looks. Good luck to him; I hope he is happily fishing somewhere, or playing a round of golf, or doing whatever people do when they are waiting for death.

Candy continued to keep her distance from me as she slithered up the promotion pole like a misogynist's wet-dream. She took on the role of deputy and was able to surf the wave of goodwill that followed Knight's demise. It was as they said. Everybody hated him. He deserved to die. His demise was a result that pleased everyone.

The next time Candy spoke to me, it was to suggest that I looked for a job elsewhere; what, I asked, would happen if I stayed? Nothing much, she said – but people suspected me of murder and that meant it was hard to progress in the school no matter how popular and timely that homicide might have been. I sort of understood that I was in this thing alone – it all went Macbeth for me after that. Even with a reasonable chap like Kingman, it wasn't really something I could have a free and frank conversation about – not as though I could play *Bohemian Rhapsody* and ask him to guess the bad thing I might have done. And by then, of course, he'd already been gone a few years. And then, I asked, wouldn't they give me a hard time in another school? I think it's just for the best she said, and promised to help me with any job I wanted. Keep positive – but one mistake and you're out of here with no reference worth asking for. That's what she said: Keep positive – one mistake and you're out! If I hadn't have been so seriously in the shit, it would have been funny.

I gave her most recent proposal as much headspace as I could. I had never really considered the concept of a future, or a plan for the future. I was pretty good at predicting the past. Eyes shut and drive through the lights was working fine.

Who did I need to atone to the most? Of all the people I've come across, it was Liam York who sprang to mind. Liam, who was now in some juvenile detention, correctly protesting his innocence. Liam was the sort of kid who never stood a chance. He was also costing the taxpayers. He would never pay tax. He would never function effectively in the society where he'd been allocated the bottom rung. That set me on course. I would teach those who needed me most. I would be their advocate in a world that did not hear their voice. I would become a special needs teacher. Where else can you go after successfully murdering a hated colleague?

It might seem rather pompous to call it a revelation, or a light bulb moment, but I thought maybe I could do something for the Liams of this world. Do something with those I had despised…this was like missionary work for the religiously challenged. So there it was, I found myself being interviewed by the legend that was Hendrix for a post in his special school. I had a glowing reference from the new head but written by Candy who was all but running the school by then. Hendrix understood it for what it was – a dignified exit. It was like I was some sort of assisted suicide out of the mainstream. We never spoke of the past.

"You can't be any worse than me," he said. "Or any better."

The only question Hendrix wanted the answer to was how I managed to blow up my VW Polo the evening Knight was murdered. Like I would know the answer to that one. He'd also changed. I couldn't quite put my finger on the exact cause or effect – but that I now know was because it was something I had never been able to do. Maybe he was a little bit more grown up, or a little more bowed down – it's hard to be a hippie when you're over fifty and starting to look more like John Cooper Clarke than Jimi Hendrix.

My last few months of Kingswater was like being an old rocker on a final world tour. I spent my time covering absent colleagues and looking at the sites where I'd shagged women and decapitated men – all two of them. Then I left for the House of Hendrix. It was closer to home and a world away from what I had known.

A few years into the job I can see the point Hendrix made about being able to do it properly. Like murder, there is no way of knowing if you can do it until you do it. Some can and some are left with the impotent weapon in their hand. There is a little less room for fuck-wit paper-boys like Knight because you cannot progress these kids at a steady rate. You fly by the instruments and you're a hole in the ground.

I found myself getting it right some of the time – and it was an okay feeling. A kid like Liam in the mainstream could tell you he was crap at pretty much everything, except football – which he was really crap at. My kids can tell you what they can do and what they want to do with their lives. It's a lot like a public school in that respect. Except these pupils are under no illusions about their capabilities.

So this is where I toiled for much of the twenty years since the killing. I now know the extent of my own ignorance where special needs education is concerned. As I rumble on to my death and/or retirement, I keep my fingers crossed that nothing much changes. New ideas are the worst. Not bad in themselves, they are just deaf and blind to the old ideas. I can hear my old man's voice saying something like *Didn't we do this in 1997?*

But now, ideas and data are the currency of self-promotion. Knight understood that as clearly as he did not understand people. And so did Candy. I googled her – she is now the CEO of a trust in Essex, bucking the trend of the gender pay gap with Multi-Academy Trusts. God alone knows who she shagged and shivved to get there.

Chapter Thirty-Two:
A Snitch in Time

It was June 2005. Candy Regent was sitting in an office – one of the many she worked from, overlooking the glorious emptiness of the world she had made for herself. Fresh from six weeks off with another un-diagnosable attack of Meniere's disease, there were always things to do and lives to destroy. Juggling with the information was the key – and never get left with damning data. That suited her fine. She was all business. She was *Capability Candy* offering up yet another delicious slice of *support plan pie*. Whether it was served hot or cold, the results were always the same. People who got in her way were just counters on a board – road-kill on the Candy Regent highway to Hell.

The current problem was in a mathematics department of a tributary school, recently failed in an Ofsted inspection by the *Bishop Consultancy*. This unit was not the cause of the failure, but there was an under-achieving teacher on a salary that could fund one and a half newbies – or a recommended *'provision for the more challenging in the school community'*. It was fund her, or a high profile soft play area. Her in-house stinking snitch had given her the heads up on this one – trusting teacher with low self-esteem easily rocked. The underachiever had been put on a support plan; guaranteed to kill 99% of all known teachers – or transplant the disease in another unsuspecting school. Unfortunately, aiming to be the 1% that gives the support plan a bad name, this non-compliant teacher had also involved her union in the personal business of her own documented shortcomings. Now there was a cussed meddling pretending to be a meeting – or worse…a mediation process. Candy had shredded all the reps in her schools, but still the unions dared to cross her path and interfere with the process of support and challenge. Looking again at the paperwork, she recognized the name of this particular area rep.

Angela Phipps and Joanne Smith, the under-achieving item of mortality, waited for the call to enter Candy Regent's office. Angela, middle-aged and rounded, tried to make small talk.

"What beautiful red hair you have," said Angela.

"Thank you," said Joanne. "It hasn't helped me much in life."

"It's probably not going to help you that much now," Angela. "But it is very beautiful."

"Do you know what she's like?" Joanne asked.

"We have some history," said Angela. "I knew her back when she was just a novice monster carrying out random acts of murder and emasculation."

"How?"

"Once upon a time, she was just a humble teacher…" which wasn't strictly true. The sign above Candy Regent's office flashed for them to enter. Above the door was the slogan CFA - *Children First Always*.

"CFA," said Joanne. "Children forever alienated." The support dance commenced. Mongoose against Cobra.

"Good morning, Mrs. Phipps." The Cobra spat first. "Good morning Joanne," added Candy.

"Good morning, Ms. Regent," said Mrs. Phipps. "Are you feeling better?"

"Getting there," said Candy. "Taking the tablets."

"Good," said Mrs. Phipps, who had dealt with many ruthless and hated CEOs. They just seemed to need copious amounts of time out – being a full time shit of a human being was clearly harder than many people imagined. Candy showed them where the seats were and then sat down herself.

"It's never an easy process," said Candy, completing the required statement of the obvious. Candy was wearing something that showed off her figure whilst being sufficiently sombre for the task of the day – which was to tear into another human being and rip out their heart and soul. Radiating power, she sat behind her desk in a beautifully fitting slightly off-white trouser suit, topped and tailed with a blood red scarf and matching ruby slippers. Angela noted that she was still beautiful. All that evil inside her had not over-cooked her looks just yet.

"Quite," she said, at which Candy clicked her shoes.

"You are looking good," Candy said.

"Thank you," she said. Angela flustered inside.

Joanne, the 'underperforming' teacher of the piece, was the only one who understood how difficult the process was – it was as if every day was an Ofsted inspection seamlessly rolling into the future with no end in sight. Every day it had seemed that there was somebody looking out for her, making sure she was doing it right. She'd spoken to her head of department about only getting the low achievers and the bad behavers – but that had gone nowhere. Unless you called being told to be *more positive* about her situation an act of encouragement and support. Now she'd folded under the unrelenting weight of eternal observation – become chronically unwell. Momentarily, she focused on a book that lay, closed, on the Head's desk, which was entitled 'How to Run your School *Efficiently*.' Initially she'd read *Run* as *Ruin*. She put that down to the beta-blockers that made everything seem dis-connected. The book was shiny blue with a gold typeface. She wondered what part of it dealt with bullying in the workplace.

"On to the matter in hand," said Candy.

She'd clearly been reading Joanne's mind and had tapped into her vulnerabilities. But if you listened to your staff it got you nowhere. There was always somebody complaining about something. And Candy had come to recognize that her greatest strength was that she'd no significant feelings for anyone she'd ever known – other than herself. Possessing no feelings had enabled her to be involved in the brutal killing of one person and the unkind dismantling of many more.

"Shall we start?" asked Mrs. Phipps. Candy did not like the way this former acquaintance was acting as if she controlled the narrative. Candy was also less easy about being in a room where women judged her. By and large, she could make a straight man do what she wanted. Strong-minded women were something else.

"We are all here for the same reason," said Candy. She paused a moment. Candy enjoyed that lie above all others. Then she continued. "We are all here to enable Miss Smith to become a more effective teacher."

The more she spoke the lie, the more she believed she could use it again and again. Eventually she would even come to believe it. Mrs. Phipps peddled in the truth.

"Miss Smith has been told that she is to be placed on a four-week plan."

"That is correct," said Candy.

"The guidelines are that support plans should be six weeks in duration." Candy tried to show an emotionally empathic expression like the ones she'd watched on non-fiction hospital programmes when a terminal illness was explained to a small child and its parents.

"If Miss Smith wishes to prolong the experience," said Candy.

"The guidelines, Ms. Regent," said Mrs. Phipps, "are there for a reason." Candy made a mental note to make sure her next underachiever was from the other union – the one that was not concerned for the welfare of its members, and one whose rep she had never met before. Candy changed the direction of the meeting – just to throw in a little chaos.

"Shall we agree on the targets?"

They looked at the feast of fraudulent reporting her peripatetic fat foul snitch had delivered her. Failure to differentiate. Failure to keep a tidy room. Failure to be in the right staffroom gossip group. The crimes were many and varied – not all could be challenged easily. People were just worn thin by the process…or wound up being whining bores. As was her way, Candy had ensured that observations were slanted against people she wanted gone. It was a perception managed numbers game. Sixteen criteria – all subjective. A one became a two. A three became a four. A committed teacher was shown the door.

Mrs. Phipps countered the paper narrative.

"Miss Smith, Joanne, was judged as underachieving because she was always given the lower-achieving groups. Another reading of the data presented shows that her groups were progressing slightly higher in Mathematics than they were in English. It appears that this was a progress triggered by my client having special needs experience."

"You had staff waiting outside my room for me to make a mistake," said Joanne.

"Did you see anyone?" Candy asked.

"I smelt her," said Joanne. Candy knew that was true. Snitch the witch's smell was famously demonic and lingered outside any room far longer than she did.

"I would be careful about what you say about your colleagues who have health issues," said Candy.

"You know who I mean," said Joanne. "She was there."

"And you did make mistakes," said Candy. "So that was just as well." Mental note thought Candy. Get Snitches to clean up her act. People on the staff where she lurked were beginning to wise up. Her foul cloud of toxic stench was so vast it probably had its own postcode. It wasn't like she was a good teacher anyway. Perhaps it was her turn to receive a support plan. Target 1 – get rid of the smell. Target 2 – lose some weight. Target 3 – drop dead.

Then came the tears from her current prey. Candy thought she might have cracked five minutes earlier. Tougher than she gave her credit for, but, sooner or later, they always went down for the count.

"I think we need to take a break, Ms. Regent," said Angela Phipps. "As you can see, my client is struggling with the process."

"Take what you need," said Candy. Hand to hand combat when lying was another of Candy's strengths. Each time she returned to this arena, she had forgotten how much fun it was to challenge their perceptions. She knew what would happen next. She watched, as a woman trapped in the depths of despair gave in to her prime states of doubt and self-pity. She could do this every day of the week, every week of the year... for half what they paid her.

A little reverse Cognitive Behaviour Therapy went a long way as well; get your opponent to over-estimate the worst case scenario and under-estimate their ability to cope with anything that might come their way. Plant a small seed of doubt around your support plan and watch it germinate. Doubt! The concept amused her as much as anxiety and stress. She was always dealing with doubt in others. It made for an easy life. Where they had doubt, she perceived certainty. Should I kill this man? Should I have adulterous sex with that man? Should I exaggerate my competence, experience and achievements to get what I want? Of course! Of course! Of course! If others chose another path...well that was their problem and theirs alone. She had read through the details; the teacher had a family to feed. The teacher had a mortgage to pay. The teacher had a credit card bill. That was her choice. Nobody told her to have a family and financial obligations. Did she think it came for free with a state handout?

She remembered the days with Paul McSmart and his family. He chose to concern himself with them after his adultery – not before. And was she, Candy Regent worth the price? Of course she was.

A world where others imposed constraints of morality and conscience was a world of opportunity. The world was her playground for her to rule...safe in the knowledge that nobody knew the depths of her depravity and soaring heights of her ambition.

Outside Candy's office, Joanne Smith tried to take it all in. The lies about her performance and the lack of empathy from the Head. And so many other things that ran around her head like a motorcyclist on a wall of death.

"Let's get you back to reception," said Angela. Bemused, Joanne could only consider one word.

"Why?"

"Why what?"

"Why does she want to hurt people so much?" Joanne had found some more words that had not been shaken out of her mind.

"She's a dark angel. You'll find her on a Venn diagram about sex and death."

"Is that a technical term?"

"Venn diagram?" There was some shared laughter.

"No," said Joanne. "If I didn't know what that was, I really should be on a support plan."

"I think she has anti-social personality disorder," said Angela.

"What does that mean?"

"It means," said Angela, "that she is a psychopath – a grade 1 listed bitch who is indifferent to the feelings of others. If you are going to have any kind of psychological impairment, it's the best one to have."

"How has she got this far?" Angela let out some breath to compose herself before answering.

"By sucking up and punching down. I used to teach science in the same school as her. There was this one kid who was fascinated by an animal called the Peacock Mantis

Shrimp. It was all kinds of pretty colours – but it could punch a hole in a crab shell. If a human was as strong it would be able to put its fist through steel plate. That little bastard feared nothing and no one. Candy's like that shrimp: pretty to look at, and fatal to be around."

"Can she kill people?"

"She probably has," said Angela. "She can do anything she wants."

"Sounds like fun for one."

"Most of the CEOs I came across are psychopathic." Angela continued.

"It's probably the only way such a job can be done. You need a person who can make hard decisions without remorse."

"Isn't there some sort of selection process that would rule her out?"

"First off, all they see are her breasts – which are very lovely of course. The perfect size and shape to ensure selective male blindness. If they ever see past those, it's too late."

"Are you saying nobody has seen what she really is?"

"She's a psychopath." Angela laughed. "She knows the value of sincerity – and she learned to fake that a long time ago."

"Fake sincerity?" Joanne asked.

"Unlike her boobs," said Angela, "I'm guessing they're real."

"Will she slip up?"

"Psychopaths are reckless people – indifferent to the consequences of their own actions and unable to learn from them." Angela shrugged. "So maybe…with enough evidence."

"And where will I find that?" Joanne asked.

"Quite," said Angela. "I think they work off the understanding that they hit you so hard the first time that you don't get up. If you do get up, you run away before they hit you again."

"Someone should stop her."

"We're still waiting for that to happen."

"Why hasn't it?"

"Like I said, she's a dark angel. People who upset her die in so many different ways."

"And you?"

"I think," said Angela, "that I amuse her. I give her validation. She likes somebody to know just how evil she is."

"Thanks."

"Never ask a question if you don't want to hear the answer. That's what my dear old dad used to tell me."

"Right."

"If I die," said Angela, "write the story and have Victoria Wood play me in the film."

"What if she kills me?"

"I'll get Julie Walters to play you."

"That's a plan, then," said Joanne.

So here she was again, seeing the first new shoots of that hardy perennial, the Candy Regent support plan package. All it needed was a shady place away from the glare of publicity and enough stupid people prepared to believe they were being given an opportunity to improve.

"Everyone has a plan until they get punched in the mouth," said Angela.

"What?"

"Mike Tyson," said Angela.

"Surprisingly wise words," said Joanne. Angela picked up the glossy brochure which was brimful of happy high achieving pupils and smiley teachers. She flicked through it before carefully placing it back where she found it. "Don't believe a word you read in that rag," commented Joanne.

"If there's one thing I have learnt about Hell," said Angela, "it's that it always has a good prospectus."

"Did you know that we were a better school before her?"

"Of course you were," said Angela. "She's taken you all the way from outstanding to good and called it proof of her good management. You can't do better than that – if you're a psychopath."

"And nobody further up has tried to stop her?" Joanne asked.

"You mean for the good of the children?" Angela asked.

"Something like that," said Joanne.

"Here is one of those stories with a moral. Once upon a time there was a Queen called Candy. Her best Knight called Duncan once dared to show her disrespect. So, late one evening, before an Ofsted, she got one of her courtiers to chop off his head."

"It sounds a bit nasty," said Joanne. "You said it had a moral."

"The moral," said Angela, "is do not disrespect Queen Candy."

"She killed him?"

"Just a rumour that never went away," said Angela.

"I was teaching in the school when it happened. A man was decapitated in his office and she got his job *and* his office. Nobody ever outright accused her – probably out of fear it would happen to them - but there were whispers about it."

"So, even if we know this," said Joanne, "nobody does anything?"

"Why would anyone get in the way of a psychopath? That really would be a really stupid thing to do."

"And yet so many people are stupid," said Joanne.

"Try stupid and brave," said Angela, "it narrows it down a tad." They were just about to leave when Candy Regent came out of her office.

"A quick word inside, Mrs. Phipps?" Angela thought carefully for a second.

"Excuse me," she said to Joanne. She went into the Lion's den. The atmosphere had changed.

"I heard what you said about my lovely breasts," said Candy. "I have to say I was very turned on." Angela froze. Latent feelings inside were set free in monstrous irresponsible ways.

"Sorry," she said.

"Never be sorry," said Candy. Angela felt as though she was levitating – such was the sheer power of Candy's sexual charisma.

"Right, thank you," Angela said. "I must be off."

"Never forget," said Candy.

"That's two things," said Angela.

"You know where to find me," said Candy. Angela left the room.

"What was that about?" Joanne asked.

"I don't have the words to say," said Angela.

"Was it something to do with me?"

"No," said Angela. Over-estimating the worst case scenario, Angela parked her feelings in some dark, shady part of her brain and tried to get on with living her life. But she understood this was not over – and that it might never be over. She and Candy might dance through eternity like a lesbian Fred (her) and Ginger (Candy) – and she wasn't even sure if that really was a worst case scenario. As Ginger had said, she was the real lead, dancing backwards in high heels – anyone could dance forward in flats. It was a fantasy that would not go away.

Chapter Thirty-Three: The Beauty of the Moment

That weekend, Paul McSmart and Joanne Smith were both invited to an eighties reunion at their university. Paul, high on steroids and opiates from a bout of Bell's palsy had decided this was an event he couldn't miss. It might well be his last reunion – and magic moments in his life were in short supply. Joanne, on the brink of losing her job, needed a diversion. He saw her across the common room and shouted across a crowd of bemused graduates who were reflecting on vanquished youth and impending mortality.

"Hey! You with the beautiful hair!" Joanne looked in the direction of the noise. She didn't recognise the lopsided rictus – but she did remember the shit it belonged to. It was the most likely of her three graduate sperm donors. He did remind her of her darling daughter. Maybe she'd tell him.

The shit bounded over to her, gave her an unwanted hug. The shit seemed eager to engage her in conversation. Clearly the turd hadn't remembered her name, or why she might not like him at all - ever.

"You don't look a day over forty-five," said Paul.

"That's because I'm forty-four," said Joanne.

"And your hair is still beautiful," he sung out in some mangled homage to a *Blondie* number.

"It didn't encourage you to stay with me last time."

"I've grown up a bit since then," said Paul.

"We'll see," said Joanne.

"Cool," said Paul. "Have a drink."

"I remember what happened to me last time you said that."

"Yeah," said Paul. "You had a drink or three."

"That so very funny."

"I thought so," he said, unaware of her irony. Unable to change the man in front of her, Joanne tried to change the topic of conversation.

"I'm a failing teacher," she said, "just about to go on a support plan."

"Cool," said Paul. "I used to be one as well. Like being on an Ofsted every waking day, knowing that you're entirely on your own, and that one false move, and its P60 time."

"I think you'll find that P60 is a tax form," said Joanne.

"Death and taxes – all we know for sure," said Paul. There was a glimmer of understanding from Joanne. That was how it was. That was how they pretended it wasn't. Or at least that was how they pretended it wasn't if they were in the Head's glee club like smelly old Snitches. Snitches, what a hateful old hag she was. She focused back on this pitiful item of humanity – heartless Paul McSmart.

"What happened?" Joanne asked.

"Bitch called Candy Regent got me to kill someone – and then she asked me to leave. She gets to be a Head…I get to be a normal boring teacher, albeit without any kind of plan." The horrible little crap knew a name that filled Joanne with fear and loathing.

"Candy Regent!"

"You know her?" Paul asked.

"She's the one failing me," said Joanne.

"She fails everyone. The union reps call her *Capability Candy*." Capability Candy sounded like the worst sort of sweet you could have; something chewy that either would choke you or turn your teeth black.

"Is that your best advice on dealing with Candy

Regent?" Joanne asked.

"Don't go near her if she's got a boyfriend with a sword," said Paul.

"She killed someone?"

"I killed someone," said Paul. Perhaps he was not the man to be given the diploma of paternity. But she could see her in him far more than she wanted.

"Why?" Joanne asked. Paul breathed out.

"She made me do it. She's very persuasive that way."

"And nobody else knows?"

"No," said Paul, "only a man who is dead now."

"Did you kill him too?" Joanne asked.

"No," said Paul. "He thought it was a good thing to have done. Said the victim deserved what he got."

"And you're telling me?" Joanne asked.

"Yeah," said Paul.

"Why?" Joanne asked. Paul paused.

"I dunno…ever since I been on these tablets for Bell's palsy, I've been telling people the truth. It's not really a very good look for me."

"It's not really a look," said Joanne.

"I know," said Paul. "But it's still not good for me."

"When did you kill this…person?"

"He wasn't really a person."

"No dissembling please."

"I don't know what that means."

"Don't lie to me. You owe me that much."

"In September 1997. It...he was a deputy head nobody liked. A couple of kids nobody liked either took the blame. I got great CPD on teaching *Macbeth* in Key Stage 3 – it really brought the text to life for me. Perfect crime really."

"And now you've gone and told me."

"She was such a fucking bitch," said Paul. "I always said if I had a terminal disease I would sort her out."

"And?"

"Lucky me! I've got cancer. I'm going to miss me when I'm gone."

"Will anyone else?"

"Who cares?"

"So what are you going to do?" Joanne asked. Paul thought.

"As a favour to you," Paul whispered, "to square the bill."

"Yes?"

"I'll say what happened," said Paul.

"She'll deny it," said Joanne.

"Shit sticks," said Paul. Even if they don't try her, she'll lose her job. You need at least to pretend you're a moral person."

"I wish she would lose her job," said Joanne, "and hopefully before mine."

"You know that nobody survives a support plan," said Paul, "don't you? They say one in three hundred – but I don't believe it. I've never heard of anybody getting through. I reckon it's as many as none. Zero."

"Why tell me that?" Joanne asked. "I heard it was fifty-fifty."

"I thought those were the odds of us hooking up."

"Very droll," said Joanne.

"I'm staying in the halls tonight," said Paul.

"And?"

"Since both our lives are in the crapper, would you like to stay over, for old time's sake?"

"You need to sell it a bit better – tell me how good it was last time," said Joanne. So, Paul thought of all the sex he had enjoyed with all the five people he'd been permitted to do it with. The best was when he was on teacher training – probably the best boobs B.C. (before Candy). She was a primary teacher who showed him the way…on top, underneath, from behind. She was up for anything – and she loved him despite knowing him. He gave her up for someone with blonde hair and longer legs. Then there was the lawyer, then the accountant. Every major profession other than medicine.

"You're up there in my top five," Paul said.

She looked at him hard; he needed to at least lie better if he wanted her, in that way.

"You've got more chance with a support plan," she said. "I'll pass on that one."

"You don't know what you're missing," said Paul. He struggled to believe his own lie.

"I think I do," said Joanne.

On her course of beta-blockers, sex was generally pretty good – but mostly she couldn't be bothered to hook up. She kissed him on the cheek. Already she could see he was looking all over someone else. It would be too much like her experience with senior management – he was hungry for sex, but not very good at it. The senior management she'd recently encountered were hungry for power, but not very good at using it effectively.

"Worth a try," said Paul.

"What's it like – facing death?" Paul remembered how Pete Conrad had described walking on the moon: *Great! Super! I really enjoyed it!* He needed to have an easy answer. He didn't have one.

"The world gets quieter. You lose that seventies cassette hiss. You find your own *Dolby*."

"Not much of an insight," said Joanne.

"You've got to be there," said Paul. "But it does make you understand it's all random. We are worlds unto ourselves – beyond us lies chaos, within us oblivion. We are faulty machines made of flesh and going nowhere. Life is a tale told by an idiot and written by a madman – something like that anyway. And we worry about it because we evolved a brain that tells us tomorrow and tomorrow we are going to die."

"PS," said Joanne. "That's not much of a pick-up line – even for a wanker like you."

"It's been working well for me lately," said Paul. "Not that I give a toss about rejection anymore. My own body is rejecting me…so why should I gave a flying fuck?"

"Thank you for sharing," said Joanne. "But no flying fuck for you."

"Goodbye, then," he said.

"Goodbye yourself," said Joanne.

"Until next time?" Paul asked. "As friends?" Just for a moment, she considered spending the night with him – or even telling him her truth. He'd at least taken an interest in her. But she remembered she had a cat to feed and that some rather nice looking photograph of a chap had messaged her on *Soulmates*.

He did have a stupid tag – *Artisan Accountant*, but then hers was – *Classless Teacher*. Perhaps another time – if that bloke turned out to be the classic knob that her colleagues and friends were sure he was. And then there was all that crap about cassettes; totally irrelevant in the twenty-first century.

"Sure," said Joanne. "Why not?" At least there were some options in her love life.

"Coolio," said Paul. She knew she'd made the right choice for her in-car evening entertainment. A Genesis album and a couple of propranolol would be far better company than this self-confessed axe murderer who thought it was appropriate to say *'Coolio'* to a woman he wanted to shag.

After she'd gone, he thought more about his death answers; he had been feeling okay on that one. There was no test to fail and no performance anxiety – you were going to die just like everyone else. For once it was a process he could not be excluded from and nobody gave your death a grade, or a level. Nobody required an education to die – no ordinary levels, no advanced levels, no degree and no diploma. Death was there for everyone, like the Open University, except it was mandatory. You just stopped functioning and somebody else was left with the paperwork. You had no future to plan and so no future to worry about. You could just be in the beauty of the moment - which is where he was when he got it. *Although I am not long for a life of sorrow, you and I are here in the beauty of the moment*; that was the chat up line that could not fail even a dying nobody.

Driving home that evening from the reunion, listening to *'Duke'*, Joanne's car left the road and had a blind date with a tree; it was death at first sight. Police at the scene concluded there were no suspicious circumstances. Prone to stress, they speculated that, maybe, she'd taken too many of the prescription beta-blockers they found in her glove compartment.

Candy Regent was able to cross another teacher off her list of expensive and experienced teachers – she really did loathe people with more educational understanding than she could ever bring to the party. Luckily that list of people was getting shorter and shorter. And as for poor whatever her name was, there would be no need for a support plan – she'd failed at life all by herself. It was another good day at the office.

She loved the term *'support plan'*. Although not strictly an oxymoron, it did the exact opposite of what it said on the tin. The process removed any residual confidence that a targeted teacher might have had; it turned them into social outcasts – colleagues were scared to go near less some of the juju rubbed off on them. And then they would become pale reflective ghosts, fading away like shadows in the twilight. Nobody on her watch would ever survive a support plan – and she intended to keep a clean sheet in perpetuity.

Elsewhere a daughter was preparing for the funeral of her mother. Josephine Smith knew that the cause of her mother's death was not beta-blockers. The cause of her death was the pressure imposed on her by Candy Regent. One day she would give Candy Regent what she deserved…the slowest death she could come up with. She would push her off a boat in the middle of the ocean; give her time to think about what she had done before she drowned.

Enchanted by the stories in Marvel comics, she came up with an alter-ego who would kill Candy Regent: *Elektra*. If she couldn't drown the bitch, she would kill her with a sword.

Chapter Thirty-Four: A Cold Case

It seems to me to have only one drawback, Hopkins,

and that is that it is intrinsically impossible.

Sir Arthur Conan Doyle

Gary, a lifer, looked me in the eye.

"Listen. You need to listen to me." He was only in his middle thirties, but had the pallor of a sixty-year-old man and the cough of a dead one. After I handed over the agreed packet of cigarettes, he started to talk.

"Me and Lump…we was fitted up for this."

My name is Jerry Brown. My late father was an art teacher known as *Hendrix*. As the killing of Duncan Knight becomes history, my old man has been a shoe-in for the murder. I'm sick of the gossip that because he did not publically mourn Duncan Knight, he must have killed the deceased deputy head. My dad was no angel, but I do not believe he killed anybody in his life. For at least some of the evening in question, he was sat with me, watching television. I remember this because he told me about being inspected and somebody throwing clay all over the place. The next morning, his school was closed.

Because my dad is dead – and he died on the job – a phrase he always liked to repeat, I now have his in-service death grant to fund my investigations into the murder of Duncan Knight. Most of the facts of the case were known and on record. Gary and his mate, Liam, were caught on CCTV walking out of school with a murder weapon wrapped in a shirt. The victim was a universally-hated member of staff, a deputy head called Duncan Knight. He had been de-capitated with a seventeenth century samurai sword while eating a pasty in his office. The two suspects had then taken the murder weapon back to their den – the shed in the garden of Gary's father. The blood of the murder weapon was on the blade of the sword and the clothing of the suspects. The two suspects had a history of petty crime, including theft and vandalism. They were also on record as having threatened the life of the victim, Duncan Knight.

Gary continued with his story.

"Everybody hated Knight. Even the teachers, all of them. He was a cunt. He would write you up for nothing – absolutely nothing. And he loved doing it. So you got a whole school of suspects. Yes. We was stupid and we did bad things. But we never killed nobody. Never!"

I had no idea if they were telling the truth, but Liam who was Gary's accomplice never struck me as a killer. He said he was with Gary that night because he was looking to get a girlfriend and Gary had promised him that would happen if he showed a bit of *'bottle'* and broke into the school that night. Gary then said something that stuck in my mind.

"We were in Bishop's office (the Head-teacher at the time) when we heard a noise of something being dropped in the corridor. When we looked, we saw the sword. It had a tassel that was still moving. It was sort of gold braid and caught the light. If we'd seen any blood, we'd never have touched it."

I have read all about how the Japanese trained to fight with swords. Successfully chopping off a man's head (even a compliant one) was no easy feat. This was achieved with a single stroke – something I suspected an adolescent of Gary's build (at the time) could not have achieved. I'd read the book by *Chris Ross* on the suicide of the author, Yukio Mishima. The team had practiced the ritual double suicide several times, but on the day, it went horribly wrong; a man's head is very difficult to sever. There was also the question of why kill Knight? It is true that the boys hated him, but Gary was hardly ever in school and Liam was in the lower half of the school where Mr. Knight had little interest or jurisdiction.

"We were just looking for kicks and cash," said Gary. "We thought we might get something for the sword. When we saw the blood, we was a bit *surprised*. We thought about chucking it in the lake, but by then it was too late to go out. The next day we was arrested – and that was that."

As far as I am aware, nobody spent a great deal of time working out whether the boys were telling the truth about how they found the sword. My problem was, if they didn't find it where they said (in the middle of the senior teacher's corridor), where did they find it? A seventeenth-century samurai sword is not the most conventional murder weapon for an adolescent. Gary himself remarked that if was going to kill Knight, he would have been *'Shivved up.'* He said he knew loads of people who owned knives and even guns. *'I could have borrowed from any of them if I had wanted.'*

Unfortunately, twenty years on, the trail has gone cold. On the night of the murder, which happened during an Ofsted inspection, a large but unknown number of staff were working late in the school buildings. I have made it my business to track these people down and re-interview them. My feeling is that the key to the case is the, hitherto, unexamined murder weapon. Establishing provenance of the sword would be a key to knowing the identity of Duncan Knight's killers.

For that, I would need to look at all the staff in the school and their access to samurai swords. I feel, as an amateur researcher, this task may be beyond my resources. The more I become involved with the case, the less I know. I think I might be on the trail of people who have killed without remorse and might kill again to keep their secret safe. I do not feel that I, or my family is safe. My quest for the truth has also had an impact on my family life. I was given an ultimatum to give up my search for the truth or lose them. I chose to pursue the truth. I am now separated from my wife and see my children only at weekends. I hate what the true murderers have done to my life. This killing is a crime that keeps on taking.

Chapter Thirty-Five: Common and Proper

I have met with no success in my efforts to even look at the killing sword. I am not even sure that it is still in existence. I heard a whisper that it was routinely destroyed after the boys were convicted of the crime nearly twenty years ago. However, some claim it's in the possession of a wealthy overseas buyer who had taken a morbid interest in the crime. Whatever the truth, the sword has effectively disappeared from public view.

    An expert in the field of swords said that its picture used in evidence led him to believe that it had been imported to the UK sometime after the end of the Second World War. In Japan, the practice of martial arts was banned. Swords with any killing potential were not allowed. Students of the ways of the warrior were only allowed to practice with swords that had very blunt blades. This sword would have been bought on the black market and then been a part of a private collection.

    My feeling or hunch is that the murderers (who I am certain were on the teaching staff at the time) acquired the sword and kept it in their possession for a number of years. The sword itself would probably have come from the storerooms of a police station. The question is how the murderer would have come by it and how would it have not been known.

    I have begun by looking at who benefitted from the crime. Certainly not his convicted killers; they have been incarcerated for twenty years. The only thing they were in possession of when they were arrested was the murder weapon. Even boys with a mild learning difficulty would have understood the need to dispose of their murder weapon. And yet they did not. They chose instead to take it back to their base and parade it as a trophy.

    My father also did not benefit. He carried on his job until he got a promotion and became head of a special school. His promotion did not depend on Mr. Knight. The deceased would have written him a good reference just to be rid of him. He is only a suspect because he dared to say what everyone felt

– and said it so soon after the murder.

Across the staff at the time, there are two individuals who significantly improved their status as a direct result of the death of Duncan Knight. They are Ms. Candy Regent, who became the head teacher, and Mr. Paul McSmart, who became the Head of Sixth for a while.

Ten years on, their lives have diverged. Ms. Regent took on the Headship of Kingswater should be and was then seconded to the Lake View High School (also in Kingswater) before becoming the CEO for the Federation of Kingswater Schools. She has co-written several books on the management of *'...violent change within a corporate sphere.'*

In contrast, Mr. Paul McSmart works in an Autistic Spectrum Condition unit. His first wife, and his children from that marriage are no longer in contact with him. When I spoke to her and told her where he worked, she was bitter. "He never wanted a wife," she said. "Just a housekeeper he could occasionally sleep with. My children came between him and his newspaper. He loved coffee and cake more than he loved them – or me. And as for working in an ASC unit… he's definitely found his tribe – even if he can't admit that to himself."

I believe that these two people are the key to this case. So, next I spent more time looking at the people who'd lost out as a result of the murder.

I returned to Wakefield to re-interview Gary. He confirmed many of my initial suspicions. Gary had been moved to Wakefield after being convicted of the murder of a prison guard. It is his claim that he was *'fitted up'* by the inmates and authorities at his previous prison, Belmarsh. Those people who still cling to the notion that Gary did kill Duncan Knight point to this subsequent conviction as proof that the earlier verdict on the then fifteen year old was correct. They say that in the child you find the man. What they do not understand is what it takes to survive a long sentence in a prison environment. Gary allowed me to record some more of his recollections of the night of the murder in Kingswater. At the time of the first trial, the evidence was not required because the case appeared closed.

This is Gary's story.

"We were in the building for a lark. Y'know, we were the Bad Man Crew. I took *'Lump'* [Liam York] with me 'cos I'd met him outside the *chippy*. He came along because he thought I could blag him a girlfriend – he was such a dozy fucker that he believed me! Got himself a life sentence for the promise of a soapy tit-wank! Ceebeebies to Seeboobies. So much for careful planning!" Gary laughed so much we had to suspend the interview for a full ten minutes. He lit up and resumed his tale. "We weren't even going to do the school. We knew there was nothing worth taking. We were thinking of breaking into the *KY* [Kingswater Youth Club]. They kicked us out the week before so we was getting our own back. Anyway, we're walking along and Lump says he remembers that Kingman (one of the deputy heads) has a petty cash box in his room. Just popped into his head. It was, he guessed, the takings from the tuck shop. So we change plans and go to the school. It was crawling with teachers. Some fucking plan we had. Lump wanted to go home, but now I couldn't show him I was bottling. So, I calm him down and we go in through the back. We smash a window and wait to see if the alarm goes off. Nothing. Lump reaches in and opens the window. He's smaller than me by a bit, so he gets in and opens the fire exit. Bingo! No alarm.

Now we are in the building. I swear we can hear a couple of people doing it. Lump reckons it was *Smartie* he could hear. I didn't know much about him 'cos he was mainly in the sixth form. Then we see the sword on the carpet. It looks like it's worth a bit. So we pick it up (like I said before). I know now it was a stupid thing to do. Then I think I hear voices coming from Knight's room. It sounded more like a woman's than a man's voice. Because we'd done this last minute, we had no disguise and Knight would clock me for sure. We all hated him, and I knew he wouldn't see the funny side of any of this.

We take the sword and leave the building. Then we sit in the woods by the lake and watch people leaving. The first one we see is *Smartie*. You know how it is when people look guilty? Well, I didn't then, but twenty years banged up teaches you that much. *Smartie* had definitely done something to somebody; shagged someone or stolen some green. He wasn't innocent.

I remember *Smartie* driving a really crappy red polo. We broke into it once – only had one cassette in it. He had nothing worth nicking – one piss poor cassette of *The Verve*. I almost felt sorry for him. That night, I watched him drive out – I can still remember the song that was playing. "*Lucky Man.*" I heard it caught fire that night – he was lucky to get out alive.

Then he stops by the gate and gets out of his car. Ten minutes later, the really hot history teacher drives out. We couldn't believe she was real – and we didn't know anybody she taught…ever. She was way out of *Smartie's* league – but they left at nearly the same time. So who knows? Like I said, he had shagged someone he shouldn't, or stolen something that wasn't his. Her hair's blowing everywhere. Beautiful hair she had…and those knockers…she was like a Disney princess with killer tits. She stops and the two of them have some sort of disagreement. It don't last long. He's punching above his weight – but respect for trying. Then they both drive off in different directions.

Me and Lump then take the sword back to the shed. Then we go home. End of. We was both innocent. We was just robbing the place. We was shat on, from a great height, by Numpties." *Shat on, from a great height, by Numpties* had the sound and feel of a *Suede* B side. It was the only light moment in an otherwise gloomy interview.

Unfortunately, I cannot get Liam to verify the story. He died of cancer five years ago. He was paroled but only spent two weeks outside prison. He'd always maintained his innocence – and that of Gary who being older got a longer sentence. For reasons he could never explain satisfactorily, it was his view that Paul McSmart had been responsible for putting him away. I found myself agreeing with him. I have now concluded my enquiries for the moment. I have sent a copy of my research to the local police station. It is my hope that this will give them the evidence they need to re-open the case.

This is the letter I got back from the investigating officers at Kingswater:

Dear Mr. Brown,

We acknowledge your concern about a miscarriage of justice. However, there has been no evidence that your father was in any way linked to the murder – other than that he was a member of staff at the same school as the victim – and made his views clear about him before and after his death. 'Hendrix' was a man with no filters – if he had done something, he would have told someone. We suggest that you focus on the positives in your father's life. Your grandfather (Digger Brown) was well known in the community and held in high respect as a war veteran; I doubt he raised a murderer.

The boys who were convicted had long criminal records and were destined for a life in crime. Nature and nurture are strong drivers of criminality; Liam's parents were well known 'faces' in the locality. Gary Smith is now serving a life term for the murder of a prison officer. We have been dealing with his extended family for over twenty years – their crimes range from theft through to extortion and murder. The Smiths are a very plausible family – until you look at what they have done in the wider community. Gary Smith's older brother is still an active criminal with drug connections to Spain and Portugal. The raw burglary rate in Kingswater fell by thirty percent in the month after these two individuals were placed in custody. There are not many innocent people in our jails. They may not have killed Duncan Knight; but we feel that, on balance, justice was done.

On the night of the murder, one of your suspects, Mr. Paul McSmart was rescued by the fire services after an incident with his car. He was checked over and sent on to St Joseph's for further tests. Your other suspect, Ms. Regent, we calculated, was probably not tall enough to have de-capitated the victim we found at the crime scene. Mr. Knight was a big man, even sitting down, she would have to have been standing on a chair to have killed him. Since the victim was clearly taken by surprise, this seems unlikely.

To pursue people simply because they were in the school on the night of Duncan Knight's murder will not yield the results you desire. If there is anything more to come out of the case (if it wasn't the boys), it will not happen because you have hounded people who were there. It is likely that, if you continue, you will lay yourself open to accusations of harassment.

We agree that there are troubling aspects to this case – but this is not your battle. In the end, most crimes of this nature are solved by confession.

Leave it and be patient...the unchained ego has a wonderful way of bringing the guilty to book.

Yours sincerely,

Detective J. Smith (no relation to Gary!),

Kingswater CID.

PS

If you have read this and still feel you need to press on, this is the address of an investigative journalist who might be interested. He's a bit of a renegade and has pissed off most of the dictatorships around the world at one time or another – but he enjoys intrigue and he is currently at a loose end. I would also add 'buyer beware' as he has a habit of pissing off other people who do not happen to be psychopathic dictators with means, motive and opportunity!

Enclosed with the letter was the calling card of an investigative journalist called Matthew Todd. He had a London address and a website which boasted threats from dictators and despots across the planet. There were also a couple of pictures of the man sporting various cuts and bruises received in the course of interviewing publicity torturers, murderers and corporate criminals. I was pretty sure the man had a death wish.

What the hell, I decided and rang the number on the card. His answerphone said he was currently out of the country, but if I left a message, then he would get back to me as soon as he could. It was another path and I was grateful for the hope. That evening I trawled through some of his greatest hits. He was certainly a confrontational chap - which raised my hopes. Maybe he could solve this case properly.

Matthew (somewhat older than I imagined) turned up and promised the earth. He agreed that there was at the very least a program to be made about what had happened.

Then this confession of sorts was uploaded onto the Kingswater School website. It remained there until the morning when it was read by the head, taken down and passed onto the Kingswater CID:

I am Paul McSmart. I am a killer and maybe a psychopath – who knows? I have only killed one person, so I guess that makes me an underachieving psychopath. However, as a person with this condition, I have suffered no regrets – occasionally I think about the boys who went down for it, but I think they were going to go down for something in this world so I saved them the bother of actually doing anything wrong.

In fact, I feel that my contribution to society has been beneficial. The man I killed was hated, and the children who were wrongly blamed were some of the worst I have ever taught. They were on a trail to jail, come what may. Win, win, as they say.

It was me. I did it. Like Lee Harvey Oswald, I did it alone (That's a joke by the way).

I was given the sword by Candy Jane Regent, or Jane Candy Regent – or whatever she is calling herself this week. She is the one who made it all happen – Randy Candy! She seduced me and made me kill that bastard – like I said, no regrets – je ne regret rien. If you are only going to kill one evil bastard in your life, you can't go wrong by taking out Duncan Knight. Everything got better for almost everyone after he was murdered.

If you want to go after those who should have done more, check out the Kingswater Constabulary; they knew it was me and they still let those boys twist in the wind. DC Grissom practically told me he knew I'd done it; but it was all too tidy with a couple of idiots in possession of the murder weapon. I was pleased to be off the hook but disappointed at the corruption of the boys in blue.

There is a cast of many incompetent and third rate people; I should know, I am one myself. But the closer you look at anybody, the less impressive they really are. The Police couldn't find two murderers in a community as porous as a school, and there was means, motive and opportunity all over the place. You'd think that at the very least they would have arrested Hendrix because he was happy that the fat bastard was not going to be able to sing anymore; I think he was disappointed too. I think he would have owned up to it if they'd asked him nicely – I really do. He's dead now and I think he would have liked that on his rap sheet wherever he was going. Killing Duncan Knight, I am sure, would give you a good reference in Heaven or Hell.

I also want you to consider the balance of my whole life. Does one act of violence nullify the career I have had after this act? Have all the people I have helped now become un-helped as a consequence of this new knowledge? I personally doubt it – but more importantly, I don't really care!

Now I must prepare myself for the only club that I cannot be blackballed from no matter what I have done. My time on this earth is done, now begins the dance of death!

Paul McSmart

April 1st 2006

The now retired DC Grissom was called in to have a look at what had been written by Paul. He said to the investigating officers that the man he interviewed in 1997 was a fool and a liar. He also was of the opinion that a woman like Candy Regent would not have shown the slightest interest in him. He suggested that the letter was as of a consequence of the mind-altering pain killers that Paul McSmart was taking towards the end of his life. Based on the retired detective's testimony and a masonic hand shake, they decided not to follow any further lines of enquiry in a case that could only bring them unrequited embarrassment.

Chapter Thirty-Six: Grey and Extinguished

From the *Kingswater News and Mail*:

Mr. Paul McSmart, a former teacher at Kingswater Comprehensive School died last week aged 45. It was reported that he died of prostate cancer, but this has yet to be confirmed. In the latter part of his career, he successfully ran a unit teaching children with Autistic Spectrum Disorder (also known as Autistic Spectrum Condition).

The Kingswater Constabulary are investigating fresh evidence concerning his involvement with the cold case of Mr. Duncan Knight; a popular and well respected teacher, who was murdered in 1997. It was also reported that Gary Smith, the surviving pupil prosecuted for the killing, has been released on parole.

The authorities have also questioned the former CEO of Kingswater Multi Academy Trust, Ms. Candy Regent, who was recently dismissed for bringing the role of CEOs into disrepute. Her alibi on the night of the murder was that she was with the self-confessed murderer, Mr. Paul McSmart. She has said that she will fight this injustice and smear on a career of selfless public service. It is clearly a case that is not yet over and done with.

Chapter Thirty-Seven:
Antiques Roadshow

A balding fifty-something, Matthew 'Toddy' Todd smelt a grim story. At least a half an hour window into lives less fortunate and maybe a chance to salve his social conscience... *nah*, just an hour and a half of television unless he sold it to a commercial channel. He'd constructed, ahead of filming, the opening sequence. It would centre on the bench that was Duncan Knight's epitaph...

'There is a bench in the north-west corner of Kingswater Comprehensive that is dedicated to the memory of a now forgotten teacher of the 1990s. It is said in whispers passed down the generations, that if any pupil should sit on the bench, they would as surely lose their head as Duncan Knight did'.

It was a tad clunky and overwrought, but it was a start. It set the scene and the mood of the puff piece he was offering up.

Poetry aside, Toddy had also been doing a little research on Candy Regent. He'd found out she'd once been sectioned during her university years. At that period, a number of men she knew had taken their lives. There was no direct proof that she had any direct involvement in any of the unexplained deaths. The other rumour was she'd been prescribed anti-psychotic drugs at school. He'd also traced her back to the time before she became a teacher and he became acquainted with the widow of a police officer who'd been more meticulous in his note taking than he was in his personal life. Detective Constable Davy Jones kept a diary during the last few weeks of his life which detailed his exploits with an unreasonably eager young lady who acquired not only a confiscated samurai sword but also a couple of forensic bio-suits that were intended to be worn at a scene of a crime. It seems they were.

Toddy found himself in a village in Buckinghamshire on an un-adopted road called Albion Crescent. A stone flew up and cracked his windshield; he hoped the journey would be worth the cost of its replacement. He stopped outside a bungalow that was midway down the rubble track. He checked the address with the sat-nav findings. If there was anything to be found here, this was the place.

He walked up the path to the door and pushed the buzzer. After a few moments, an elderly woman answered the door. She opened it only as far as the chain would allow.

"Are you Mr. Todd?"

"Yes," said Toddy showing her his BBC gate pass.

"Come in," she said, uncoupling the chain from the door. Once inside, it felt so old and smoky that he was sure he could hear Kent Walton softly commentating on the fixed wrestling that preceded the football results of his youth. So many names of places he would never visit, Queen of the South which wasn't even a place, Stenhousemuir that was, and Partick Thistle that he always read as Patrick Thistle. Then there were the wrestlers themselves: Les Kellet, Kendo Nagasaki, the Royal Brothers, Jackie Pallo, Mick McManus. But the television that hummed away to itself in the corner was not monochrome and showed *Midsomer Murders*.

He was shown to the front room. A cigarette was silently burning to nothing in an ashtray. In this house he could imagine how men died at fifty-six. It was cozy and toxic at the same time – just how he liked it. She turned and looked at him – implants for teeth she guessed. Not too sure about his very high hairline either.

"My husband was no worse than any of the others," she said.

"On my third marriage," said Toddy, holding up his hands. They got younger every time.

"He treated me with respect – he got me. Trouble was he treated a few others with the same respect – he got them as well."

"Like I say, I'm not one to judge…"

"He kept it out of the house. For a copper, you can't say fairer than that."

"Yes," said Toddy.

"I didn't know any officer that wasn't shagging someone on the side," she said. "If you were CID, it was part of the job description." Just like the BBC, thought Toddy – but we have better expenses and better-looking women.

"I see," he said.

"But that last one…she didn't play by the rules…she took him out of his comfort zone…she made him break the law."

"Can I record this?"

"Why else are you here? I'm done with the ways of men."

"Fair play," said Toddy, faintly outraged at the idea that she thought he would. She was far too close to his own age group. He set up his minimal recording gear and let her become a talking head.

"He came home the last evening white and blue. I knew he was up to something. He gave me his notebook and told me to put it away for safe keeping. It was like he knew it would come in handy. The next day they came round and told me he had died in this flat. Her flat. Natural causes they said. Well, I knew it was more than that – but what can you do? I was worried I might lose some pension rights, so I kept quiet. Watched that smug little bitch leave town with a sword and a couple of forensic suits. Then she was gone. Out of my life. Then her name comes up again with that killing a couple of years ago. And still I thought, leave it alone, girl. But then I read about those boys who were sentenced. My Davy always said that it was dodgy testimony rather than evidence that convicted most of them who came up before the beak. Then this stuff with that teacher, Mr. McSmart? And that poor boy looking to clear his father. And her going through the massed ranks like a dose of salts. This is where two and two make five."

"Very good," said Toddy. Next she produced an old leather briefcase from behind her sofa.

"It's all in there," she said. "Davy Jones's lock-up. I suggest you take a good look."

"You trust me?"

"Watch your step, my boy." She laughed like a stage witch. "I still have friends who owe me a favour."

"Okay," said Toddy. He knew the score. He pointed the camera at himself and lowered his voice to a whisper. "So...we now have some hard evidence that this is not the open and shut case it looked to be twenty years ago. The sword that killed Duncan Knight still has a few more tales to tell." Then he trained the camera on the case. "I think we need to see what's inside." Toddy turned the camera off.

"What now?" the old girl asked.

"We take a good look at what he wrote in those last three weeks." Toddy was relieved that the late detective was a methodical man. The diaries were in year order, filed inside the case like so many compact discs. He picked out the last one. It started in January 1987. He went carefully through the pages until he got to September.

'Gave a maid a blade in return for favours offered. Took a sword from the stockade. Japanese origin. Probably won't be noticed. But if it does get used for anything iffier than a Knighthood in a porno, this is what it looks like.' The picture attached to the page with brown crusty paper glue was definitely a close match for the murder weapon. It might even have been the murder weapon.

"I think we have a story," said Toddy.

"Yes we do," said the old girl.

"I can give you five thousand up front," said Toddy. She waved him away.

"My wretched boy, this is not about the money. I got more money than I can spend in the time I have left on this rotting planet. I'm from a generation that quietly holds to real values. This is about setting the record straight. This is about the awkward truth." Living in a largely post-truth world, this sounded surprisingly false to 'Toddy.' But each to their own - he chose to go with the old girl's flow.

"Yes. The truth."

"In the old days, they would have hanged her – like Ruth Ellis." In the good old days, he thought, they would have burned or drowned her for being a witch. Better safe than sorry.

"So true." She was not yet done.

"The truth, Mr. Todd, the whole truth and nothing but the truth." All he could see was eighty-something Jack Warner, creaking at the knee, pretending to be a policeman on the beat. Telling the truth. What a concept!

"So, Mr. Todd, are you going to aim for the truth?"

"Sure am, mam."

"Don't get cute with me, just go for it!"

"The truth it is."

"I do hope you are more real than your china teeth, Mr. Todd." She looked at him slantways. "Lovely as they are, sitting there in that rotten craw of yours."

"I paid a lot for these," said Toddy. The old girl changed tack.

"I believe it was Martin Luther King who said that injustice was a threat to justice everywhere."

"I'll write that down," he said. "It's a good one to tell

my boy. He's studying Martin Luther King as part of one of his media courses." He had no idea about the quote – but it sounded plausible and he did write it down for his son John. For more than a few moments, Toddy felt as though he was in a bad movie with a shot-away cast of has been celebrities. But then he realized he'd been listening to the sound of authentic anger and a last-ditch effort to free some kind of meaning from a world of soundbites and bullshit masquerading as entertainment. Through the fumes and the fag ash, it felt inspiring - like a sweet breath of fresh air. He would go for it - and keep the five thousand for sundries for wine, women and song.

Chapter Thirty-Eight:
If You See Her, Say Fuck Off

With his trusted camera-person, Snuffy Jones, in tow, the chase was now on. Snuffy got his nickname from saying *'Snuff'* when he'd listened to as much of his partner as he could bear in one take. Snuffy was a bulky man who made his several stones over-weight partner look petite – for a middle-aged man as vain as Toddy was, that counted for more than competence. Their quarry was an overachieving history teacher who may or may not have been an accessory to a murder.

"*Highway 61 Revisited*," said Snuffy. This was the opening gambit to the wind-up game he played with his partner, shit Dylan songs with great titles. It always pissed Toddy off. Dylan was not to be criticised on any level, for anything. He said nothing. "Any Dylan album, or song, after 1975," added Snuffy. There was a pause. "You know I'm right," continued Snuffy.

"I think you mean all rock music since 1975," said Toddy.

"That doesn't explain *Wish You Were Here*," said Snuffy.

"Fuck off, we've got a job to do." Toddy felt the thrill that was the start of any quest no matter how pointless, doomed and stale it was. This was why he got out of bed at noon for a shade under a hundred thousand plus benefits - fucking BBC skinflints. Their secret was to doorstep and make it seem like investigative journalism. To paraphrase the great Bob Monkhouse; once you learned to fake reality, the rest was easy.

The first stop on the jaunt was the grave-site of Paul McSmart – or more accurately, more or less the place where his ashes had been scattered – *over and done with* as his ex-wife said at the time.

'As you can see,' said Toddy, 'dead men tell no tales.'

The camera panned around the crematorium grounds. A squirrel ran for cover and a pigeon took to the sky. Nothing indicated Paul McSmart had ever been here. So, for an authentic feel, they had brought along a marble effect flower pot with stuck on gold letters that spelt out the word **PAUL**. It was a shitty thing to do and they knew they would both go straight to hell – but unless they lied like this, nobody would ever believe their story.

'This is the final resting place of one of the suspected murderers of respected teacher Duncan Knight. It is, for us, the beginning of a search for the truth in what may well be one of the biggest miscarriages of justice since Craig and Bentley.'

The scene set, the partners in crime drove off for their next soundbite. Its job done, they left the marble effect flowerpot at the crematorium pretending it had something to do with the memory of Paul McSmart. Their next stop was all too real.

"Fuck my old boots," said Toddy, "No wonder we have a literacy problem in this country." They'd fetched up outside a police station that now doubled up as a library and a town hall. It offended every one of Toddy's sensibilities about education, crime and government.

"What kid would go and borrow a fucking book in the shadow of Plod?" Snuffy looked at the building.

"I can't see any books in there," he said. "It's all fucking computers and DVDs." After a decent pause to agree a general indignation, Snuffy got ready to roll and Toddy found his media voice.

"Here we are at the very police station where the murder weapon was procured in 1987." Inside the police station, rebuilt after 1997 in a frenzy of urban regeneration, there was no single person with an attachment to any of the events being investigated. They looked out at two balding, middle-aged, boy-scouts trying to set the dead embers of a camp fire ablaze.

"Should we tell them to sling their hook?" one officer asked the other.

"You want to be part of a current affairs program about bent coppers with a taste for violence?" the other replied. A question had answered another question. Two minutes later, the journalist and his cameraman were gone.

They fetched up next at the educational establishment at the heart of the affair. Snuffy aimed his camera at the school building. It was approaching sunset and everything was bathed in a nostalgic glow.

"This is the scene of the murder. From our vantage point we can see the original office of Duncan Knight. I believe it is now a study room for pupils. Nearly twenty years ago, it was where teachers were preparing for the new Ofsted inspections that were part of the new drive for excellence in education. Further down from Duncan Knight's office were those of Candy Regent and Paul McSmart. We would have liked to have taken a closer look at the murder scene, but have been denied access by the school." The claim was not strictly true – but it made for a more exciting narrative. There was really nothing to see here or there.

The two men then moved on to the last known address for Candy Regent. They posed outside a five-bedroomed mock Tudor house.

"Here we are at the home of Candy Regent. We believe that she is in." Toddy then proceeded to walk up to the door of the house. His feet crunched on the small stones in the drive. He wheezed before he spoke again. "I am going to knock on the door." There was no response. After fifteen minutes of waiting, Snuffy turned off the camera and they wandered back to their vehicle. Twenty minutes later, a car drove out of the property.

"French piece of shit," said Snuffy.

"We are now giving chase to Candy Regent," said Toddy. The Citroen C3 stopped at the local Tesco Express and a man got out. They'd no way of knowing who he was. If they'd done their homework, they might have discovered it was Candy Regent's current squeeze – his danglers were on probation. With Toddy and Snuffy in pale pursuit of a red herring, Candy Regent walked out of her own house and into a waiting taxi. Tediosity. But they were only men. She knew what she could do to them. It was just a matter of when the doggie bag came out.

"The old car decoy trick," said Snuffy.

"You know where to go next," said Toddy. They broke a few rules and saved a few minutes.

"It's usually a train station," said Snuffy.

"It takes a lot to laugh, it takes a train to cry," said Toddy.

"What?" asked Snuffy.

"New game," said Toddy. "Great Dylan songs with shit titles."

"I think you mean shit Dylan songs with shit titles."

"Have you ever listened to the album?" asked Toddy.

"Only lying in a pool of vomit at the dog-end of a student party," said Snuffy.

"So the answer is yes," said Toddy.

The taxi dropped Candy at the train station. She walked a few steps and glimpsed sideways.

"Fuck," she whispered to nobody. There they were. Heads like hard-boiled eggs waiting for breakfast; Tweedledum and Tweedledee. It would be off with their heads if they annoyed her any more.

"Ms. Regent!" A voice called out to her. All high explosive and pin-sharp rage, she looked properly in their direction.

"Yes?" she answered.

"Did you conspire with the late Paul McSmart to kill Duncan Knight?"

"What sort of a question is that?"

"A reasonable one," said 'Toddy.'

"That rattled her cage," said Snuffy. They were only half right. She composed herself as she walked away. She turned and looked back at them with eyes cold and dead. She saw a pair of fat and frightened potato men, two zeros chasing after nothing they could begin to understand or cope with.

"Are you suggesting that a woman is incapable of killing a man on her own…if she so chooses?" They knew a killer line when they heard one.

"What about your relationship with Paul McSmart?"

"You found out where I live. I'll find out where you live," said Candy. Toddy was slightly uncomfortable.

"Is that a threat?"

"Call it a promise," said Candy.

"I think it's a threat," said Toddy.

"Call it what you like. Now call off your attack dog. I have a sick and demented mother to visit." There was a pause… then she stalked into the middle distance. Perfect camera shot. A body to die for. Toddy sang out a tuneless song from his latent adolescence. Unexpectedly, she walked back to them. Her manner had completely changed.

"I think we might talk."

"When?" Toddy asked.

"Give me your number." He handed her a calling card. He looked at the name. It said Jane. *Jane Candy Regent*. She was more opaque than Lee Harvey Oswald.

"Thank you."

She walked off again.

"Queen Jane Approximately – great title and great song." Snuffy tutted in response.

"You and fucking Zimmerma,"Snuffy responded. He got the reply of the consummate Bobcat; the navel-gazing male trapped, forever young, between the age of nineteen and twenty-two.

"He's always relevant," said Toddy. "Always clear where others took the easy path."

"But mostly when you're feeling sick in the head."

"Yeah, I guess so."

"Will she shaft us or shag us?" asked Snuffy.

"I dunno. But I think we have part one of our story," said Toddy.

"And part two?" Snuffy asked.

"Not bothered about that," said Toddy. "Let some other bugger join the dots."

"Too right," said Snuffy. "She scares the shit out of me." They had met their fair share of male psychopaths; what she had just gifted them was as close to a confession as they could hope for. Unfortunately, Toddy lived for the thrill of the chase. She was clearly dangerous – but now he felt he was on a promise of some description.

"There is something about her," said Toddy. Snuffy had seen that look before. He understood that nothing good would come of it. He also knew that would not change anything with his mate. He could only warn and watch as Toddy contemplated a last drugged dance with a praying mantis.

"You just stay out of her knickers, old son."

"You know me."

"I do. You'll be after the best a man can get."

"What's the worst she can do to me with one of those?" asked Toddy, giving his old comrade a farewell hug.

"I don't want to know the answer to that, old friend."

"Yeah." Toddy received a new text message.

'Hi. I really fancy a hot toddy tonight xxx.' They both knew who it was.

"Say you're too unwell to go out with her," said Snuffy.

"No can do," said Toddy.

"It's your funeral," said Snuffy.

"I'd better buy my own dead flowers," said Toddy.

"Yeah," said Snuffy.

"Am I in a new relationship?" Toddy asked. Still looking at his phone, Toddy considered a Facebook update.

"Only if you think you've finally found yourself," said Snuffy.

"I think she gets me," said Toddy.

"She's a psychopath," said Snuffy, "so I'm sure she will…eventually."

"Keep calm and fuck your mum," cautioned Toddy.

"You'll have to dig her up first," said Snuffy.

"Hasta la vista, amigo."

"Ciao."

"You never said that before," said Toddy.

"I never thought I would never see you again," said Snuffy.

"Smoke me a kipper," said Toddy. Snuffy looked up to the sky – this required something more serious than a *Red Dwarf* quote.

"I can hear the *Idiot Wind* blowing around your skull, old sport."

"It's a great song."

"No, it's not – but someone has got it in for you."

"Not before I get it into them," said Toddy.

Chapter Thirty-Nine: Viagra Falls

The next evening, Candy Regent knocked on the door of the London flat of Matthew Todd. He'd brought fresh flowers and warm whisky. He was expecting her. He was not expecting her to have a better than life-like sex toy in tow. It hung off her shoulder looking, to the predator in Toddy, appealingly intoxicated and ready to peel and feel.

"Have you met my friend?" Candy asked.

"Where did you find her?"

"Japan. I love all things Japanese," she said. Underneath the coat, the Japanese love mannequin was unclothed and occidental. Like the pervert he was, he looked her up and down. The texture of the skin was better than human. He tweaked an ersatz nipple. The breasts were exquisite…to look at anyway. She was a red head like Nicole Kidman. How did she know he loved red heads? He was with Springsteen on that one; a red-headed woman was really the best a man could get.

"Not quite a Nexus 6," he said. "But she looks pretty real to me." The psychopath in Candy could practically taste the blood of her victim; for different reasons, she was as aroused as he was.

"Sex with a replicant," said Candy. "That's one more thing to tick off the bucket list." That she knew what he was thinking shook him.

"Yeah. Alien sex. The final frontier."

"Sometimes I like to play with her," said Candy, unbuttoning her coat to reveal that she was wearing marginally more than the doll. It was an old trick - but she was real! The lace enclosed something more than silicone. The lesbian android hybrid concept had an immediate effect on Toddy - even though he could see it was pretty stupid for a woman to use a sex toy like this.

"You do?" his throat was dry.

"When I can't get what I really want," she said, "I pop in a dildo and off I go." This was nearly too much to bear. They were both enjoying the lie. Even though it made no sense, he forgot his fear.

"No you don't," he said.

"Oh, yes I do," she replied.

"Really?" Toddy asked.

"Yes, really." She thrust the pouting silicon mouth in his direction. He peered into the slippery lips. Expertly, she rubbed the bulge in his trousers. Though distracted, Toddy looked quizzically at her distorted smile.

"Why is it wet?" Toddy asked, "the doll.".

"Why wouldn't it be?" At this point, the sentient being that sometimes lurked in Toddy could see something not quite kosher.

"Why," he asked, "are you wearing latex gloves?"

"Because," she said, "they make me feel all warm and moist – now show me what you can do to her – be the hot toddy of my darkest desire." He was never to know that this killer queen had laced every opening with as much opioid medication she had been able to find at her dying and demented mother's house.

"You really do it with her?" He'd clearly forgotten the plots of *Snow White, Body of Evidence* and *To Die For* – movies he'd listed as some of his all-time favourites on *Wikipedia*.

"And I'll do it with you. But you just have to try her first," said Candy. "Just for me…please." She stroked his forearm. He felt stupid and turned on in the same moment.

"Put my old boy into that?"

"Yes," said Candy. "You know…the old chestnut…the sixty-nine." His heart raced. This was the magazine position of all his boyhood wet-dreams. In the laboratory of human response, everything ended in a simultaneous orgasm and there were always fag adverts on the back cover.

"Then I can do the same to you?" She smiled like the wicked witch she was.

"Have you taken your rocket pills?" He'd prepared that part of assignation as carefully as an idiot would.

"Yes."

"Good boy!"

"So…same to you…after the android?"

"Only if you live that long." Again blind to nuance, he was up for it.

"Does she have a name?"

"Ophelia. You know…from *Desolation Row?*"

"Of course." Queen Candy had done her homework more than approximately. She'd absolutely nailed him on *Wikipedia*. He was a movie buff and sci-fi fan whose favourite movie was *Blade Runner*. Bob Dylan was his favourite singer. A little more self-awareness and he might have even saved his own life. If only he had remembered plotlines and lyrics.

He put his real tongue into her artificial crevice and started to lick. It felt stupid to be trying to give pleasure to a lump of industrial totty. He looked at Candy; she gave him a smile of encouragement. He carried on with the charade. Then his mouth started to go numb. Why was cunnilingus like being at the dentist? It was a joke with no punchline. He hated being at the dentist. Then he fell into a darkness beyond the realm of Morpheus.

When he came to, he was unable to move or speak. She was standing over him, naked – apart from the latex gloves, with a bottle of liquid morphine in her hand.

"Spoiler alert," she said. "Now you know the real reason for the gloves." She poured the marvelous medicine into a small cup and gently opened his numbed lips.

"There," she said. "Another dram of this should see you into the limitless night." She watched as he fell asleep looking up at her.

"You know what? Blink if you can hear me." He blinked.

"I think you really do have a death wish. Blink twice if you agree." He blinked twice.

"How lucky you found me."

The last thing he would see on this planet were her almost perfect breasts mocking him like gentle hillocks where he would never roam. Between them he thought he could see a silver skull grinning at him like the grim reaper. She was the mother who smothered. Men and breasts! That was all they ever saw of her before it was too late; stupid men who thought the world owed them something more than a comfortable death. Soon, she knew he would stop breathing altogether. She envied him his peaceful onward journey, bastard that he was.

"I'm so sorry it couldn't have been more painful." He blinked twice. He had become, in *Pink Floyd* speak, *'comfortably numb'*. Only now she was not looking at him. She was having her own moment of self-actualization. She felt good. Really good. It was like an oxytocin rush; the business of killing people who were inconvenient to her was way better than enduring bad sex with them.

She stepped over his rigid member.

"And now you even have somewhere to hang your hat. And one more piece of advice – never trust a younger woman who finds you attractive. In your case, Toddy, never trust any woman who finds you attractive." She was funny. He really wanted to laugh – but it was like an itch he couldn't scratch anymore. She had his danglers in a doggie bag. "Hasta la vista, baby." And she even knew his favourite action hero.

She put on a head-scarf that disguised any distinguishing feature and dragged her sex doll out of the flat. Anybody that saw the pair of them would, she knew, only remember the strange red head with the funny walk. How many more, she wondered, before she could live a life without killing? She hoped there would be a few.

Pausing at a bridge on her way home, she dropped the death doll into the river and carried on driving.

"Sink or swim, Ophelia dear."

One day someone might rescue her and wonder why a sex toy was wearing rubber gloves. Nobody was going to rescue Toddy. He was on his own.

Tomorrow she would visit her demented mother and return what was left of the medication she'd appropriated. With luck, the old bat would be also be dead and lying in a pool of her own excrement. Days like these made her feel glad to be alive; the buzz from watching a person die was like no drug she'd ever taken. It was so beautiful she decided she'd kill her mother the next time she saw her. She was not yet certain if she would suffocate her with a pillow or let her overdose on her medication. Choices. Choices. Death was full of choices.

Chapter Forty: Red Herring

Fifty-five year old Matthew 'Toddy' Todd was found dead at his home in Battersea yesterday. A neighbour sounded the alarm when he failed to collect an Amazon delivery. He'd been deceased for at least a week. A bunch of roses was found with his body. The initial cause of death was given as a heart attack. He was investigating a number of high profile cases both at home and abroad. A spokesperson for the Police said that it was a potentially difficult case because of the *'Number of enemies he routinely made in the course of his employment at the BBC'*. The Police also said they were looking to question a couple of women, who were seen, arm in arm, near his flat in the week before his death was reported. Eyewitnesses describe one of the women outside his property as an attractive red-head who walked with a slight limp.

The BBC department for current affairs agreed that his latest program should never be aired because it contained nothing more than circumstantial evidence. Police also interviewed Candy Regent, one of the last people to see him alive. At her request, they took a sample of her DNA. An official confirmed that her DNA was not present in the deceased's flat – or on his body.

His colleagues at the BBC described him as a man with an instinct for causing trouble in the cause of a good story - rather than troubling himself for a good cause. One journalist privately said that, behind his back, the pet-name they had for him was '*Shoddy*.' The self-same nickname was used at his boarding school by several of the masters - for failing, amongst other things, to complete his prep in the correct manner. He leaves an estranged wife, two further ex-wives, five children and seven grandchildren.

Chapter Forty-One: Breaking News

'It has been established that Mr. Matthew Todd, a BBC television journalist, was poisoned. A toxicology report has shown traces of a range of opioids in his system. It was mooted that they were introduced via his penis and his mouth, where the concentration of the drugs was at its highest. Russian, Korean and Israeli sources have denied any involvement in his death. A spokesperson for TASS was quoted as saying that it was regrettable that Mr. Todd passed away as a consequence of a liaison with a woman of the night. However, it fitted a pattern of indulgent behaviour; here was a man with an addiction to the black market in oral sex. It is evident that he died as he lived – with a chemically enhanced erection and a grin of bourgeois gratification that begat his shoddy values.

The reporter suggested British authorities confine their search for his murderess to their own house. From the best surveillance available, the reporter suggested they might best look for sexually-active females aged between twenty-five and fifty who wanted him dead. It is a long box not open to approximation. They might start by checking for whom he bought flowers. The reporter opined that they could not be any more specific.

Chapter Forty-Two: Living Your Values

In what the *TES* called a landmark decision for an employment tribunal, Candy Regent was awarded substantial, undisclosed damages for the loss of her CEO post, and the harm done to her reputation by the BBC, mainstream print media and twenty disgruntled former colleagues. Completely fire-proof, she laughed all the way down the stairs. Alone, she crowned herself.

"I have been a Regent for too long. Now I will be a Queen."

At street level, in a statement read out, in her absence, by her solicitor, Queen Candy had this to say to waiting journalists willing to take the risk: *'If I had been a man, none of the issues I faced would have been considered prejudicial to me being considered as competent and responsible. I would have simply been identified as a strong leader prepared to ruthlessly engage with what was required to raise educational standards for the pupils in my care. As it is, in some places it has been whispered that I am a psychopath – that I have an anti-social personality disorder. I am no more a psychopath than I am a murderer, but such is the need to malign strong women in our society, that these are the accusations I have faced in the course of simply doing the job I love to the best of my ability.*

There has been too much written and spoken about my private life. I have recently lost my mother to dementia – but instead of sympathy, I am ridiculed for having any kind of life beyond caring for her in her final days on this planet. I was so pleased that she did not know the pain I suffered from the toxic publicity generated by macho tabloid media. Again, this kind of prolonged intrusion is not something a single, hetero-sexual male would ever have to endure. I look forward to being able to rebuild my career without the constant prurient gaze that has been focused upon me.

I hope that in my new role as a Values Based

Education consultant, I will be able to operate without the patriarchal intrusions of the media, the unions and those misogynist individuals in the world of education who still act as though a women's place is solely in the classroom. Only by being allowed to operate without the constraints I have alluded to, will I truly achieve my true potential in my chosen area of expertise.

I shall be the change I would like to see in others. I will provide curriculum care based on core human values and led by pupil needs. I intend to be quite ruthless about that.

Finally, I would like to thank those people, friends and colleagues, who have stood by me and allowed me to get my professional life back on track.'

She particularly liked the last paragraph, although it was a complete fiction. She had no friends and colleagues, although certain stinky Snitches had only supported her out of a paralyzed animal fear. And that was the way she wanted it to remain in any future employment. As her words of warning were being spoken to the world, Queen Candy left via a side door, climbed into a waiting taxi and resumed her career in education management.

As she watched the streets of London flash past, she had an idea that would not go away. To be a serial killer was rather passé; there were so many of them and there was nothing in it for her if she got caught. She did not yearn for a life of notoriety behind bars. To be a female Charles Manson held no appeal for her. No. She'd killed happily – but now it was time to move on and earn herself some real money before she lost her looks and died. Yes. She would climb onboard the best gravy train there was for a person who did not wish to work any harder than she needed to. She would become an MEP…or, at the very least, an MP. The career change would also guarantee her the company of like-minded souls on her journey to oblivion.

Chapter Forty-Three: Regicidal

"Fuck! Fuck! Fuck!" Jerry Brown, son of Hendrix, watched the whole sorry spectacle unfold on his tablet. She'd killed and killed and walked free. It was true. The world was not his friend. Here was a woman who had all but been found guilty of three murders he knew of, leaving the clutches of justice with compensation and an even higher-paying job than before. And people still suspected his father of killing Duncan Knight because he dared to laugh at the whole sorry story.

Bringing her to justice became his hunt. He was like Ahab chasing down *Moby-Dick*. Sick of his conspiracy theories long ago his wife had asked him to leave the family home. Flush with cash from his father's in service death grant, he'd set himself up in a motel from where he planned a sting that would rid the world of Candy Regent.

He searched through his downloads for Jimi Hendrix playing *'All Along the Watchtower,'* his old man's favourite song. For two and a half minutes all was well in his world. Jerry Brown looked up to the sky. He wasn't sure his old man was anywhere that he could guess. In death as in life he remained elusive to his own flesh and blood.

"I tried, Dad, I really tried." It was at times like this that the words really did make sense. Then he had the stupid idea of confronting her. He was his father's boy. He would do it. He had no idea how.

He just knew he would.

Chapter Forty-Four: Danglers in a Doggie Bag

There was knock at the door. "It's open," said Jerry Brown.

Candy Regent, wearing a long raincoat, entered the room.

"You've been expecting me," she said. What he was not anticipating was almost complete amnesia about his motives for luring her here. She took off her raincoat. She was wearing nothing else but a pair of thigh length boots.

He did not notice she was carrying a bag of knives and swords as well as a change of knickers. He forgot to turn on the very expensive surveillance equipment he'd squandered his inheritance on. He remembered that he'd not had sex in six months.

She looked at his penis. It was clear he was not doing any real thinking about the clear and present danger he was in. But it was a pity to waste it. Shag first and kill later had the advantage that men didn't give a monkey's if you killed them after sex; it was a fair cop.

Get Kingswater – your local law enforcement voice.

A man identified as Jerry Brown was found decapitated in a motel in Kingswater. Police do not yet have a motive for the murder – although a significant amount of surveillance equipment was found in the victim's room. DNA taken from the scene indicates that Mr. Brown had unprotected sexual intercourse shortly before he died. The murder weapon has not been found and no witnesses have been identified. Mr. Brown had been investigating the death of Duncan Knight who was killed in a similar fashion in 1997. He leaves a wife from whom he was recently separated and two young children.

Chapter Forty-Five: It Was All of Me!

Candy Regent paused at her happy bridge over the Thames. All was dark, quiet and still. In the distance, a clocked chimed three times. With the moon shrouded behind a cluster of clouds, she dropped her beloved *Katana* into the river. There was a tiny splash as the blade sliced through the still waters. The unkindest cut. She was sorry to say goodbye to her babe – but it was the right thing to do. "You really must stop doing this," she said to herself.

"But, Queen Candy, you like doing it," said another voice in her head.

"I do," she said to herself. "I really do." The other voice continued the dialogue.

"And, Queen Candy, if you like doing it, then it must be the right thing to do."

Another voice piped up, which sounded like her snitch. "Yes, my lady, if it is right for you, it will be right for everyone else." Candy laughed.

"Apart from the people we will kill," she said.

"It's only what they expect of you," said the voice of her snitch.

"A lesson to the others," Queen Candy added.

"I think we have reached a consensus," said Candy. All the voices were certain that she should not stop now.

"Yes. Yes. Yes. You carry on killing. Don't let the fun stop." The future would be such an adventure. As the moon revealed itself, she laughed and laughed. Life was fun when you came off your meds. The pills she had chosen not to take for the past month were also in the river with the sword she had used to kill Jerry Brown. He'd made her reflect too much on her own behaviour - and just like his old man before him there was never any learning. He'd also found her a tad too irresistible in the flesh. Those were the sins that did for them all in the end.

Chapter Forty-Six:
Flesh Pastures

For a few moments on the bridge, the laughter had turned to tears of joy. She held on as the water poured out of her eyes. If anybody had been looking, they might have thought she was about to jump into the water. And just for a second, one of her voices thought that was an idea worth considering.

"Excuse me Madam?" Was that a young male moderating voice in her head? Thankfully not: it was a police officer - green as grass, doggie bag in his pocket. It looked like his hat was falling off his head. This would be too easy.

"My mother has just died," she said. "I don't know whether to laugh or cry."

"Can I help?" She gave him a cool look up and down. He could help in the trouser department.

"You could help me get home," she said. "Before I do anything really silly." The police officer had already made his own observations based on youth and ignorance.

"It would be a pleasure, Madam. My shift has just finished anyway." Theatrically, he turned off his work phone and placed it in his back pocket.

"Thank you," she said and smiled her killer's smile, not that he noticed.

"Shall we get you off this bridge?" he asked. "It's rather chilly." She linked her arm in his. As they walked, she asked him a few questions.

"Do you have any hobbies?" He looked up at the stars.

"I like to read about serial killers." That was perfect. She smirked inwardly – a nod to the voices in her head, all of whom were looking forward to her garden growing.

"I hope you are not one yourself," she said.

"No Madam," he said. "I just find them interesting."

"Do you watch the news on television?" she asked, pulling him a fraction closer.

"No Madam," he said. "It's all lies and disinformation."

"Quite," she said.

"But I am a good judge of character," he said. "My mum always said that." It was a bum note, but she would forgive him that on a night like this.

"I think we have much in common," Candy said. He smiled.

"Yes Madam." He was due a lucky night.

"By the way," she said, "my name is Candy. Candy Regent. I am a values-based consultant."

"My name is Jerrad," he said. "And I have no idea what you are talking about."

"Nice name," she said. "Jerrad." Perfect, she decided again. Just perfect.

"I love the necklace," he said. "I have a thing about skulls."

"I think you were checking out my boobs." Caught out, he laughed.

"Guilty as charged," he said. "They are worth a look."

"You have no idea," she said. Stupid young men with (hopefully) flawless bodies, low expectations and natural erections were one of Mother Nature's better ideas. She currently had no idea whether he would live through the night. Already she had forgotten his name – PC Dick or whatever he was called. She would have a quick meeting with the voices in her head. She counted them out, one two three – including me. That was a sufficient number for her meeting to be quorate. Quick! She needed an agenda. By what criteria should he live or die after his time in her royal bedchamber? They spoke as one.

"Performance management!" Well that was obvious. She could have come up with that all on her lonesome. Perhaps it was time for her to go back on the meds. The little people in her head had been listening; they did not like what they were hearing.

"Please don't," pleaded one of the voices. Now she could see them; the pretty maids all in a row – apart from Snitches of course. But then she was once a real person in her life.

"We like it when you kill people," said another. "It makes us happy."

"You're not a Queen, you're a *Qwunt*." This was a familiar *male* voice from her middle past. She knew him right away. It was Hendrix – and that, *Qwunt*, well that wasn't even a word. He'd come back to haunt her without asking permission – Yes! That was Hendrix all over – an acquired taste she no longer desired. Now she was definitely going back to the meds. She would kill him like she killed his balls for brains boy – or mace him with medication at the very least. Trying to get her done for murder after trying to get off with her. Who did he think he was? He was Hendrix, and before the drugs took hold, he wanted the last word. "You're a Foxy Lady… which is why they should never have put you in charge of the henhouse." But higher authorities than Hendrix had put her in charge of several henhouses with very predictable results.

As for PC Plod, or whatever his name was, he would be appraised like anyone else she dealt with. His three targets would be total satisfaction (hers of course), gratitude and attitude in the morning (his of course). Contrary wise, there would be no support plan if he failed to achieve any one of these fair and just outcomes – just silver bells and cockleshells. One mistake anywhere and she would invoke a capability procedure, or as she liked to call it, the *Mantis* option.

She wasn't all bad, for she would make him say his

prayers before bedtime. What she had not done was consider fully the consequences of murdering a young police officer who still had something to live for. It was a classic error of her personality disorder. She also did not know that the late, great Hendrix was more than just a solo voice in her head to be stilled with pills; he was very much a part of her future and was destined to have one more spin of fortune's wheel.

Before she hacked him to bits, PC Plod had provided her with a very welcome distraction – but now it was time for him to leave. As for his performance management targets, he was a little less than awed after she had shagged herself to a standstill. She would stick to the elderly and infirm in the future – gratitude was better than attitude. He dared to rate her, and then he only gave her an eight out of ten. Nobody gave her an eight out of ten and lived to tell; she was definitely an eleven on looks alone.

Dropping him off at the bridge, she sung out an improvised tune remembered from a sexist television advert from the dawn of time about breakfast cereal.

"There are no men in my life, one I killed with a sword, the other with a knife – but they both have Candy on their mind." She watched for the bubbles, but it was too dark to see anything. If she had lingered a little longer, she would have had time to correct her sloppy roping and knotting skills.

"I am a genuine cereal killer," she said to all the voices in her head.

"No, you're not," said one of them. "I am." She recognized the dissenting voice. It was Hendrix going for an encore after his boring solo.

"You again!"

"You killed my boy!"

"It was what he wanted."

"It'll be your turn soon."

"Go away Hendrix. You were no fun when you were alive and you're no fun now."

"You wait until they hear my story," said Hendrix.

"Dead men tell no tales," said Candy.

"I told this one before I died," said Hendrix.

"You couldn't organize a bunk up in a brothel."

"Dream on, sister."

"You know why I never did you?"

"Scared of my equipment?" She was going to say something to Hendrix, but became aware of a real person standing next to her. Another police officer. A female police officer. A very attractive female police officer.

"I think you need to come with us to the station."

She looked around. *'Us'* was two further male police officers not far from two police vehicles. If it wasn't for the fact they were arresting her for murder, this would have been her biggest sexual fantasy being played out at her favourite time and location. The female police officer cuffed her and gently led her to a van.

"How did you know?" Candy asked.

"I was supposed to see him tonight. I was going to ask him to move in with me."

"Lucky escape," said Candy.

"Yes."

"I wish I'd met you instead," said Candy.

"Would that have been his lucky escape?"

"You're good," said Candy. "You're really good."

"You do know you'll be going to prison?"

"Looking forward to it," said Candy. "Gives me a chance to sort things out."

"It's a nasty place full of bad people," said the female police officer.

"I like a challenge," said Candy.

"It's not like a failing school," said the female police officer.

"You're not just a pretty face," said Candy. "You have done your homework."

"Like I said, it won't be like school...packed full of stupid men who can't see past your body."

"They don't stand a chance," said Candy. "Not a snowball's in Hell."

"In we go," said the female police officer, opening the door of the van. Candy was now in the cage inside. With the female police officer sat next to her, she sensed an opportunity of sorts.

"Is it me, or is it getting hot?" Candy asked.

"I think it's you." One of the male police officers clambered into the back of the van.

"Come to watch us?" Candy asked.

"She's all questions, this one," said the male police officer.

"I'm good for two," said Candy. The male police officer laughed. In a second Candy realized her lack of judgement. She'd been so focused on the seduction of a straight woman, she had failed to factor in the sexuality of a male police officer – something she had always taken for granted. His danglers were not there for the taking.

"Equal opportunities," he said. "Even the police take all-comers. So yes, I'm here as a gay man to make sure you, as a sexually omnivorous female, play by the rules."

"It's a fair cop," she said.

"I see myself as more of a brunette," he said.

"Of course you do," said Candy. The remainder of the journey to the police station was sexually uneventful, allowing Candy time to think about what she could do next. Now that being made a Dame for services to values-based education was a goner, she decided it would be a good move to cash in on her notoriety. She knew just the person to help with her latest cunning plan: Angela Phipps. Together, the least they could achieve was the writing of a best seller about her life and crimes. Angela Philips was where she would find her path to whatever came next in her random story of sex and death.

Killer Queen

Chapter Forty-Seven: The Hendrix Chronicles

Right. Fuck! Which way up? Right. Okay. Sorted. So I'm saying this and getting down exactly as is.

In 1997, Candy Regent and Paul McSmart killed Duncan Knight. I know this because Paul McSmart told me he did it the day after. I know he was telling the truth because he was so shit at lying. As far as I can tell, Candy Regent seduced him into murder. If you knew her and Duncan Knight, you'd get how easy that was. Never trust a woman with a perfect body or a virgin with a clipboard.

They both had the same alibi – they were shagging each other when it happened. Candy told Paul she had found the sword in the lake at the bottom of the field – if Carlsberg sold you a singing crock of shit, it would sound like that.

Paul knew it was bollocks – but he wanted in on all levels. From his description of the weapon, it sounds like one of those swords my old man brought back from Japan after the war – you could circumcise a flea with that blade. All the blades had form for something, and if they had been handled by experts you wouldn't know they had done anything wrong.

Anyway, dad gave his to the old bill after I nearly slit my mate's throat with it when I was about eight years old. Many of them were handed in for pretty much the same reason. So I would look where Ms. Regent spent her formative years. I am sure you will find she had access to an array of weapons sometime back in the past. She was what my sweet mum would call *an old man's darling,* so look for some sad old boy giving his life and a blade and a blow job – or even just the post-dated promise of one.

After she offed Knight, she carved herself out a career hurting anybody stupid, or ignorant enough to get in her way. But boy was she savvy. She always made sure other people did her dirty work. Counting on my fingers and toes meant I lost track of how many people I knew she ruined over the next few years. Usually she went for people who wanted to do a good job – they were the easiest to nobble. I also think that she was being looked after by people higher up the totem; Kingman thought pretty much the same. In the whole time we were in the same school, I cannot remember any kid talking about a lesson they'd had with her. It was as though she never taught a single lesson anywhere – and yet there she is making judgements on others...

The tape stops.

Here's the fucking joke. I am typing onto a freaking iPad so you can hear the words that somebody else should be writing down. This illness has stopped me talking. Anyhow, I am now worried about my boy. He's an idiot like me. Such a lot of people think Duncan Knight's death was down to me because I wasn't sorry he was dead. He was a mean fucker who deserved to die – but so was Pol Pot and I didn't kill either of them. But my boy...he has this quest to exonerate me – as if proving me innocent of something I didn't do will cleanse me of the very real sins I did commit. Life's not like that in my experience. You cannot undo what's been done. I think Bob Dylan may have said that. You just have to roll with the punches and put downs – such is man.

Here's the thing...Candy Regent is going to be everywhere that people die. She's an Angel of Death – an apex predator who smells your weakness. Do not underestimate that power she wields. But one day, sooner or later, she will slip on a banana skin. She over-rates her ability to cope with the shit she stirs – because nobody has caught her out. It's like pyramid selling but for murderers – you keep on passing the buck to somebody else. One day the bubble will burst and people will ask how it happened – how was it possible for a monster to walk the streets and be praised for the good work she did. Trust me, there are many monsters out there, we do nothing because they are beautiful monsters who are well-connected. I would guess she will go too far – kill a copper or a journalist maybe. Look what happens to anyone she doesn't like – or is related to. I'm guessing they are all pushing up daisies, or zonked out on Xanax.

So why the story? I have put this together so that, if anything happens to my boy, this will be read and somebody will do something about her. Just join the dots, people.

I was hoping to write more – I was hoping to figure out a way of keeping my boy safe. Instead, I am writing this in the vain hope that justice will be done.

Last thoughts? I wished I had shagged more women and taken more drugs. Mind you, the in-service death grant is looking pretty healthy – a literal plum. Nice to have something to leave behind for the boy. Now I'm off to that gig in the sky. Hendrix over and out.

Chapter Forty-Eight: Circle of Death

A book proposal by Angela Phipps:

Candy Regent (born Jane Crippen) was described by medical social workers as a very unusual young person. At the age of fourteen, she was the prime suspect in the killing of a number of cats in her neighbourhood.

Rather than be tried in any court, her guardians agreed that she be prescribed the experimental drug *Diproxipine* and recommended cognitive behaviour therapy (CBT). Though now discredited as a result of more recent clinical trials, *Diproxipine* was an anti-psychotic drug developed in 1977 that was hailed as a game changer in the treatment of anti-social personality disorder. It turned out to have an entirely opposite effect, diminishing the hallucinations of psychosis, but enhancing morality-free decision-making abilities.

Jane Crippen adopted the name Candy Regent after a period of detention as an adolescent. She changed her name legally before attending a university that wishes not to be named in this synopsis. Because she was being legally protected as a ward of the court, Candy was allowed to resume her life with this new identity.

What is now clear is that the medication had a disinhibiting effect on Candy. It allowed her to consider that any act that appeared to improve her life, or give her pleasure, was acceptable and that the death or disadvantage to others was simply acceptable collateral damage.

It is not known exactly how many people she conspired to have killed – or killed on her own, but it appears to have been at least five with several others dying in mysterious circumstances where she was the common factor. This total is something I will be discussing with Candy in a series of interviews which will form the bulk of my future writing.

Her downfall appears to be the carelessness of her

last known killing and the emergence of a document called *The Hendrix Chronicles*. The document provides some corroborative evidence for Candy Regent being one of the killers of Duncan Knight in 1997.

Presently, she is in jail for the killing of Jerry Brown and PC Jerrad Smith. Jerry Brown was found decapitated in a motel and Jerrad Smith was found floating in the River Thames with multiple stab wounds. Police divers who searched the area also found a ceremonial sword. Despite being in the water for several hours, forensic scientists were able to extract enough DNA to match skin and blood on the sword to Jerry Brown and Candy Regent.

There was also a harrowing recording of Jerrad Smith being murdered. He had managed to switch on his phone before he was stabbed to death.

An eye witness was also able to identify Candy Regent as the person seen pushing a large sack into the River Thames. The sack itself was weighted, but the fastening was not secure, so it sank to the bed of the river and was located at almost the exact location of the sword that was used to murder Jerry Brown.

Police described the suspect (at the time) as being calm and flirtatious. From my experience, this is how she dealt with all issues of a serious nature where the police were involved. She was possessed of an iron will not to be distracted by issues of grief or guilt.

It is said that success has many relatives and failure is an orphan – it appears that at the point of her incarceration Candy Regent became the motherless child she always wanted to be – overweight and happy in her own skin.

In prison, the strength of her personality disorder again prevailed. She became a person that prisoners and staff either feared or respected. It even appeared as though she had turned a corner. Eventually the old Candy Regent/Crippen became dominant. A young vulnerable prisoner was found dead in her cell. CCTV images identified as those of Candy Regent showed that she was the last person to see the young girl alive.

Candy Regent is now being held in solitary confinement. However, she will be eligible for parole in ten years' time. Currently, she edits her own fanzine - *KTs (Killer Tits)* - and answers messages from males from around the world.

Chapter Forty-Nine: All the World's a Jail

Dear Angela,

Thank you for asking me to write a foreword for your marvelous book proposal. I am sure we can work together to set the record straight. A book about Candy Regent! You always did understand me so well. We should have spent more time with each other. Who needs men?

So here it is – from the model prisoner.

It is stupid that they think they can contain me. All my friends and relatives live in my head. All the people I have ever known or killed live in my head. All the people I will ever know or kill, they live in my head too. You live in my head!

Inside story; I first knew I could kill anyone after I had an abortion. Cats were easy. People are a different proposition. I had just left university, shagged a shit-load of coppers and one of their little tadpoles made it all the way upstream. I like policemen, but they are not the best sorts to have around the house and I've never liked children of any age. The whole thing was a bit raw – but in the end it was no worse for me than having a tooth out. A week of eating paracetamol and watching daytime television and I was ready to face the world. If I could kill something inside me, killing anything else was going to be a doddle.

And now I am here. Home Sweet Home. Lots of pills from the quacks and lots of cake from my new fan base. A little factual error – my maiden name, if you will, was Crispen *not* Crippen – a little Freudian slip on your part (tee hee). I will take the description of being overweight – but Angela, darling, I was always comfortable in my skin.

Everyday people who want to get into my head come and visit me. I am so much more interesting than the people I have killed or hurt. And yes, I have learnt to say that I know it was wrong to kill – but these are relative and subjective concepts. Right for who? Wrong for whom?

Release me and I will kill again. ☺

Only kidding!

Maybe.

Kind Regards.

Queen Candy of the West Wing.

Chapter Fifty:
KTs

Breaking news:

A radical crypto-feminist group called the *KTs* have claimed responsibility for the escape of Candy Regent. At least one of the team penetrated the security of the prison by masquerading as a member of the WI. The subject of the scheduled WI talk was green alternatives to conventional funerals. Candy Regent was apparently smuggled out of the jail in a cardboard coffin. Inside the room where the talk was held, the police found a number of discarded items with a total weight of a mature adult female. A witness confirmed that the coffin had been crayoned with the lyrics of *Please Release Me* and a picture of a character identified as a red costumed female super-hero. It appeared that, because of spending cuts, basic security in the prison was compromised with nobody carrying out a roll call of prisoners - or checking what was inside the departing cardboard coffin.

Chicken soup supplied to duty officers by members of the WI was also found to contain traces of Xanax which may have led to an atmosphere conducive to a prisoner being able to leave the premises so easily. The people responsible for allowing the escape of Candy Regent blamed the whole event on mind control; they described the woman responsible as somehow controlling their thoughts as they helped her out of the high security building with a coffin far too big for one person to carry. They even said she had told them her name: *Elektra.* A spokesman for the police said it was highly unlikely that one woman would have been able to accomplish such a job without help.

Elektra the escapologist became an overnight sensation; sales of the 2005 DVD picked up after the film starring Jennifer Garner was a box office flop. Comic books were re-printed and a new series of stories based around the resurrection of an English Elektra was published in 2008.

A group of women calling themselves the *Elektra Natchios Nation* said in a statement that, *whilst it was unlikely that any male law enforcement officer could duplicate the task, there was the clear and complete underestimation of the power and resources of a single motivated female – with or without the ability to manipulate minds.*

Security was improved after the event; an opposition spokesperson described it as being *Too little too late*. The minister for prisons agreed there were some issues that needed to be sorted out; the WI is neither permitted to carry out talks in high security prisons nor supply chicken soup to duty prison officers.

Candy Regent has become something of a folk hero. Many people believe she is innocent of the crimes she was convicted for – suggesting that is simply the revenge of the patriarchy. As this news is going to press, a number of female actors are being lined up to play the role of Candy Regent. A screenplay based on the synopsis of the unpublished book by Angela Phipps is believed to be in production. It has the working title of *KT*s.

The present whereabouts of Candy Regent remain unknown. There is speculation that she is heading for Brazil where extradition laws are different. She has also been sighted in a number of different English coastal towns in the Kent area. It is not known if she has any previous family connections with the south-east.

Chapter Fifty-One:
Just like Elektra

On a small boat heading across the channel and safely out of her prison attire, Candy Regent was properly introduced to her rescuer. She saw something in the woman's face that she could not place.

"You look familiar to me. Do you have a name?"

"Elektra," said her rescuer.

"No Daddy to hold your hand?"

Elektra shook her head. She was not that sort of Elektra.

"I work alone." It appeared that the escape had been a one-person enterprise all along. What might have taken ten males had only required one female. Candy was impressed – perhaps she had finally met a woman after her own heart.

"So," said Candy, "it was just you?" The woman turned the engine off and jumped down to where Candy was.

"Yes." Candy was about to say some carefully chosen kind words – but suddenly, her heroine looked very young and very angry. The wind swept strands of red hair across her face.

"You might not know me," she said. "But you may have met my mother, Joanne Smith." Wearing a green bikini with a pattern of scales, Candy was sunning herself on the bow of the boat. Joanne Smith was not the person she was thinking of. It was somebody else altogether.

"I meet so many people," she said, pulling her knees up to her chest. The woman continued in a tone that was not entirely sweet to Candy's ears.

"You met my mother in a school you ran. She taught mathematics." Candy nodded. It was not even a woman she was thinking of. She rattled through the filing cabinet in her head.

"I have worked in a great many schools. I meet a lot of mathematics teachers. It's a core subject you know." She looked at the woman who was now on the foothills of an emotional overload.

"You put my mother on a support plan." Candy nodded again – that narrowed it down to everyone subordinate to her, so hardly at all.

"Sometimes people need a little support."

"And sometimes," said the woman, "that is just enough to put them over the edge." For Candy, people put themselves on the edge - not support plans. To suggest otherwise was to be part of the blame culture that she had fought all her working life.

"You know what they say," said Candy. "Sink or swim." Too late, Candy realised she was not balanced in a way that was safe for her environment.

"Arhhhhh!" The woman screamed and pushed Candy off the boat, something Candy hadn't anticipated.

There was a splash. Candy sank like a teacher on one of her bespoke support plans.

"Au Revoir!" Elektra called out to her as she started to drown.

Candy sunk, then re-surfaced and swam for her life. Paul! That was who the young woman reminded her of: the late and very compliant Paul McSmart. At least she hadn't got her head chopped off. There would have been no way of knowing what direction to swim in. The woman, too easily satisfied that Candy would die a slow cold death, turned the boat about and headed back to the English coast. Candy watched the boat and the sun disappear over the horizon. Unsure of what dry land was the closest, she took a chance on her immoral compass and started swimming in the same direction. The extra weight she had gained in prison helped her stay conscious and afloat in the cold water.

Many hours later, Candy Regent dragged herself onto a nameless sandy beach fringed with coarse grasses that grew on the dunes. She had no idea where she was. It could have been Kent, Essex or maybe even France. All she knew was that she was still alive – her and the voices inside her head.

As she lay there, crusted with kelp and gasping for breath, an old man and his Alsatian dog walked past, taking in the late evening air. The dog barked. He saw her flat out on the sand; she was his pension pot - a vision of aquatic erotica delivered to his beach by an unknown providence.

"My God! Are you a mermaid from the sea?" He shouted out to her. She composed herself and gave him her salty-sweet siren smile. England – it would be much more straightforward to kill and move on. Right now she was anything he wanted her to be – but she was an air sign, not a water sign.

"Yes." He returned a toothless leer that told her all his Christmases had come at once. The dog held his ground – but the man rushed over, took off his coat and looked her up and down. She'd all the right bits in all the right places. This was the retirement he had been hoping for. She was all he had ever dared to dream of. She was perfection. She was his.

"Let me help you out of your wet clothes." She wasn't wearing all that much. And what she was wearing had dried out pretty quickly. But she knew what he meant.

"Thank you," she said.

"Let me take you home and get you dry."

"That would be good," she said.

"I always knew," he said, "that one day I would find a mermaid on the beach."

"Do you live alone?" Candy asked.

"Of course," he replied.

"Close by?" Candy asked. His faithful dog, trained to recognize danger, growled out a warning that the man totally ignored.

"Yes." She reeled him in with the smile that no straight guy over sixty-five had ever managed to resist. Sheer enjoyment! Like an old cigar advert from the sixties, it spoke of deserted tropical islands and other James Bond fantasy moments. He paused a moment, as if waiting an instruction that he hardly dared believe would come his way. Next came the knockout punch.

"Then please carry me home and dry me off." His faithful dog barked out another warning – but there was no saving him from himself. She had his danglers in a doggie bag.

"You have made an old detective inspector very, very, happy." Candy knew she had hit pay-dirt with this old boy – more inspector than detective. She could see now that he was a copper who'd enjoyed better times – even if he could no longer properly remember them.

"It's what I do best," said Candy, ignoring the canine beast. "I live for your happiness." She could see tears in his eyes.

"Is that true?"

"Yes," said Candy, touching his arm. "Just enjoy me." He was going to have sex again! He could almost feel himself going into her. He farted with the excitement of it all.

"Oops!"

"Nothing to be scared of," she said.

It was true. Geriatrics 101.

There was going to be at least one elderly person dying today who'd never died before – and when you were as old as this wealthy chap, death was just a matter of patience and timing. He would be at one with the cosmos just as soon as she figured out his finances, and she knew precisely how she would find her way to those.

Standing over yet another dead body, she'd liberated enough money to do what she wanted for as far into the future as she could see. The first thing she would do was buy another necklace. She was lost without a silver skull around her neck. When she was very young, she had read how Mary, Queen of Scots had a watch in the shape of a silver skull that she carried as a reminder of her own mortality.

Under cover of night, she buried the man and his dog in the sands where they'd found her. She'd never killed a dog before. As for the old boy, he'd seen her naked. At his age and his condition, he was lucky to have done so. Now she was off to meet her destiny in London. She had found herself in the strange situation of actually missing another human being. Angela Phipps was on her mind. It wasn't about sex. Sex was easy. She ran through all the possible combinations and alternatives she could think of. Having eliminated those, she came to the conclusion that she was in love. It gave her a shiver of excitement. She knew this weakness would be the end of her if she allowed it to – and maybe that was how it should be. Life had once again become an adventure – a ride to the abyss and beyond.

Chapter Fifty-Two: Sweet and Salty

It was the start of a normal working day in the union offices. Angela Phipps opened her email.

It was well over a month since the escape and subsequent disappearance of Candy Regent. It was a story that had started to sink off the front pages of nearly all the national papers with the exception of *The Mail*, who had somehow managed to link her disappearance to dementia, immigration and falling house prices in the south-east.

A woman using the address of Joanna Smith had sent her a message.

Dear Angela,

I thought you would like to know that Candy Regent no longer walks the earth. I was responsible for setting her free from prison and then pushing her off a boat in the middle of the channel.

I am considering whether I tell the authorities at least some of my story.

Best wishes.

Elektra

Angela had a sense that this was not the end, and might not be even the beginning of the end. There was something so powerful about Candy Regent that did not mesh with her drowning off the coast of England. The numbers did not add up. It was actually very unsatisfactory, Candy Regent was like some sort of mythical beast that knights went on quests to kill – and often perished in the attempt; she could not possibly have died in such a mundane way. It was unthinkable.

Sooner or later, Angela knew that something would back up her hunch. Then something else happened. Another email popped up in her inbox.

Her heart raced. She knew who it was without even looking. She licked her lips in anticipation of the adventure ahead.

Hiya Angela,

I am sure you know who I am. That's right. Your old friend Candy Regent.

The written words gave her a tingle she had seldom experienced – a sexual shiver she wanted to feel again and again. She remembered the last time she had felt that way. The Joanne Smith case. And yet she knew it was wrong – evil in fact. But there she was, reading words on a screen and walking around an abyss of debauchery that she wanted to fall into…to succumb to. Momentarily, she wrestled back control from the unchecked forces unleashed inside her. She laughed; this force of nature could compromise and corrupt a saint. What chance did she have? She read on.

Please don't be scared, my darling Angela. You are literally the last person in this world I want to hurt. You get me. You and I have a shared destiny. I think you always understood that – even when we were enemies. I might even be in love with you! As for my biography, I liked most of what you wrote about me – but it is unfinished business. It needs to be written and published.

Don't worry for me, I am safe and well.

Together we are going to write my story – or at least the fun bits! I have always enjoyed the company of police officers. In fact, my daddy was a Deputy Commissioner in the Met. How did you think I was able to slip under the radar so easily? Let me start with the case of a Detective Jones in September 1987. I was just a young graduate then and my only previous crimes had been the killing of a few stray cats. But I had dreams of doing much more – even though I did not know who I truly was. Now I know. I am a psychopath and this is my story...

Angela went back to her inbox.

Dear Elektra

I am sorry to tell you that Candy Regent is alive and well. I have just had an email from her. So I would say that the next time you try and kill her...do a better job – bring weapons of mass destruction perhaps? I think we need to take this matter further. If you feel strong enough to arrange a meeting with me – please get in touch.

Regards Angela

She then emailed Candy.

Dearest Candy,

I think we need to meet again. Destiny demands it.

Please tell me where and when.

Love Angela x

She felt a glorious kick of emotional overload as she hit *'send'*. Like the start of a love affair, she had no idea how this was going to play out – or what she wanted from either Candy or the mystery daughter. She only knew this was the most excitement she could remember in forever.

Chapter Fifty-Three: Part of the Union

Angela had dressed for the occasion in stiletto shoes and dark stockings. She knew the shoes would be no use when it came to running away – but if it came to that she knew she was a goner. Her heart pounded with first date and death anticipation. Everything in her life was vanilla – except this. Her husband was kind and predictable; she knew it could be a great deal worse. Her kids were doing well at school and university; she was looking into a void of irrelevance and obsolescence. One day too soon, she would not be part of the union; the adventure of helping others would be well and truly over. Still she'd no idea of what she wanted – she'd never had much more than a girl crush on a prefect at school, and Candy Regent was a long stretch from being anybody's idea of a role model. Maybe Nicole Kidman would play her in the film of the book she was going to write about this if she lived through it. She dismissed that vanity very swiftly – in her heart she knew she knew that someone as powerful as Kathy Burke would nail it. Maybe Nicole Kidman could play Candy Regent – yes, she could project the correct levels of beauty and cold, calculating sexuality.

The emails had carried on, back and forth with Candy and the mystery woman. It was as much unsafe fun as Angela could recall - ever. It was also an adventure she would not recommend to anybody in a professional capacity – a semi-Sapphic dalliance with a sexy serial killer was not the best way to improve net happiness in a person's life. But it was working for her.

Angela had taken the standard dating advice and made sure that somebody knew where she was going. That somebody was not her husband; part of his charm was that he was too simple a piece of mortality to understand why she was doing this. Angela was having a very tricky task explaining all of her motives to herself; it would have been impossible for her fella. But there was at least one person who understood – even though she had never met her and only had it on her own intuition that the person was who she said she was.

Angela got off at the designated tube stop. North London. Mackerel pinky sky. Very Queen Candy – glorious pink flesh with a salty undertow. Momentarily a line from one of Nicole Kidman's films popped into her head. If she had to choose between Richmond and death, she would choose death. Angela could not afford either London or Richmond in life or in death. The address she was given was a flat in a mansion block – something she'd seen in films where Americans are allowed to see how life is in London. It was a place where a nineties Hugh Grant might have hung out with his chums – or maybe where Paddington Bear lived with the Brown family. All of these references running around her head added to the unreality of the whole stupid scheme. She looked up to see if there were any chimney sweeps with atrocious cockney accents – there were none to be spotted.

"*Chim chiminee*," she sang softly to herself.

She pushed on the buzzer.

"Angela." She recognized the purr. The door opened and another person pushed past.

"Careful," said Angela. Nothing was said. Angela walked up the first flight of stairs. All she could hear was her own breathing. The person who had come in with her had disappeared. It pushed her anxiety levels still higher. She knocked on the door.

"It's open," said Candy. "Come in and make yourself at home." Angela walked into the lounge.

"Where are you?" she asked.

"In the kitchen," said Candy.

"Okay," said Angela. A few moments later, Candy came out.

"Wow," said Angela. "You scrub up well."

"I haven't been called a scrubber since I was fifteen," said Candy. "But since it's you, I'll let you off."

"What did you do last time it happened?"

"I let daddy deal with it."

"I see."

"But I'm a big girl now." She was dressed in stilettos and a long black dress that shimmered as she moved. The sleeves and skirt were slit to reveal her near flawless skin and stunning curves. She knew full well the power of the image. Enough was revealed and enough was concealed. In appearance at least, she was divinely edible.

"What now?" Angela asked.

"Were you expecting tea and crumpets?"

"No," said Angela.

"I want to play some games, Honey," said Candy.

"What sort of games?" Angela asked.

"The best sort of course" said Candy, pulling some pieces of sash cord from out of a pocket that Angela did not see was there. She walked over to Angela, gave her a gentle kiss on the cheek, and pushed her in the direction of the reading chair that was in the corner of the room. Angela noticed she was wearing a chain with an exquisite silver skull pendant.

"Will this hurt?" Angela asked.

"It won't hurt me," said Candy. "But if you are worried, we can have a safe name that you call out if you want it to stop. I'm sure you won't." Angela eased her herself into the chair. The breath seemed to escape from inside her, creating a suffocating vacuum of fear and longing. She managed to gasp out the sentence she had rehearsed the night before.

"So, if in the middle of this I shout out *'Tony Blair'* you'll stop what you're doing and untie me."

"That's a funny one," said Candy. "Sure. Tony Blair it is." Candy tightened the cords and Angela found herself immobilized and entirely at the mercy of a women she knew was more of a killer than a lover. Candy started to stroke Angela's shoulders. She felt the cold silver skull on the necklace brush against her. Next Candy moved her hands downwards towards the cleft in buttocks. Slowly she moved her hands back up to her breasts and stroked them gently. Angela shuddered and surrendered to that exquisite moment; so this was where the thrill of sex and the drive to death enjoyed their fatal liaison. Then, suddenly, her hands moved again.

Angela started to choke.

"Gordon Brown," she said. Candy's nimble fingers were now tightly around Angela's throat.

"Now hands that kill kittens can be soft as your face with...I forget the rest. That was the start of a story that got me excluded from my first secondary school. Daddy fixed that too for his Candy Jane. That was when I decided I would be a teacher..." Angela called on all her reserves of will and strength.

"Gordon Brown!" she shouted. Candy smiled.

"Wrong call, my lovely, not that it's going to make any difference now!"

"Why?"

"You thought you were special to me, didn't you?" Angela nodded.

"Well you are, Angela darling. And now you're going to join all the other good folk who live in my mind – Satan's elves if you will. And you know what I think...if you could choose between somebody beautiful killing you and somebody ugly killing you...well I know what I'd prefer..." Angela could feel herself slipping away. Kitten killing hands? Satan's elves? Murderers ranked by looks and charm?

Had Elektra forgotten the safe word? Where was she?

Please. Not like this. Please.

No...

"Just as Jesus died for your sins, I will sin for your death." Candy continued as Angela lost consciousness. Yet Candy was so involved in the business of murder, that she was oblivious to some strange noises in the spare bedroom.

Killer Queen

Chapter Fifty-Four: Gordon Brown

A figure in a dark red coat flew out of the spare bedroom. Something in her hand caught the light as she moved across the room.

Candy looked up in time to see a Japanese sword bearing down on her. She caught a glimpse of the face of the person with the blade.

"You again!" In a moment of peace, she watched it fall towards her neck – it was definitely Paul Smart's daughter. She knew that look of concentration and rage. She was going home. Backed by a thousand years of craftsmanship, the blade cut fast and sure.

"Sayonara!"

In an eternal moment it was done; sex and death were cleaved apart. The killer queen was stilled. He head lay several feet from the rest of her – still stunning. Beauty in death was what she had always wished for. Then there was a silence that lasted into eternity as the living took stock of the dead. Then sounds of breathing could be heard, and gradually the vibrations of the outside world took back their place in the natural order of things.

"I got her this time," said the woman in the dark coat. Angela, covered in blood, looked up at her saviour.

"Where did you get the sword?"

"Bitch! I'm Elektra. I can steal anything from anywhere!"

"I think you gave her the death she wanted," said Angela.

"Is that bad or good?"

"It just is," said Angela. "There are no moral measures

for this."

"Right."

"Whatever it is, this is definitely women's work," said Angela. "No straight man alive could have thought it through and then carried it out."

"Absolutely."

"I need something different to wear out of here," said Angela. The woman in the dark coat had a rummage through Candy's wardrobe. She threw Angela a long mac.

"She definitely won't be needing a raincoat where she's going." Angela looked more closely at the woman.

"You have the most beautiful red hair," she said. "Like your mother."

"You know what they say? Red heads do it best."

"I'm just glad it's over," said Angela.

"It is over, isn't it?"

"Of course it is," she said. "Look at the mess." Angela chose to go with the comfort of a lie.

"Yes," said Elektra. "Nothing could live through that."

"And you owe it to your mum to make something more of your life," said Angela.

"I will. I promise you I will."

"Good girl," said Angela. She went over to the body for one last look. The bloodied necklace was now lying somewhere between the head and the torso of Candy Regent. Succumbing to an impulse, Angela picked it up and put it in the pocket of her raincoat.

"What was that about?" Elektra asked.

"A momento," said Angela. "A *memento-mori* in fact."

"I think it would be better to forget this happened," said Elektra.

"Funny girl," said Angela. "They haven't got the drugs or therapy for that."

"I'm going to medicate with wine and chocolate," said Josephine.

"Killer heels too," she said looking down at the shoes Candy was wearing. Angela stepped over Candy's torso.

"You're not going to take those as well?" Josephine asked.

"That would be weird," said Angela. "Besides, she's not my size."

"That's a bit too much background," said Josephine.

"Know your enemy better than you know yourself," said Angela. Leaving the sword in the bloodied room, they left the death flat and walked out of the building.

"I wonder what the police will make of this," said Elektra.

"I think they'll be glad she's finally gone," said Angela. "I know I will."

"Is she?" Elektra asked.

"They say evil never dies," said Angela. "But you gave it your best shot – if she comes back, it's down to me."

They reached the underground station that they hoped would deliver them from evil. The omens seemed good; everything was almost as it was before; only the pink afternoon sky had surrendered to a bloody sunset.

"I think this is where we say goodbye," said Elektra.

"I wish we could be friends," said Angela.

"I wish you were my mum," said Elektra.

"Do you have a real name you could share with me?" Angela asked.

"Josephine."

"That's a beautiful name," said Angela.

"This is heartbreaking," said Josephine.

"No tears," Angela.

"Too late," said Josephine. They hugged and then, unravelling in opposite directions, both tried to resume their normal lives.

By agreement, they never spoke or saw each other again. Both of them took a small part of Candy Regent home with them that night. Josephine was rattled by how Candy had looked deep into her when they were connected by the arc of her blade. Angela was far more damaged than she wanted to admit to anyone, least of all herself.

The case of the death of Candy Regent remained open. The papers recorded that she had died as a result of a sex game gone wrong. That maybe there was a lesbian relationship, maybe there were more than two people involved. The case would return to the public eye every few years – kept alive by clickbait and regular *Daily Mail* exclusives. Candy became the new Joyce McKinney – her actual life, which was far worse than the journalists could ever comprehend, became almost completely irrelevant.

The police were just content that she was not out there anymore killing young and old officers. As in the case of the murder of the journalist Matthew *'Toddy'* Todd, there were just so many suspects; they were simply waiting on a confession that would join the dots.

The *Panorama* story of Candy Regent is available as

a DVD from the BBC archives. A sequel is being planned by Matthew Todd's son, John, who is also a filmmaker. Working alongside his father's old partner Snuffy, they re-investigated some of the people and places that made up the cold case – much of the evidence was missing or hadn't been looked at properly. John Todd claims he has discovered that Duncan Knight had arranged for a team of hitmen to take out Candy Regent and Paul McSmart. This is in part confirmed by testimony from a partnership who called themselves 'Burke and Hare.' They'd travelled down to the school on the day after Duncan Knight was killed. Unable to locate either Mr. Knight, or the two thousand pounds deposit they were to be paid for the job, they went home. They also confirmed they were in negotiation with the deceased for the killing of the current Head of the school, Ms. Bel Bishop. John Todd has also said that he will be looking to interview DC Grissom, who led the case in 1997, about whether cash or evidence of a contractual agreement was found anywhere.

Chapter Fifty-Five: Goodbye Candy Jane

Elektra wrote a graphic novel about a female psychopath who becomes the CEO of a Multi Academy Trust and kills off older staff as a cost cutting exercise. The publishers suggested she make the central character a man - as it would then be a more believable tale.

She rejected the advice and self-published *Divine Blight – the story of a Killer Queen*. Josephine Smith/aka Elektra is still working as a supply teacher in Wandsworth.

Angela considered burning her manuscripts and deleting her files – but then who would ever believe any of this happened? She put them in a bank box for safe keeping – to be opened after she was no more.

Eventually, every physical trace of Candy Jane Regent was erased from her life. Except for the necklace with the silver skull, that amnesiac souvenir she'd been unable to put down from the moment she'd left the death flat. She even hoped that the necklace protected her from the forgotten past. She was wrong. However hard she tried to evict her, the seed of Candy Jane Regent had germinated in Angela's diseased and damaged psyche - cold as ice cream, but not as sweet. Gradually a dialogue that didn't need broadband was re-established. To begin with, it was there in the dormant hours of the night – then it bloomed in her mind like a flaming toxic flower. Incrementally, it became bolder and bolder – then finally demanding and dominant.

What could she do to still that voice in her head? How could she drown out the sound? Were there any other choices?

Over the next few months, she tried to still the parasite inside her. It was going nowhere. It had nowhere to go. Initially her sex life picked up – but that was the only upside and proof positive there really was more to life than bedtime fun. She finally understood there was nothing else that she could do. Candy Jane Regent was in her and she was, hour by hour, becoming Candy Jane and that good sex was not enough of sweetener. There was no saying goodbye to Candy Jane – she was certainly not a candle in the wind.

At work she would find herself checking out the young staff she worked with; wondering which ones she could seduce and corrupt. She understood the price of everyone and the value of nobody. One day she found herself planning how she could get a promotion by killing her boss, how she could own her house by killing her husband, how she could get rich by killing her mother. She was multi-tasking attempted murder and sexual abuse – and then normalizing the whole bloody exercise. These were plays straight out of the Candy Jane Regent book of tricks. It was time to be decisive. When she was sure Candy Jane was not listening, she sat down and planned out how to say goodbye to everything she had ever loved before it was destroyed by the monster in her mind. The incubus that continued to whisper into her ear soft stories of death and betrayal. That person trusted you. You could destroy them. That person loved you. You could abuse them. Everybody was a counter on a board, a shake of the dice or a spin of the wheel. The excitement was seeing who you hurt and what you could get. And it was exciting – that was the worst thing. There was fun to be had in killing and hurting. There were many victories and few defeats. And you never had to feel bad about any of it because it was never a part of you. The world was just a toy you played with and threw away when you got bored.

What was the worst case scenario of letting Candy Jane Regent into her life on any level? Becoming Candy Jane and losing her true self.

Chapter Fifty-Six: Redemption is a River

On a moonless night, Angela Phipps stood shivering on the bridge. Her car was neatly parked. Her make-up was immaculate. Her coat pockets were full of rocks. Having written a farewell note to her family and drunk a bottle of Irish crème liqueur, she knew she had to jump before it all came back up again. Dying was one thing – being sick and disheveled in public was something else altogether.

Over the past year, she'd gone through all the options, electro-convulsive therapy, CBT, legal drugs, illegal drugs, cake and carbs. Nothing worked. Candy Jane Regent remained an under-stain on her soul. Watching the John Todd documentary about the whole sordid affair was the tipping point – the tsunami of social media it unleashed had been too much for her to bear.

Wearing Candy Jane Regent's bloodied silver skull necklace, Angela spread her wings and embraced the waters of oblivion.

Chapter Fifty-Seven: Sugar Free

As her life thrashed before her, she was happy that most of her memories had been good ones. As she hit the water, the necklace fell away from her – headfirst she reached down grabbed at it. The silver skull seemed to wink at her, encouraging her into the inky depths. Under the water and sinking, she was able to let herself go…to surrender to the eternal kindness of death's release.

When her body was recovered the next day, the silver skull necklace had gone. The police report stated that she'd left all her jewelry in her car. The keys to her car were in her coat pocket when she jumped. She had left a spare set at home, along with a note for her husband saying she had always loved him – but could see no way out of the pain she was in.

It's for the best, she wrote. *I did try, but I cannot go on. Sorry my Sweet. Don't forget to feed the cat and please stay off the scotch and widow women for a couple of weeks.*

Chapter Fifty-Eight: Evil Never Dies

(By Josephine Pauline Smith)

Twenty-seven-year-old graphic artist, supply teacher and WI member, Josephine Smith, has produced a wonderful graphic novel about a flame haired female Van-Helsing for the millennium. In a style she describes as *manic realism*, her heroine battles the modern vampires who have learnt to deal with daylight and are spending their immortality as CEOs of Multi Academy Trusts.

Angelina Phillips is the main character, a middle-aged firecracker who works by day as a union rep and by night as a vampire hunter. In this story, the vampires cannot be killed by a stake through the heart – they have to be de-capitated to be truly sent back to hell. Angelina achieves this with *Ursula*, her mythical sword of truth- discovered in a lake by a school and a magic crucifix she stole from a freshly killed vampire bitch.

As well as killing CEO vampires, Angelina has to save many of the teachers who have become vulnerable to these adaptive creatures of the night. Teachers over a certain age, teachers who didn't fit, and teachers who knew too much were those that Angelina had to work the hardest to save.

This battle against evil is not fought without a cost. The final exchange between the queen vampire and Angelina provides the core of the book. If you see the vampire as a monster who cannot be forgiven, she lives forever. If you see her as a victim, she is sucked into anonymity.

In the end, Angelina has to sacrifice everything she holds dear to keep the world of education safe. It is believed that some of the inspiration for Ms. Smith's story came from the life and death of Candy Jane Regent, a one-time CEO of an MAT who was previously associated with the unsolved murder of Duncan Knight in 1997. This is an allegation that Ms. Smith has denied. In a recent *Guardian* interview, she said that it *'would be wrong to single out one person as the sole example of educational vampirism when in fact the whole system was riddled with this type of parasitic life form. I took my inspiration from the case of the late Angela Phipps, a union rep who had worked with my mother before she died. She fought the real life CEOs whose corrupt practices still pollute our educational system. If you do not believe me, look at the news of the Multi Academy Trusts; hardly a day goes by without some 'Sir' or similar caught with his or her nose in trough – and those are just the stories you get to hear about. I could tell you case after case of good people ruined by these creatures. Evil will always exist. As good people it falls to us to ensure it is contained and in plain sight.*

Education should not be a numbers game run by the free market and we should never allow our children to be viewed as products or pawns on a chessboard. I feel ashamed that our system rewards the powerful and fails the weak as a matter of course – that is the greatest evil and it is entirely down to a succession of vampire governments since May 1979 who were more concerned with bloodless efficiency improvements than the welfare of living human beings.'

Chapter Fifty-Nine: Grave News

On a cold wet night, there was a knock on the door of Josephine's luxury West London flat. She looked through her spyhole.

"Who is it?" She could make out a man. If she could have seen further down the corridor, she would have seen another man with a camera.

"My name is John Todd. I'm an investigative reporter for the BBC. I've come to ask you about the murder of Candy Regent."

"How do I know you're a reporter?"

"Because I know you're a murderess." Josephine had quite a few cold callers since her graphic novel took off – many of them said the same thing. Actually, so far nobody had been as formal as to call her a murderess – she quite liked the label.

"Do you have any evidence?" Josephine asked.

"I know you sometimes call yourself Elektra," said John.

"One of my alleged dads liked Marvel comics – that's not evidence."

"So why Elektra?" John asked.

"She's majorly damaged – but she takes no shit from anyone."

"The first year that Elektra appeared in any comic was the year you were born," said John.

"Big whoop, I knew that too."

"There's more." He had so much hard evidence. He had really done his homework. He could even tell her who her father was – if she wanted.

"So who was my father?"

"Paul McSmart," said John.

"And how do you know I killed anyone?"

"An extra at Pinewood remembers you looking at a Japanese sword." John had all the answers.

"Everyone likes a sword," said Josephine. "Not just Elektra."

"Before you walked off with it," said John, "and used it to kill Candy Regent."

"You can buy a Japanese sword on the internet," said Josephine.

"But you didn't," said John. "I checked that one out."

"You do know a good deal about me," said Josephine. "Did you know that bitch hounded my mother into an early grave?" Of course he did, that, and so much more. He'd been looking at her picture for so long he'd fallen in love with it. Now he was weary of the battle for truth and justice.

"My father was killed by Candy Regent," said John Todd. "She was a murdering fiend. I don't want to bring you in for killing her. I want to thank you for killing her." Exiled no more by pain of bereavement, they connected. He looked back and gave a thumbs up to Snuffy who took the evening off. He knew Toddy's boy was safe with this one.

"Say it then," said Josephine.

"Thank you, Elektra, for killing the evil Candy Regent in Camden Town with a Japanese Sword."

"That's a novel chat up line," said Josephine.

"I thought you'd like it," said John.

"I'm tired," said Josephine.

"Me too," said John.

"I need somebody who understands," said Josephine.

"I know," said John. "We are both lost." Those were the words that unlocked the door.

"Wait a moment." Josephine let him in. John looked at her. She was not a killer; just like him, she was a victim. She was more than her picture, so very much more.

"I need to be healed," she said. "Please don't hurt me."

"I will never hurt you." She held him. They just seemed to fit.

"Good," she said.

"I know what you can do with a sword and a smile," he said. She laughed and kissed him.

"And I know what you can do with yours."

"Do you believe in love at first sight?" John asked.

"I want to," said Josephine. She never knew how empty her heart was until he filled it. She felt giddy and safe. There were very few people who understood both the how and the why, maybe only him. She had met so many chancers in her search for what? A fling? A fantasy? A father figure? She had no idea anymore. But now that search was about to be called off.

The woman on the page and the real woman were dancing a reel in John's head. A schoolboy poem, long forgotten, jumped into his head.

It was love at first sight.

Well second.

He wanted to marry her.

Well he wanted a bit.

They set up home together.

Well he stayed the night.

That may or may not have been his original intention, but in the end he never left after that first night and nobody died to make it so. She stole his heart and he was happy enough not to press charges. Everything had a flow. What had been rough was now smooth.

In the next few months the extent of John Todd's research bore a less bitter fruit; he was able to put Josephine in touch with James and Sarah – the other known children of her father. From having no family other than her mother, she gained a brother, a sister and a bunch of nieces and nephews to spoil.

The story of Josephine Smith and how she killed Candy Regent was going to be edited out of the forthcoming DVD, podcast and digital download. He had the whole story, right down to her ashes being placed in a salt urn and buried at sea. He knew that Angela Phipps would be posthumously happy to take all the credit for slaying that particular dragon, although no evidence could be provided as to the provenance of the killing sword. Indeed, this was one of the common issues of evidence that linked the first and last murder. The mystery of both swords was a broken link in the chain of evidence that allowed the conspiracy theorists in through the back door; some of the instant experts had seen it as evidence of a modern day Jack the Ripper.

The reality of Candy Regent was actually more banal; recent information released because of the GPDR laws had shown that Candy Regent had gained an initial promotion because of the lobbying of a former head of the now discredited Cradcrock consultancy. That head subsequently died in circumstances that have never satisfactorily been explained. Duncan Knight, who was assured that he would be the consultancy mole, was passed over for the job without any explanation of why this had happened. When Candy Regent went rogue and started her killing spree, the consultancy continued to collude in her ascendancy rather than admit that they had employed a psychopath. In many ways, it suited their purposes as they were looking to create a flatter management structure in the schools they oversaw – such a school offers less resistance to consultancy looking for the kudos of continual change. The fact that a good many other CEOs and educational leaders are also psychopaths, provided an ideal cover for Candy Regent, and a further reason for the consultancy not to risk her ire.

So where does the blame lie? It could be said that you cannot blame a psychopath for taking full advantage of the weakness of others – that it is what they do. It appears that perhaps the business model of consultancies is at fault. Teams who invade a territory, take it over and then leave others to deal with the damage. And as for the truth, we live in an age of very successful liars; every so often one of the minor liars is ritually sacrificed to keep the rich and powerful liars safe from everything except perhaps the judgement of history.

But that was not how it was for John Todd. He was looking now at the smaller picture – which is what you have to do if you wish to survive. One woman had taken his father's life. Another woman had given him a reason to live. He knew it was not all about him and that eternal pain and suffering could not be balanced against fleeting mortal happiness. But that was how it played out for the two lovers who were now able to shut out a world that had taken so much from them.

Sometimes something good comes out of something evil.

Glossary

A book about teachers and teaching seems to carry a great deal of jargon and acronyms. They get in the way of understanding the process of education precisely because that is their purpose. The following are a few that are found in this novel, and may confound the general reading public.

ASC: Autistic Spectrum Condition which is a more PC way of saying ASD which stands for Autistic Spectrum Disorder and carries a sense of autism being an illness.

Academy Status: a school that is independent of the local authority and can do what it wants which is usually to pay head teachers more and class teachers less.

A-Level: Advanced Level study of a subject; an advanced examination that used to be done in two years with a single pass/fail exam. Now education is more accountable to money rather than standards, the respect given to the qualification has diminished radically.

Accountability: a modern watch word of the unaccountable who run the educational world.

A Banda: an old machine for reproducing classroom resources, in use until around 1982 when it was replaced by photocopiers; the fluids used were mildly intoxicating.

CPD: Continuous Professional Development which is something that should happen organically.

CPVE: Certificate of Pre-Vocational Education, which was used to bridge the gap between leaving school and youth unemployment.

Capability Plans or Procedures: what a management team puts in place when they feel confident enough to have you dismissed for incompetence; it is usually actually a matter of financial restrictions and/or personality clashes.

Challenging behaviour: when a maniac destined for a future of life imprisonment wrecks your room because he/she does not like you telling him/her to be quiet when a lesson begins.

Core Values: what every decent human being has except for the person espousing them. Core values include honesty, compassion and reliability. They can also appear as inspirational slogans when a school leadership team is populated with former physical education teachers.

Curriculum Development: the process of changing something that works and replacing it with something that does not work. Eventually the services of a Consultant are required to put everything back where it was previously. This guarantees a promotion for the change maker and a substantial fee for the consultant. Often they will be the same person.

CSE: Certificate of Secondary Education, an examination which was used in secondary school without the capacity to deliver O-Levels, involving a shambles of shoddy coursework and soft exams, it was worth nothing unless you gained a grade one. It was replaced by the GCSE in the mid-1980s.

DT: Directed Time where a person with more time on their hands explains how you will do the job you have been doing very successfully for a long time. It is also a justification for making teachers work longer hours as in *'that's part of directed time.'*

DT: Design and Technology, known in the olden times as woodwork and metalwork.

Differentiation: Where every child gets the work they can do independently with a degree of challenge that does not have them wrecking your classroom. Done properly you use up all your directed time and die sad and lonely. A failure to differentiate to the taste of SLT (who seldom, if ever, differentiate their own lessons) is a staple of the Capability Plan and its evil sibling the Support Plan.

Expectations management: A situation where the teacher is more likely to be put on a support plan than receive a performance-related pay increase.

Final Salary Pension: a modern myth of the teaching profession; a once generous scheme to support hard-working teachers in retirement, enjoyed by lucky ex-teachers recruited in the high rolling eighties.

GCSE: General Certificate of Secondary Education, which replaced CSEs and O-Levels. It had coursework which could easily be farmed out to a third party (unsanctioned cheating) and is now being phased out.

GNVQ: General National Vocational Qualification, which was to bridge the gap between youth unemployment and A-level. It was a mix of coursework, classroom misery and multiple choice.

HLTA: Higher Level Teaching Assistant, the unicorn of special needs teaching. Everyone has heard of them and can tell you how beautiful they look in a classroom. Nobody has ever seen one.

Inclusion: not excluding pupils because they spoil the view – or, more importantly your data set.

Inclusion Unit: a place to keep pupils you do want messing up your stats by being externally excluded.

Key Stages: the point at which a pupil has progressed in a school, for example Key Stage 3 is years 7-9 (in old money, 1st, 2nd and 3rd years of secondary school).

LSA: Learning Support Assistant, also known as TAs (Teaching Assistants/Teaching Angels).

MATs: multi-academy trusts which are larger and more corrupt versions of Academies – often identified by gender imbalances in pay and huge numbers of consultants often related to senior management.

MLD: moderate learning difficulties.

NRA: National Records of Achievement which is what you are given instead of GCSEs.

O-Level: Ordinary Level, in the good old days an exam of some status taken at 16 if you did not take CSE.

Ofsted: Ofsted, or Office for Standards in Education, later Office for Standards in Education, Children's Services and Skills, the butt of numerous jokes.

Permanent Exclusion: a pupil who cannot go back to their school and is therefore sent to a PRU, formerly known as being *expelled*.

PRU: pupil referral unit, pupils who cannot access mainstream education, who go there as do teachers who like to break up fights.

PGCE: a post graduate certificate of education, a qualification which allows a graduate to become a teacher. It is less enjoyable than university and facilitates the transition from fun to futility.

Rigour: A meaningless word used negatively by a school manager to malign a subordinate's work/preparation – as in your plan *lacks rigour*.

Robust: Another meaningless word used negatively by a school manager to de-motivate a subordinate by criticising their work/preparation – as in your differentiation was *not robust*.

Support Plan: the weapon of choice for head teachers who feel that failure to worship them is a form of dissent. The support plan does the opposite of what it says on the packet; it fails to support you in almost every conceivable way unless the head is foolish enough to assign you a competent mentor. Done properly, nobody should survive a support plan.

SLT: acronym for Senior Leadership Team; the bare bones of an SLT is usually an absentee boss, one stooge and a person who runs the school.

TES: The *Times Educational Supplement*; in the days before the internet, teaching jobs were found by reading it weekly on Fridays.

Whiteboard: see blackboard; an interactive whiteboard is an electric blackboard.

13.03.19